Praise for *Raising Parents, Raising Kids*...

"This insightful and practical book by seasoned psychotherapist and parent, Dawn Menken, portrays parenting as an emergent and adventurous process, one that requires our wakefulness as parents. With concrete examples and useful tips, *Raising Parents, Raising Kids* helps parents to become in tune with their child, a key to deep parenting. Addressing issues ranging from emotional intelligence and dreams, to bullying, couples' conflicts, and more, this valuable guide provides essential insights and down-to-earth tools to serve the sacred task of parenting."

—Tobin Hart, Ph.D.
Author of *The Secret Spiritual World of Children*

"At a time when both parents and children are becoming overwhelmed by technology and the busyness of modern life, Dr. Dawn Menken is deeply attuned to the importance of developing and nurturing the inner lives of children. Peppered with anecdotes from her practice and personal life, the book paints compelling pictures of how Dr. Menken works with children to engage them more deeply with their emotional lives, and provides concrete activities to help readers do this important work with children as well. I found myself reading chapter after chapter and nodding, yes! This is a crucial book for parents and educators of this millennium."

—Jenn David-Lang
Editor of *The Main Idea*

"Dr. Dawn Menken offers a sensitive and insightful understanding of how children experience and understand their inner and outer worlds. In *Raising Parents, Raising Kids,* she describes a range of dynamics that challenge children, parents, and families in both home and school life. By reaching below the surface through case illustrations and explanations, Dr. Menken guides the reader in how to validate the positive development of the child, skillfully offering useful tools and techniques to aid parents and children in their relationships with each other and with the world."

—Ingrid Rose, Ph.D.
Author of *School Violence*

"Dr. Dawn Menken writes with great knowledge and passion about how to work with the critical issues children and parents face in today's world. *Raising Parents, Raising Kids* is a significant contribution to the growing field of process-oriented family therapy. Dr. Menken writes with great clarity and her new book is full of wonderful stories and examples that offer valuable tools for anyone raising or working with children either as parent, caregiver, or professional. I wish I had had this book when I was raising my own children."

—Gary Reiss, Ph.D.
Author of *Families that Dream Together*

"Dawn Menken's reader-friendly book teaches us how to appreciate and flow with the unique journey of each parent and child. Her book is full of lively and easy-to-understand examples. She not only supports the inner wisdom and dreaming of children, but also addresses social issues that are relevant today. Her down-to-earth style and sensitive, therapeutic wisdom make this book important for everyone to read since each of us is at one time or another a parent, elder, teacher, or child!"

—Amy Mindell, Ph.D.
Author of *Metaskills*

"Dr. Menken's profound respect for the child-parent relationship highlights the mystery and mutuality which are critical to both child and parent becoming themselves together. While many children are taught the necessary rules by their parents, Menken shows how they are nurtured at their roots by the authentic movement and unfolding of this precious bond.

Raising Parents, Raising Kids not only addresses a total rainbow of possible parent-child interactions, dilemmas, and predicaments, but also offers an absolute pot of golden wisdom, practical advice, and heart for each one."

—David Bedrick, J.D., Dipl. PW
Author of *Talking Back to Dr. Phil*

"This powerful and insightful book shows how to creatively explore parenting issues and see them as a process of mutual learning leading to a deeper connection between parent and child. With many case examples and creative and fun practical tips and exercises, this book teaches awareness, shows the creativity of parenting, and helps raise an emotionally intelligent next generation. A powerful addition to the literature on parenting—a must read for parents, aunties and uncles, teachers, psychologists, and anyone working with children!"

—Silvia Camastral, Ph.D.
Child Psychotherapist, Australia

"I thoroughly enjoyed reading Dawn Menken's book and feel it is a must read for all parents. Every chapter spoke to me as a parent and an educator. The chapter on bullying, both for victims and bystanders, is especially innovative, timely, and powerful. With a great sense of humor, humility, and personal experience, Dr. Menken teaches us that our children are our best teachers and we can learn so much from them when we listen. This is easily one of the best books I have read on parenting and I offer my highest recommendation."

—Brian Anderson
Elementary School Principal, Portland, Oregon

"In *Raising Parents, Raising Kids,* Dr. Dawn Menken portrays parenting as a continuous evolutionary process, a unique and sacred path that parents and children take together. We raise each other as children and parents, every step guided by life's mystery and the parent's and the child's inherent wisdom. This book invites the reader to rethink what parenting means placing it in the larger context of social, historical, and global issues. As a medical doctor and mental health counselor, I encounter on a daily basis how vital it is that we all learn to parent ourselves, our children, our communities, and the environment. Dr. Menken's book is a must read for everybody who cares about the state of our relationships and our world."

—Pierre Morin, M.D., Ph.D.

Coauthor of *Inside Coma* and

clinical director of Lutheran Community Services Northwest

"Dr. Menken's amazing book, *Raising Parents, Raising Kids*, is a much-needed wake-up call, challenging us to turn away from the distractions and diversions of the outer world and turn inward to cultivate our rich and nourishing inner worlds. This book is a treasure trove of insightful stories, advice, and guidance for parents, therapists, teachers, and all of us interested in growing our inner lives, and becoming more emotionally and spiritually intelligent. In a very concrete and easy-to-read style, Menken addresses conflict, bullying, jealousy, power issues, and a host of other topics relevant to parents through a lens of process-oriented psychology, *Raising Parents, Raising Kids* is a powerful reminder of the sacred journey of parenting, whether we are parenting children or our own inner lives."

—Julie Diamond, Ph.D.

Coauthor of *A Path Made By Walking*

raising parents raising kids

Hands-on Wisdom for the Next Generation

Dawn Menken PhD

Foreword by Arnold Mindell PhD

BELLY ⬤ SONG
press
Santa Fe, New Mexico

WITHDRAWN

Published by: Belly Song Press
518 Old Santa Fe Trail
Suite 1 #626
Santa Fe, NM 87505
www.bellysongpress.com

Cover image: Howard Menken
Book cover design: Howard Menken
Interior design and production: Ann Lowe

Raising Parents, Raising Kids is factually accurate, except that names, locales, and minor aspects of some chapters have been altered to preserve coherence while protecting privacy.

Printed in the United States of America on recycled paper

PUBLISHER'S CATALOGING-IN-PULICATION DATA
Menken, Dawn.

Raising parents, raising kids : hands-on wisdom for the next generation / Dawn Menken ; foreword by Arnold Mindell. -- Santa Fe, NM : Belly Song Press, c2013.

p. ; cm.

ISBN: 978-0-9852667-4-5 ; 978-0-9852667-5-2 (PDF) ; 978-0-9852667-6-9 (Kindle) ; 978-0-9852667-7-6 (ePub)
Includes bibliographical references and index.
Summary: A cutting edge approach to parenting, based on process-oriented psychology, that goes beyond the conventional "how to" book. Using anecdotes from the author's practice and personal life along with practical tips and exercises, this book for parents, educators, and counselors covers such topics as children's inner and emotional lives, power and autonomy, and cultivating a life of meaning. New inroads are made to address power struggles, conflict, bullying, diversity, and social issues. Explores typical challenges to the parenting relationship, parents' own personal growth, and inspires the joy and wonder of the parenting experience.--Publisher.

1. Parenting. 2. Child rearing. 3. Parent and child. 4. Child development. 5. Child psychology. 6. Bullying. 7. Interpersonal conflict. 8. Parents--Life skills guides. 9. Parents--Attitudes. I. Title.

HQ769 .M46 2013   2013940350
649/.1--dc23   1310

1 3 5 7 9 10 8 6 4 2

Also by Dawn Menken

Speak Out! Talking About Love, Sex and Eternity
New Falcon Press

 **acknowledgements**

My dreams had hinted at the ecstatic experience that awaited me once I would become a parent. And although my dreams were somehow prophetic and uncanny, I did not anticipate the beautiful child that would come into my life. My deepest gratitude goes to my son, Theo Ackermann, for opening up new paths that I could hardly imagine and for guiding me in the awe-inspiring world of parenting.

I am also grateful to and feel enriched by the many parents and children that I have worked with over the years. Thank you for your inspiration, heartfelt expression, and courage. It is my hope that the stories used in this book will be encouraging to others.

My approach to parenting and working with children and families is based in the paradigm and theory of process-oriented psychology, also known as process work. I am forever indebted to its founder Dr. Arnold Mindell. I have cited his works throughout the book, however my entire way of thinking is steeped in process work and is reflected in my approach and writings. No words can adequately express my profound gratitude to him for the gift of his spirit that has inspired his life work and has enriched countless others.

Many thanks to Julie Diamond, Jan Dworkin, Renata Ackermann, Amy Mindell, Silvia Camastral, Jessica Hunsberger, and Ruth Menken for instructive, helpful, and encouraging feedback. I want to thank the Process Work Institute in Portland, Oregon and the students who came to my first series of classes, in which many of these ideas were initially presented. Thanks to Sarah Jade Steinberg for a first edit of this manuscript. I am deeply indebted to Julie Diamond for her vision, enthusiasm, and skillful editing. Big thanks to Howard Menken for the beautiful cover design. I am extremely grateful to David Bedrick and Lisa Blair of Belly Song Press; their enthusiastic support and expertise to bring this book to press has warmed my heart.

I want to thank my loving partner, Renata Ackermann; it has been a sacred and profoundly meaningful journey to be on this path with you.

 **contents**

foreword

Parenting is a central issue in today's world. Our attitude towards parenting determines not only how we deal with our children, but also how we deal with ourselves and with those around us in our local and global communities. Good parenting can contribute to reducing the harm we do to ourselves and others and, at best, help create a more sustainable planet.

Raising Parents, Raising Kids is a most process-oriented approach to children, parenting, family life, and community. Throughout the book, the child shines forth, appearing not only as the learner, but also as the teacher helping parents grow. Dr. Menken shows that parenting is, in part, something we can learn from the child. She emphasizes the need to nurture and explore our inner lives and reminds us of the mystery and meaning of life. She highlights the inherent wonderment and natural spirituality of the child, illuminating the child's own sense of the universe.

Dr. Menken suggests that having children and becoming a parent is a calling and it is not necessarily the right path for everyone. She advises that each follow her or his personal dreaming. For those who choose the parenting path, her work illuminates details about different parenting styles, typical conflicts between parents, and offers new ways to resolve them.

Raising Parents, Raising Kids awakens us all to our capacity for "elder-ship," that is, our potential for parenting our planet. Dr. Menken inspires us with practical examples and creative solutions to the common problems parents face, whether social issues, conflict, or just everyday family life and school situations. I personally believe—and know—that learning how to work out conflict issues should begin in the earliest phases of life, in kindergarten, if not earlier. Menken's book enlightens us to the many ways this is possible.

Reading this book, I was brought back to my own childhood and found resolutions and insights into my personal history. Dr. Menken's capacity to appreciate the unique spirit and experience of each child is a gift not only to parents, educators, and caregivers, but also to any of us who are compelled to unfold and come to know our deepest selves.

—Dr. Arny Mindell
Yachats, Oregon
March 2013

 **introduction**

This book birthed itself effortlessly and with great joy, and finally, with urgency. My path as a parent was present before I gave birth to my son. I have always enjoyed my work with children and families. I am continually inspired and delighted by the open and unpredictable nature of babies and young children. I appreciate the unique voice, the courage and vitality of older youth, and I have strong feelings about our schools being genuine places where kids thrive in their pursuit of learning, and can experience the great diversity inside themselves and in the world. The parent inside of me has presented herself repeatedly throughout my life in my desire to care for, understand, and appreciate all beings as part of the human family.

Parenting is about making relationship; and although this is obvious, we can lose sight of this basic path. Relationship is about curiosity, exploration, and learning. Can we meet our children with curiosity and discover who *they* are? And can we give our children the opportunity to get to know us as well? Too often we think children need molding; we fill them up with our values and perceptions. While it is true that they learn from us, they also thrive and flourish through our loving attention and our interest to create a good relationship.

Parenting is also a process. By this I mean that parenting is an experience. It is a continual evolution and not an end state. When we view parenting as a process, we are open to flowing with the unpredictable nature of experience. It means we are always growing. As a process-oriented practitioner I help people follow and embrace their experiences, the familiar as well as that which is unknown or emergent. My approach stems from the work of Dr. Arnold Mindell, founder of process-oriented psychology.[1] A process-oriented approach embraces the mystery of life and acknowledges each person's unique nature. Therefore, what feels like a good direction for one parent and child will not be a good fit for another.

This is why there are so many parenting books! One book or one direction is not any better than another; it is a matter of what resonates for you and your child. This becomes immediately apparent when new parents are confronted with a variety of approaches to sleeping and nursing! Being able to follow your own inner process, your feelings, deepest beliefs and dreams, as well as those of your child, should be your guide. The relationship between you and all of the complex and sometimes conflicting feelings you may experience is an entry into the world of parenting. Even Dr. Benjamin Spock, who published his seminal book in 1946, which has been revered and disputed, had the following message to women, "You know more than you think you do."[2] While it is true there is a lot to learn about parenting, this statement encourages parents to trust their deepest feelings and inner wisdom, that which is beyond conscious knowing.

In my approach this means not only supporting conscious goals and ideals, but also unfolding and supporting the less known and mysterious world. Following process means exploring what we already know, including those experiences that are less known, emergent, and at the periphery of our awareness. Therefore, this book is not a "how-to" book, but a book that supports parents, caretakers, and educators to follow the unique path of their parenting process and the unique path of their child's development.

CHILDHOOD DEVELOPMENT AND PROCESS

It is important to track the development of your child and there are many informative books that can help you with that. At the same time, I encourage parents to follow the individual developmental process of their child. Certainly books on sleeping, nursing, or tips to deal with the toddler or teenage years can be enormously helpful. Yet I invite you to entertain the idea that your child and your relationship with your child are unique and have their own special paths. Your child's nature, your own inner experience as a parent, your dreams, and the relationship between you and your child are your best guides.

Being in tune with your child's inner development is one of the joys of parenting. And so is observing how your child perceives the world, formulates experiences, discovers new abilities, deals with challenges, develops self-awareness, and relates to others. It is thrilling to watch our children grow and develop and to celebrate their milestones. Our curiosity, attention, and delighted reactions nurture their growth and reinforce their learning.

Development and learning are always happening, and when we can hook into it, our experience of parenting becomes more enriching. My son was always an energetic and physical person, and when he was between the ages of two and four, he would enjoy going for a run with me. I had a sense that it looked pretty odd from the outside—having such a young child jog next to me—and certainly, this would not be right for all children. But it suited his nature and his energy. He also had a lot of stamina for hiking. However, at around age four, that began to change. His attention was less focused on the pure physicality of enjoying a run or a hike. His mind needed more engagement. He began to count; counting animals that we saw, counting how many steps we had to climb. After he mastered counting, hikes became opportunities to practice different motor skills, like throwing rocks. Could we hit a target or skip a stone? These are all certainly ordinary events, but when you see them in the context of your child's development they can become quite extraordinary adventures.

FOLLOWING THE PROCESS OF THE CHILD

If we are awake, children show us the kind of parenting they need. Everyday is a lesson in how to parent; nothing extra need be created. Life itself creates lessons and challenges. Nature teaches us about sunshine and storms, gentle and strong winds. The unfolding of life and the natural development of your child will show you the way. If only we can follow it!

Each of us has our own intrinsic direction, something ineffable that leads us in the discovery of life and furthers our inner development. To follow the process of a child means to unfold their inherent wisdom, support their unique nature, and be open to explore the fun and trouble that emerge in this journey called life.

One day, when my son was four, he and his friend were running up and down our block, a little too far for my comfort. The other boy's mother and I kept calling for them to come back. They ignored us, and after a few calls, we jumped into action, ran after our boys and scooped them up. We said goodbye to our friends and I took Theo into the house. "I want to talk to you," I said. "Okay Mama," he said and went straight to his room and brought out a little chair into the living room. He directed me to sit in the chair. He then brought another chair for himself and sat down directly across from me. He looked right at me and said, "What do you want to talk about Mama?" I told him I get frustrated when he doesn't listen to me because cars and streets are dangerous and I get afraid for his safety. He looked at me thoughtfully and said, "Oh, I won't do that again Mama. I will listen better. I'm so sorry."

That was a huge learning moment. His process showed us the way to approach this situation. He demonstrated to me that he could set up a container for a discussion. He could be serious, respectful, and have an important dialogue. Those two chairs were very important to him. He kept them in the living room for three days and told people when they came in the house what they were for. He showed me a method of how to parent him, how we could talk together and how important it is for him to set up the proper container. These are subtle signals that guide us in the parenting of our children.

Throughout the book, readers will find a multitude of examples of how to follow the innate wisdom and direction of their child's process, while discovering and exploring their own parenting styles. I use a variety of examples of children of different ages and share many stories from my own home life because these are often more intimate and might not come up in a private practice setting. My son, Theo, has given me his permission to share our experiences. It is important to me that I have his permission and that he feels respected and empowered in anything that I share publicly. Identities that I share from my work with children and parents have all been altered to ensure confidentiality.

My hope is that this book inspires the reader to follow the process of children, to notice what seems more unusual, incomprehensible or mysterious, and then to approach a child with curiosity and wonder. This attitude in itself is parental in that it cares for all dimensions of a child.

Raising a child means raising a parent. We celebrate the birth of children; I also want to celebrate the birth of parents. This book is meant to excite you about parenting, to grow yourself as a parent, and to develop a more intimate relationship with your child. I am particularly passionate about parenting that supports children's inner lives. Too often, inner experience is disavowed and not appreciated as a nourishing force that sustains us. I also address "power" as central to parenting—how to explore and appreciate the power dynamics that emerge with children and offer tips to help parents use power wisely.

This book will also engage readers to think about how their child relates to the world around her. I explore how to make social issues, diversity experiences, and the present-day effects of history and oppression relevant. I offer ideas and support for dealing with bullying, including tips for victims, bullies, and bystanders. I have also included a conflict resolution toolbox that offers useful pointers for all ages. A section on the process of parenting addresses those who are considering parenthood, the growth of parents, as well as some of the typical couple's issues that emerge in the parenting relationship.

Enjoy this sacred journey!

the inside scoop

Nurturing the Inner Life of Children

I have a special place inside my mind. It feels like a warm sun.
I wonder if it is the same sun inside that is outside.
—Maya, age 7

Children ask themselves big questions. They might not always verbalize them, but they reflect, wonder, and respond creatively in play and fantasy. Young children are deeply engaged with their inner worlds, inspired by imagination and creativity, and much closer to the spirit that moves them. As adults, we marvel when we hear our child's ingenious formulations of how they view the world and themselves. As they mature, often times, their sense of wonder and curiosity lessens.

In a world that often values material possessions, reason, and linear thought over imagination, spirit, and play, it is challenging to find support for valuing our inner lives. And yet, it is our deep connection with ourselves that gives life meaning. The following two chapters are about nourishing and cultivating the inner life of children, and, as a perk, our own.

WHAT IS AN INNER LIFE?

An inner life is full of imagination and creativity. It includes subjective experiences and feelings that we marginalize. While an important part of parenting is educating your child about the physical and social world, it is just as essential to educate your child about the world of imagination, feelings, and dreaming. To only emphasize the rational and material world of our experiences neglects the dreaming world of possibility.

For example, take a six-year-old boy who complains about other kids in his class being stronger and bigger. From a rational standpoint he is right; others are physically bigger. But when he comes into my office he grabs the biggest bear and stomps on all the other stuffed animals with it. In his fantasy life, or dreaming mind, he *is* the big, strong bear. His inner fantasy and playful instincts draw him to select an animal that reflects his power, an experience he misses in his everyday life. His inner life teaches him to express himself and use his powers. He also has recurring nightmares of a giant. The dream world informs him that he is not just a six-year-old boy, but a giant with great powers. The dream world is always trying to awaken us to connect with all of who we are.

An inner life means being open to all of who we are. Can we value our unique nature and cultivate a curiosity about the parts of ourselves with which we are less familiar? This means being fluid, being able to change, move, learn, and explore. Society values some behaviors more than others. Hence, when we raise our children we may tend to only value those behaviors and traits that culture supports and neglect or discourage qualities that are more unusual or less familiar. We need to nourish the uniqueness in our children and embrace all of who they are.

An inner life means exploring and knowing our emotional wholeness. We need to teach our kids about emotional intelligence, the ability to be aware of what they feel, to have the courage to express feelings and to notice what others feel.[1] Too often I find that emotional intelligence isn't valued enough in the parenting process. For instance, in a typical family conflict, the daughter says something nasty to the mother. The mother sends the daughter to her room for being disrespectful. This teaches the daughter that certain language is bad and she will be punished. But she will still think those thoughts about the mother. Sending the daughter to her room does nothing for the relationship between them. Teaching emotional intelligence would mean showing the daughter that her words hurt. The mother can express her feelings, not to make the daughter feel guilty, but as a genuine consequence of a hurtful statement. Parents rarely show the hurt they feel in relationship to children. Parents get angry and they punish, but rarely do they show hurt. When parents show their genuine feelings, kids learn they have an impact on another human being. They learn empathy, they learn relationship skills, and they learn how to get along with feelings and with others.

In addition, it is important to teach children about emotions and the ability to notice them in others. For example, I do a lot of work in the playground: two children have taken the hat of another child and won't give it back. I ask the two kids to look at the one without his hat. "Does he look happy?" I ask. "No," they answer. "How do you think he feels?" I ask. Now we are talking about feelings, and we are learning to notice other people's feelings, not just our own.

An inner life means that we emphasize learning and meaning. Is our life meaningful? Have we learned something? A successful life is often defined as getting somewhere, acquiring things, winning and losing, good and bad. Success is also about meaning and learning. These are essential components in life, because when times are tough, and life doesn't go your way, when friends hurt you or you lose a game, fail a test, or someone dies, there is always wisdom to be discovered. Giving children the tools to value their inner lives supports them to learn to parent themselves and draw meaning from the challenges of life experience.

Nurturing an inner life requires a special kind of attention, a second attention.[2] Young children naturally have it. This is the part of you that notices feelings, fantasies, and dreams. It is the inner awareness that can focus on irrational and subjective experiences. Children naturally have this awareness and it comes out in their play. For example, a five-year-old boy comes into my practice and notices a piece of golden material. He goes over to it and puts it on his head, and says he is now a princess with flowing long hair. He begins to move and sway like a princess. We all have little flirts and fantasies like this, but rarely do we allow ourselves to notice and act on them. With kids it is all part of a game. An older boy has already marginalized that awareness and will think it's foolish. But he will go home that night and dream about a princess. The younger child's second attention is still active and grabs the chance to engage and play with fantasies.

SECOND ATTENTION AND DREAMING

With an active inner life the veil between dreams and reality is permeable and fluid. For instance, consider this conflict between four-year-old Jake and six-year-old Sam. They are in a room with a couch and chairs.

Jake: This is a stone.
Sam: It is not. It's a pillow.
Jake: It is a stone, a great big stone.
Sam: Can't you see Jake it is a brown pillow!
Jake: It is not! It is a big stone!
Sam: Mommy—tell Jake the pillow is not a stone!

Who is right? Both are. Sam is speaking from the perspective of consensus reality. The reality we all consent to; the "real" world. Sam is adamant about his view; he is now in school and is learning to value this view of reality. Jake's worldview is more marginalized, although accepted in young children. He is in the world of dreamland where imagination and creativity are just as important and real to him.[3]

Supporting children's inner lives means supporting our children to dream. By dreaming, I don't just mean nighttime dreams, but also feelings, fantasies, and the imaginary world. As we get older, these experiences are disavowed, which is why they emerge in our nighttime dreams.

As we can see in the conflict between Jake and Sam, young children naturally live in the world of dreaming. Their second attention is intact, which allows them to slip easily into fantasy and play. Our first attention picks up the important cues that emphasize and reinforce the material world. Our second attention is that creative ability to dream and take things further than what seems apparent. Second attention is important even for adults because it includes our ability to see beyond the material world and value perceptions that seem "other."

Thus, second attention gives us the ability to see many perspectives at once. It gives value to the seeds of creation, spinning them further by embellishing them and taking them seriously. The artist doesn't just paint from his known skill-set, but gives value to what happens spontaneously or even appears as a mistake. His second attention is at work, led by his imagination, feeling life, and fantasy. When a musician improvises or writes a piece of music she dips into the world of dreaming, the ineffable feelings and spontaneous impulses that allow her to connect with her deepest self.

Most parents are terrific in helping children to develop their first attention. But how can we support children to maintain their second attention, their natural dreaming intelligence? What does this look like as a parenting style? It means we value and engage with them in dreamland. We remain curious and enter their world. Remember the boy above who saw a piece of golden cloth in my office and said he was a princess? We can support his second attention by joining his world, and saying things like: "Yes, that is beautiful hair dear princess. I love how it sways in the wind. Can you feel it? What is it like?" As your play progresses and you also engage with this dreaming reality, your second attention might notice another role in the drama; suddenly you are a dragon going after the princess. Entering into play and fantasy is a way to develop second attention.

When we correct children's perceptions by continually reinforcing consensus reality, we cut off a child's ability to dream and be creative (and we cut off their ability to relate to and accept less known parts of themselves). Such parents will say, "That's a piece of cloth, it's not hair," or "that's silly." Instead, try to pick up your own dreaming. Step into the dreaming world together with your child in the form of fantasy, art, or music. Use your second attention to notice the feelings that you dismiss and creatively dream with your child by following your own spontaneity. Dare to be silly and to step outside of cultural norms that define reality!

LIFE AS AN ADVENTURE

Parents can get totally inundated with domestic life. The tasks and chores that must be completed seem far from the world of dreaming, imagination, and creativity. Young children help to remind us that the world of dreaming is happening everywhere. Suddenly, errands become adventures! We are not going out to do mundane tasks; we are off on an adventure! We don't know what will happen or whom we will meet. We might find ourselves walking on ledges trying to escape villains. We might pick flowers and express our love. We might meet a mesmerizing street performer who will capture the fancy of our child. The world is ripe with discovery and adventure.

While we rush around, doing errands and getting things done, our kids are living outside consensus reality in dreamtime. If we joined them, maybe our stressful day of errands could be a lot more fun and relaxing! When we dream together, we may realize that we don't have to push to get through the day. Life is not just a checklist of chores; in fact, errands can even be quality time with our children. When we remember that dreaming is everywhere, domestic life becomes creative instead of burdensome.

Experiment with letting your child take the lead. Once in a while, try to put aside your urgency to hurry and get things done. Instead of dragging your child from one errand to the next, follow her attention and let her take the lead. Sometimes the world presents us with jarring, surprising, or unpleasant experiences. But these too are moments of adventure, full of potential meaning and learning.

I remember being out in the city when my son was about four and he had to pee with no bathroom in sight. He just couldn't hold it and so I let him pee on a tree. Right then, a man stopped his car and scolded us. I defended us and said that even though he may have a point, the way he spoke to us was nasty and hurtful. Theo felt pretty badly, and I comforted him and told him that I don't like people interacting that way. He agreed. This was a great opportunity to use our second attention to learn from what happened. So we explored this man as if he were a part of our adventure, a nasty villain that interrupted our fun! But how could we use and learn from his energy or message? We played around together, each of us acting out the man yelling at us. In Theo's imagination he transformed into a policeman. The "policeman" said that little boys had to be more aware of their bodies and that Theo was growing up and had to check in more about his peeing. Good point and good learning, and an example of how we can extract meaning and wisdom from life's more unpleasant circumstances.

THE WORLD OF DREAMS

Paying attention to your child's dreams nurtures children's inner lives. We discussed dreaming as experiences that do not necessarily go along with concrete reality, but represent the realm of feelings, imagination, and creative thinking. All of these experiences can be found in our nighttime dreams too.

Kids love dreams. Even if you don't know much about dreamwork, you can apply a basic premise: *everything in the dream is a part of you.* Dream images that seem most odd, unusual, and frightening are parts of ourselves that we don't identify with yet, or don't know much about. Therefore, dreamwork lends itself to the spirit of exploration and discovery, qualities that are at the heart of play. Most children love to play and enact their dreams, draw them, or re-create them in movement and fantasy.

Dreams often become a problem for children (and parents) when they are frightening. Nightmares are scary because they show us experiences that are less known to us. It is our normal identity, however, that is scared, not our totality. Once we step into the scary figure, play it out, and explore its energies, we are less fearful.

Many children between the ages of four and nine have a significant dream they remember throughout their lives, often a nightmare. Many of us can remember a central, significant or repetitive, intense or scary dream from childhood. These dreams are central to the essence of who we are and tell the story of our life myth.[4] These big dreams occur to young children just when they are becoming more aware of the outer world. The child identifies as small and young and sees everyone else as bigger. No one sees the great powers of the child, even the child herself! Therefore, it is often at this time in life that big powers appear in dreams and challenge the small and young identity. These powers are expressed in dreams as animals, monsters, "bad guys," or as awesome, magical, and unbelievable experiences. It is the children who are these awesome animals, allies, and powerful experiences—they just don't consciously know it!

In the light of day it is fun to play with these dreams. Your curiosity and sense of play can make nightmares less frightening. Ask the child to play out the witch, the big wind that blew them away, or the dog that bit them. Play around and get to know the special powers that these dream figures contain. Join the play and pace your child, watch for their feedback. Remember their fear is due to not having enough of an experience of the dream energies.

For example, I worked with a seven-year-old girl who dreamt that a witch was chasing her. She was very scared to even tell me the dream. I asked her what was scary about the witch. She said that the witch was flying through the air and was about to grab her with a giant-sized arm when she woke up. She would then scream and crawl into her parents' bed. I helped her with the fear by making a friendly environment where even witches are welcome. I moved my hand and swooshed it through the air and asked her if that was how the witch flew. She nodded in agreement and I said, "I like flying around like this with my hand, would you like to try it too?"

A flying hand was not that scary, so the girl joined me. We flew our hands around and sometimes crashed into each other. Pretty soon we decided we wanted to fly with our whole bodies. We stood up and began to swoosh around my office, arms wide, as if we were flying. I told her that I loved being a witch with her. We were having fun and I was intentionally pacing our play together so that she continued to feel comfortable.

I then felt free to suggest another step, "Let's fly around together and grab someone or something."

She squealed with delight, "Yes, let's get that monkey!" She swooped down and grabbed my monkey puppet. She flew with the monkey and then dropped it and said she wanted to get the turtle. Next came the cow, the panther, the donkey, and then the dog.

She was really enjoying grabbing the animals and by this time her energy had completely changed. She was not afraid, but rather bold and very directive, qualities that she usually did not identify with. In fact, at that time in her life she was having trouble at school making friends and the witch energy was showing her that she could be assertive; she could grab people and things that interested her.

Next, I told her I would pretend to be a child at school and asked her how the witch would make friends with me. She flew around the room, stopped in front of me, reached out her hand and said with great enthusiasm, "Come play with me Sabrina!"

The witch taught this girl how to be more assertive and to go after what she wanted. This was not a quality that came easily to her in everyday life. She was more fearful and felt unable to ask for things. As she gets older and becomes an adult, this dream of the witch may take on even greater meaning, as she feels challenged to go for things that may be less popular and conventional, but more aligned with her deepest aspirations. Indeed, the symbol of the witch is otherworldly, not the most conventional attribute for girls and women in our culture. Therefore, it is hard for her normal identity to embrace. The over-sized arm in the dream represents her ability to reach for what is sometimes experienced as unreachable.

Dreams show us experiences that are at the edge of what we feel we can do and hint at where we are growing. Just playing around with energies and qualities, without interpreting or thinking about them, can be fun and helpful to your child. She will pick up and integrate into life what she feels is possible.

TODDLERS AND DREAMS

Dreams show your child's development. One night I awoke to my son speaking in a far-away but clear voice, "I peed in the potty. I did it! Yeah!" An hour later, he muttered, "No diapers."

These are important things that a three-year-old dreams. He had been peeing in the potty at home for the past half-year taking gradual steps in his learning. Pooping in the potty had only happened a few times. However, he had not yet risked leaving home without a diaper and unfailingly would ask for a diaper when he felt a bowel movement on its way.

That morning, inspired by his dreaming, he did not wear diapers. We went out for brunch and he proudly walked out of the house for the first time, free and easy. His pants barely stayed on him without the extra material. At the restaurant he used a public toilet for the first time, and then a second time. Each time he was so proud and excited by his accomplishments that he yelled out like he did in his dreams.

WORKING THINGS OUT IN DREAMS

Kids work things out in dreams like we all do. Dreams bring new patterns, new experiences, and answers that can't be found through rational thought. It is fun to work with kids on their dreams through their play and support them to explore new experiences that are emerging in their dream worlds. Dreams allow us to work out problems and challenges that we may not yet have the answer to in everyday life.

Take a six-year-old boy who had recurring nightmares of a lion chasing him. We had explored the energy of the lion in our play together and he enjoyed the experience of strength and confidence. He said he was a protector against "bad things." One day he strutted into my office and proudly reported that he dreamed of the lion chasing him, but this time when the lion came to snatch him he raised his up his arms and roared. He exuberantly acted out the dream for me and claimed he had new powers. His mother also reported to me that first grade seemed to be going really well, that he seemed more confident and felt more at home in the school. Connecting with the energy of the lion allowed him to make big inner changes that were also reflected in his dreams and put a halt to his nightmares.

Remember that dream-life is always present at night, but also in the unpredictable experiences and life events that occur during the day. One weekend when my son was seven and a half, he was crashing into everything. He accidentally broke a window and crashed a clock down to the floor. He had always been an energetic child and very physical. We had been trying to get him to be more aware of how he used his physical energy. He had an easier time identifying with crashing but less with the things that he crashed into. In other words, he had good knowledge of himself as an active and kinesthetic child, but didn't know his quieter or stiller self, and felt little patience for such states.

That night he went to bed and reported the following dream in the morning. "I dreamed I was a starfish and I was glued to the sand. I was lying on my back looking at the sun. It was nice and warm. I thought I would be bored, but I began to dream."

I was fascinated and excited by this dream and by his experience of a new part of himself. The experience of the starfish that lies still, glued to the sand and can gaze at the sun and dream, was a new part of him. Like many energetic kids his age he experienced himself as active and energetic. Less known was the experience of a starfish, feeling and dreaming.

FAMILY DREAM TALK

Dreams are doorways into new and exciting worlds of experience. It can be challenging at first to find the way through that door without much experience working with dreams. Our everyday minds are usually surprised by dreams since they seem weird or terrifying to us. This is because the dream brings up energies and experiences that are outside of our known identity. Therefore, information is presented symbolically in order to circumvent the exceedingly discriminating conscious mind. The main point of all this dream theory is to have an open mind! If you can be curious and open about the strange images and energies in your dreams, you can have fun with dreams with your family!

For instance, take a child who dreams of a man with a big brain who is controlling everything. Ask your child to imagine being a man with a big brain—this is a child who needs support to use all of her brainpower. Or in another case, a child dreams of a tiger chasing him. Play with the tiger energy; make claws and pounce. How could this energy be useful in your lives?

Dreams can also give us answers to questions we have. Just recently, my son played in a challenging basketball tournament where his team lost all of their games. Afterwards, he shared with me that in his mind he was wondering if he was able to play with such physically strong players.

He said it was a question he was turning over in his brain. I said that maybe the answer would come, and maybe he would have a dream that night. The next morning he dreamt that he was climbing a ladder to the top and was very proud of himself. He then remembered his question from the night before and recognized the meaning of his dream. "Yup, I certainly think I can play with these players," he beamed. As he told the dream and connected with that energy, his whole demeanor changed. The dream had given him a new confidence that he needed. 'Climbing to the top of the ladder,' became our insider family motto for the season.

DREAMWORK PLAY

Parenting the whole child means following dream-life, even if you don't know much about working with dreams. You needn't think about interpreting dreams; just play with the energies, figures, and experiences in dreams. Let your fantasy and imagination take you into other worlds. Young children naturally dip into this world and show us the way to discover and explore ourselves. Here are some suggestions on how to explore your child's dreams:

1. Include dreams in your every-day life. Enjoy sharing them in the morning.
2. Listen with a curious and playful attitude.
3. Take note of the figures and experiences that are unusual, frightening, or foreign. (These are usually not the figure of the dreamer, unless, of course, the dreamer is doing something unusual or out of the ordinary.)
4. Encourage play and exploration of these unusual figures and experiences by acting them out, drawing them, or moving like them.
5. Find the energetic essence of these dream experiences, play, enjoy, and befriend them!

THE BODY DREAMS TOO![5]

Encouraging children to experience their bodies is an important way of nurturing their inner lives. Our bodies absorb much of what our conscious minds disavow. Therefore, when we encourage kids to notice their body experiences, we support greater health and more self-awareness. Check in with your children and ask them how their body feels. Ask about different parts of the body and help them put together body experience with emotions and feelings. Ask them, "Is your heart beating really fast—are you excited or nervous? What kind of an animal would that fast heart be? Oh it's a horse, a wild one that wants to run around." When we relate to our younger children with such curiosity and put attention on body awareness they internalize this kind of focus as they mature. They are more able to notice how their body feels and understand its connection to emotions.

The body is a great anchor for our experiences and can help kids be aware of their emotions. Take ten-year-old Eliza who came to see me because of her rages. She would fly into rages at school, scream and kick the other girls, and hurt herself and others. We explored what brought on these rages. It was challenging for her to track what the trigger was because she was responding to extremely subtle signals from other children. For example, one girl would turn her back on her, or another would give her a "funny" look. She didn't consciously notice these things, but would just fall into a rage.

Our work revolved around noticing these cues and then interacting more directly with her peers. We role-played a variety of situations where she practiced and expressed herself instead of flying into a rage. "Why did you give me that kind of a look? Did you think I said something unusual or did I hurt you?" Or, "It hurts me when you turn your back on me. I would like to be included." Eliza had to learn to trust her perceptions and to give language to them. And finally, she needed courage to voice her experience. This seemed to be the most difficult part for her. I asked her where in her body she felt courage. She said that in the back of her head there was a tingly place where a wizard lived who was very brave. Here was a physical anchor for Eliza that she could rely on when she was challenged in her relationships with other girls. The tingly sensation in her head would remind her of the wizard and her courage. The next time I saw Eliza she was full of stories of how the wizard was helping her in her relationships.

THE DREAMING NATURE OF BODY SYMPTOMS

A delightful and kind nine-year-old girl was having some trouble at school with some rougher kids. She was an avid nail-biter and dreamt of an alligator with big teeth that was snapping at her. We played alligators together and she especially enjoyed my alligator puppet with large teeth. She snapped and bit all of my other puppets thoroughly enjoying herself. Within her dream and the compulsion to bite her nails was the one who could stand up for herself. She needed to grow her own "teeth"—an ability to take a stand and say "no" to others. The dream of the alligator gave her a fun way to explore this energy and enabled her to explore a new part of herself that also relieved her nail biting.

This example shows how dreams are connected to our body experiences.[6] The energetic qualities of our body experiences are dream-like in that they are mirrored in the visual imagery of our dreams. Body symptoms and experiences are dreams waiting to be explored. Everyone has body symptoms, young and old. Doctor visits and medicines are essential, as well as the whole range of alternative and health care practices available to us. In addition, we can learn about ourselves and at times even clear up body symptoms by also approaching them as a dreaming process.

A thirteen-year-old girl who suffered from allergies had the chance to work with me on the dreaming process of her allergies. Stella was allergic to a bunch of things including grass, dust, and cat hair. Her eyes, ears, and throat would get terribly itchy and she would feel congested. The itchiness was unbearable for her and she could hardly keep her hands out of her eyes. We decided to explore the itchy feeling. I took a pillow in my room and we imagined it was a head, designating places for her different facial features. Her job was to then show me on the pillow how the itch expressed itself in her eyes, ears, and throat. I wanted her to be the "itch," not just the victim of it. She used her fingers and began to gently "tickle" the affected areas of her allergy. "Let's imagine that itch was a person or a creature, what kinds of qualities would it have?" I asked.

"It is an annoying person!" Stella exclaimed.

"Yes, I know you are normally not annoying, but let's fool around and be *really* annoying," I suggested. I joined her and we began to be terribly annoying and bothersome; we tickled the pillow and ran away and we began to plan annoying schemes against her siblings and kids at school.

"This reminds me of some of the boys at school," she said. "I find them terribly annoying. They play pranks and try to embarrass me and my friends. I can't stand them!"

We discussed the situation at school and I learned that Stella ignored the boys and endured quite a bit of harassment. "I notice when we fool around together and imagine being annoying you smile and we seem to have fun. Do you notice that?" I asked.

"Yes, it is much better to be the one who annoys than the one who has to take it."

Stella was more identified with the part of her that "takes it," doesn't react, is easy-going, and doesn't make waves. Less known to her was a part of her that would react more and be "annoying" and stand up against things she doesn't like. At thirteen, she wanted boys to like her and, as a result, tolerated too much. This was a huge piece of her development as a young teenager learning to navigate the social world. Her ability to go against the grain, take a stand, resist peer pressures and social expectations was central to cultivating her self-esteem. The rest of our session focused on how she could do just that. We role-played different situations where she was not just a passive victim but could react to things as well. In one school scene she blurted out to the boys, "If you like me, how about if you just tell me instead of being so annoying!" She was thrilled to reveal the unspeakable truth and was excited to react more at school.

I saw Stella a month after our session and she proudly reported a bunch of situations where she was speaking out and "annoying" others. Her allergies had also seen some improvement and she found herself needing less medication.

Obviously, working on body experiences and symptoms can be rather complex, and you also need help from doctors—this work is not a medical substitute. However, playing with the body's energies and tapping into their wisdom can often bring some healing effects. Here is an exercise to try.

EXERCISE: WORKING WITH BODY SYMPTOMS

1. Ask your child to describe her body experience in detail.
2. Notice there are two experiences. One is what the symptom itself does and the other is how it makes your child feel. For example, if your child has a headache, the headache makes a pounding experience, but your child feels hurt and wants to lie down.
3. We want to play with the experience of the symptom itself. Ask your child to show you what the symptom does. Does it pound, create an itch, put pressure, make heat, make a stabbing pain, create dizziness, etc.?
4. Have your child become the symptom maker. She can do it on a pillow, on your body, on a stuffed animal, or whatever your imagination comes up with.
5. Play with that energy with your child. Make it into a game; use your imagination and fantasy.
6. Explore how that energy might be useful to your child. How can she embrace and use that energy instead of feeling victimized by it?

THE BODY AND THE INNER PARENT

Body-based experiences are a way to deepen the expression of love and connection and can help children when we are separated from them. Young children sometimes have a difficult time with transitions and fear separating from parents. Even older children, although they might not express it, on occasion feel this as well. Those moments are opportunities to help the child keep contact with us even when we are not present. Can we give them an inner experience of "mother" or "father" inside of themselves?

Find out where in your child's body "you" are located. "If Mama were to live inside of your body, where would she be?" Ask them what that body area feels like, the sensations and temperature. Does it have a color? Asking these kinds of questions helps your children to explore the physical and psychic sense of an inner parent. The feelings, colors, and images are experiences of you that your child can rely on when you are not present. Reinforce this experience by saying you will always be there. When you are on the phone, particularly with parents who are separated or divorced, you can say to children who miss you, "Can you feel me inside of your heart? I am there. My arms are holding you tight, always. Did you hear me today at school? I was sending you a special love message."

Speaking like this with your kids helps them to develop a bodily sense of who you are inside of them. Likewise, I say to my son, "You are always in my heart, I feel you there. It makes me smile in the middle of my day." They then pass this gift of expression on to others. When my son's pre-school teacher had to move and leave the state, she said she was going to miss the children. My son piped in, "Don't worry teacher Sara, you will always be in my heart."

As a new mother it dawned on me that I had a central parenting goal. My task was to support my son in developing an inner parent that could support his wholeness.

Being an older mom and aware of my own mortality gave me a sense not only of my importance in my son's life, but also of a presence that was beyond my physical being. How does he and will he parent himself? How can I support and model for him the kind of inner presence that gives an eternal sense of well-being and nurtures his wholeness?

This is a crucial therapeutic life issue for many of us. How do we parent ourselves? Being in practice now for over 25 years, I can say that most people work on this essential question in one way or another because most of us don't parent ourselves all that well. We have internalized parental voices or feelings that aren't supportive and most of the time we aren't even aware of it! We also incorporate institutional and societal views into our inner dialogue that don't necessarily support our deepest selves. Just think about how you talk to yourself when you look in the mirror! Most of us look through a cultural lens that measures and evaluates our appearance and we suffer terribly under that scrutiny. Many of us lack the inner parent who can nurture our deepest feelings, encourage us in our curiosity, and support our creativity. Too often we are run by inner criticism, harshness, and cultural norms that don't help us to grow and experience all of who we are.

By cultivating your child's inner life you help to create a model for an inner parent. The way you support your child's feelings and fantasies and the curiosity you encourage and model towards what is unknown will help your child to feel nourished and at home in his own skin. This special kind of attention and love sustains our children as they internalize our parenting.

One of my proudest moments happened when my son was about four years old. He was really sick one night and vomited. Afterwards he said to himself, "Good boy Theo." It was one of the first times I really noticed an independent parenting attitude in him. Something caring and comforting was present inside of him. I felt my work was done! (Not really, but in that moment I felt very gratified.)

Finding the inner parent might create a more relaxed attitude around death or during those times when we need to leave our children for whatever reason. Tell your child that you will always be there, no matter what. Our connection with them is beyond our physical bodies. We are eternal parts of our children that will never die. For many of us these are deeply held spiritual beliefs. But regardless of your religious or spiritual beliefs, you are present for your child when you are not around. Your voice and parenting style are present in your child in the way she talks and cares for herself.

As soon as my son could make sentences, he would speak of death as just a different form of contact. In his view, we would always be together; I was always an inner experience that he would feel close to. Of course, like every parent, I agonize over what will happen should we become separated. Another part of me, however, knows that I will always be with him.

Mama when you are one hundred years old
You won't fit in the house
You will be too big and live in the sky
You will be a bright shining star
And shine down on me
You will fly around and come visit me[7]

My son spoke and then sang these words when he was four and a half years old. I was amazed to hear him express such feelings. Yes, somehow our contact remains, even when my body doesn't fit in the house. In other words, my body is not a material body anymore, but a spirit, an eternal presence that is much bigger than my mere body could ever be. This sense of me will always live on in him.

When we foster this sense of an internal parent we give our child the tools to support their own inner life. When cultivated, this inner guide assists children to meet life with an attitude of openness and creativity and a curiosity to explore new experiences. This awareness gives a child a deep sense of belonging and connection and it opens them up to the richness that is inside of them.

heart and smarts

Fostering Emotional Intelligence

*It's good to be unique because you don't have to do what
other people tell you, but you can follow your heart.*

—Miles, age 10

Teaching kids to have an inner life means supporting our children
in their emotional experiences. In addition to supporting our child's
intellectual and social development, we also need to prepare them
emotionally and relationally. Many of us grew up in homes and families
where emotions were repressed, and, our world reflects a reality in which
our emotional wholeness is not always supported. Therefore, it is a big
challenge to support our child's emotional life as well as our own.

PUTTING LANGUAGE TO INNER EXPERIENCE

Emotional intelligence means being fluid and at ease with our
feelings.[1] It means we can track and express different feelings as they
arise. Young children are naturally masters at being fluid with feelings
unless they have been put down or threatened. Before school age, children show a range of emotional expression, although they might not
have the language for what they are feeling. They move relatively quickly
through a range of feelings: anger, hurt, need, and love. As children

get older they get the message that some feelings are taboo or socially forbidden.

Children need a language to express their feelings. They also need body awareness to notice the physical side of the emotions they feel. You can teach them this language by asking, "Is your heart racing? Do you feel like hiding? Do you notice your voice getting louder? You are moving away, is that because you are afraid?" Help your child describe and put language to their experiences. Offer them different possibilities: "Do you feel scared, nervous, sad, or shy?" You can make faces or gestures to show them the kinds of emotions people feel. There are some great books that focus on noticing and expressing feeling, some with beautiful illustrations of the different faces that go along with emotions.[2] Elementary schools are increasingly valuing feelings and including education around feelings and emotions in their curriculum.

When we can show and express our feelings even to our youngest children, we model an essential and basic awareness. We show that feelings are valuable and relevant in our relationships. Too often a child will ask us what we feel, and we say "nothing," or we put them off, or tell them not to worry. We don't take the time to simply explain what *we* are feeling. "Mommy is feeling frustrated because she can't get her work done." "Daddy is disappointed because he really wanted to spend private time with Mommy." Kids may even surprise you with their compassion or advice.

At the same time, kids are amazing in how they can discover new language to express feelings and body awareness. They come up with awesome, powerful, and poetic expressions to describe what they feel. I remember one day when my son had turned five and had been sick for a few days; we were having a yard sale, and he was inside watching TV. I came in to check on him, and he asked if I would stay and play cards with him. I said, "For sure, I'd love to." His eyes filled with tears. I asked him what he was feeling. He said, "My tears are not sad; they don't hurt. It is a love cry because I am so happy that you are staying in to play cards with me." His poetic description of his tears melted me. And his discovery was awesome—it was the first time he found himself crying not connected to pain or hurt. He found his own unique way of expressing the experience of being touched by love. "Love cry" has been a standard expression in our home ever since.

There is such a fine feeling distinction between different kinds of crying. He was learning what it was like to cry out of gratitude, love, or joy. Previously, crying had been about pain and hurt. Now he was differentiating crying from pain from crying from joy. His awareness came from believing in his inner experience and body feelings, and giving them voice. Teaching body awareness and helping children formulate and express their emotional life leads to increased emotional intelligence.

GIRLS, BOYS, AND FEELING

To this day, despite all the work that has been done in the area of gender awareness, my experience informs me that there are certain feelings that are more supported for boys, and others more for girls. Obviously, these things vary depending upon your culture, ethnic background, and the country you are from.

In general, in the U.S., and many other cultures, girls are still discouraged from expressing anger and being direct. Girls still receive the message early on to be "nice," to accommodate, and to not hurt others. Boys get less support to show sensitive feelings, tenderness, and still get the message that crying is weak. Obviously, this is not true for all, and many families are raising their girls and boys to embrace their entire emotional selves.

In *Odd Girl Out: The Hidden Culture of Aggression in Girls,* Rachel Simmons demonstrates that the culture of meanness and bullying between girls results from girls not being supported to have direct conflict with each other.[3] Consequently, girl aggression can be particularly nasty in its more covert expression. Relational aggression in which girls bully by isolating and spreading rumors is difficult to defend against, especially with the proliferation of social media. Conflicts between girls can become very entangled, even at a young age.

Seven-year-old Eve is good friends with Zella, but Zella is also friends with Sally. Zella and Sally have known each other since birth, and Eve and Zella know each other since kindergarten. When Zella is playing with Sally, Sally says Eve can't join in. Eve tells me she feels terribly hurt and doesn't have a chance to play with Zella. Though Zella feels badly about it, she can't tell Sally because it would hurt Sally who might get angry with her too. Have you lost me yet?

Many girls seem to more easily care-take and protect others, sacrificing their own feelings in the process. Because girls (and boys) are not encouraged to have a direct conversation and possibly risk potential disagreement, these kinds of feelings incubate and seep out through gossip and other forms of indirect communication, which inadvertently ends up creating more hurt and misunderstanding as the conflict escalates over time.

Girls are not the only ones having difficulties expressing anger. Boys, too, can be told not to express anger, or, are given the message, directly or not, that anger is the only emotion they can express. Rarely do children or adults learn how to express anger in a way that also supports relationship. Most of us are taught to overlook small hurts and upsets that often precede anger and we don't express those feelings until things build up to bigger explosions. Then we feel justified to "let someone have it." We let many opportunities pass us by to express our unhappiness or hurt until we are just so vengeful we end up having a big blow up. Anger is not an end in itself, but an important momentary emotion. It can be an invitation for more connection.

EMOTIONAL FLUIDITY

Encourage children to express anger and notice what happens next. This is crucial not just for children but for adults too. It's important to model for children the ability to move fluidly through different emotional experiences. This is a big part of emotional intelligence: that we can get angry, and then after expressing it, we change. And when we are on the receiving end of someone's hurt or anger, we are able to listen, change, and be affected. Anger is often just the beginning, and noticing what else we feel, is something children—and adults—need to learn. Our ability to engage with children genuinely through different feeling experiences helps to support emotional health and build life-long relationship skills.

Take twelve-year-old Jesse who is furious with her good friend Eliza. Apparently, Eliza had promised Jesse they would get together on Saturday. Eliza cancelled and said that her mother needed her to stay home. At school on Monday, Jesse heard that Naomi and Eliza had gone to the movies. Jesse was so hurt and angry she could hardly concentrate on her schoolwork. The next day at school, Jesse did not know how to talk to Eliza so she avoided her. When I saw the two girls, I encouraged Jesse to tell Eliza how she felt. Jesse was angry; the floodgates opened, as Jesse revealed many incidents where she had felt rejected by Eliza. Anger then turned to tears. Jesse tried to push away the tears and stay angry, but I asked her why she was crying. Jesse said she missed Eliza and expressed how important she was to her. Eliza then began to cry. I asked her what made her cry and Eliza said that she was touched by Jesse's feelings, but she also felt badly about something that was hard to say. She then admitted that she felt terrible because Naomi had invited her to the movies and that she really wanted Naomi to like her, so she cancelled her date with Jesse. The two girls continued their conversation moving through feelings of anger, hurt, betrayal, the need for love, and finally reconciliation.

Anger can also be the expression of frustration, particularly for kids. Kids get frustrated at not being heard, being overlooked or misunderstood, and being unable to complete a task or keep up with others.

Help kids to unfold the feelings in anger. Don't prevent anger, but engage or dance with it. If we don't support our children to express anger directly, they become frozen, develop a chip on their shoulder, or become self-loathing.

Take a teenager who goes into his room and won't talk to his mother. She says he can't play games on his computer until he does his homework. He is not easy to be with and carries a massive chip on his shoulder, barely greeting his mother and then retreating to his room. He freezes his mother out and displays feelings of disdain towards her. He can't express his anger. He has blown up a few times, but then cloisters himself away. In our session, I began to speak for him in a passionate and louder voice, "You don't understand me. I am angry with you. You just don't get it. You don't get me!" My prompt helped him to tell his Mom that he felt she didn't understand his passion for computers and gaming. He was incredibly creative and excited about gaming. She couldn't really understand and appreciate it and instead used it as a weapon to punish him. She didn't see the intelligence and creativity he had around it. This was the main thing he was angry with. Not doing the homework was a way to battle her, but deep down, he wanted to be seen for the amazingly intelligent and creative young man he was, and that he was making all of these wonderful things on the computer. His mother needed to open up and see something she couldn't appreciate and understand. After she did this, the freeze melted.

As you can see, it's critical that we help our kids to unfold their anger and frustration. Too often we just turn off from our children when they are angry. Try to listen to anger and hear what is underneath it. Hear the passion, need, or desperation. Oftentimes, underneath anger is hurt. Sometimes there is a need to be appreciated or to be seen as powerful. Anger often needs to be appreciated and felt. If we go against anger or forbid it, it usually escalates.

FORBIDDEN FEELINGS

Most cultures tend to support feelings of strength and power more than feelings of hurt or sadness, which are equated with weakness. Vulnerability, sensitivity, and inability are sometimes viewed as liabilities. As a result, people do not express such feelings except in the most intimate of relationships. In my view these are wonderful qualities that are marginalized and their beauty overlooked.

We need to teach kids that it is not just okay to cry, feel sad or inadequate, but it is human, and beautiful. Learning to stand for all of our humanity, including frailties and sensitivities, as well as our strengths and power, is essential. Many adults disavow these aspects of themselves and, as a result, children learn to as well. They learn to value the strength that is connected with willpower, accomplishment, and physical prowess. However, the strength of sensitivity is often over-looked and not celebrated. Yet, these vulnerable emotions have their own power; they move hearts and minds, and give us deeper connection to the essence of ourselves and others. It is this emotional power that allows us to express the need for tenderness and connection. It creates intimacy, the vital ingredient for sustaining and nurturing relationships.

Imagine a child who can stand up with strength and conviction for her sensitivity, saying things like, "That hurts me, please be more kind," or, "Please include me; it hurts to be left out." If that child is then met with teasing or unkind words, she could respond, "Teasing hurts. Why would you want to put me down? Does it make you feel powerful? I find it mean." Your child might not be well received, but she can feel good about herself. Standing strong for feelings promotes healthy self-esteem.

Imagine a child who says with pride that he doesn't know how to do something and feels good about asking for help or a child who isn't aware of the coolest music or trend and feels the self-confidence to assert it. Imagine that in the midst of conflict we don't have to pretend that we are cool and unaffected. We don't have to play hard to get and withhold love, but can see our ability to express love as a strength.

I am so thankful to J. K. Rowling for giving us a teenage hero whose greatest power is his love. Harry Potter is brave, strong, and clever, but he survived the attack of Voldemort, the evil wizard, because of the love he received from his mother.[4] Dumbledore, wizard extraordinaire, explains to Harry that such a love has given him a deep power that can never be penetrated: "Your mother died to save you. If there is one thing Voldemort cannot understand, it is love. He didn't realize that love as powerful as your mother's for you leaves its own mark. Not a scar, no visible sign . . . to have been loved so deeply, even though the person who loved us is gone, will give us some protection forever." I am hopeful that this message is not lost on the billions of readers who have been inspired and delighted by Rowling's books.

FEEDBACK AWARENESS

Teaching emotional intelligence to children also means helping them notice feedback from others, specifically emotional feedback. This is what develops empathy, sensitivity, and social skills. For example, imagine you are one of a group of parents on duty on the playground, and the kids are playing tag. The kid who is "it" is really slow and has been trying for a long time to tag someone else, but can't. He is getting more and more frustrated and begins to cry a little. Another parent comes in and says, "How about if someone else is 'it'?" That is fine. But additionally, you could say, "Hey, do you guys notice what Sam might be feeling?" Then the kids will notice and talk about it. "Well, what do you think we should do?" Then the kids come up with suggestions. They want to comfort him or they decide someone else should be "it." As parents, we quickly make decisions and suggestions based on the feedback we see, but we can help our children to notice feelings around them.

Here are some simple questions to help build a child's awareness of emotions:

- Sally is standing outside of the circle. What do you think she might feel?
- Joe is moving away from those kids. Why do you think he is doing that?
- What kind of a face or expression does Uncle Charles have? Do you think he likes it when you charge into him?

Not only will your child learn to be more aware of her own feelings and those of others, but she will also learn to express herself and engage people. She will be able to make suggestions and reach out to others. She can then include Sally who is standing outside of the circle: "Sally, would you like to join us?"

EXERCISE: EXPLORING FORBIDDEN FEELINGS

In order to nurture and appreciate the diversity of expression in our children, we need to be more open to our own feeling life. The following is an exercise to explore the more marginalized feelings in your family.

1. Which emotions are marginalized or not really expressed in your home?
2. What do you have against those emotions and feelings?
3. Can you appreciate these parts of yourself? Many of us are against certain feelings because we are afraid of them, have been hurt by them, or just don't know enough about them.
4. See if you can open up to those feelings in some way or consider exploring them with some outer support.
5. Imagine playing like a child. Children try on all kinds of roles and emotions in play. We have a lot to learn from them here. How about "playing" angry or hurt. Ask your child to join you.

Children often express feelings that make parents feel uncomfortable. They can pick up the disavowed and forbidden feelings and this usually creates tensions within the family. For example, Daniel is a physical and spirited five-year-old. He can be volatile, aggressive, and loud. The family feels he is a disturbance. When I work with the mother it quickly becomes apparent that she has little contact with her own loud, assertive, and more physical nature. She gets on quite well with her older son who is quieter and more like her. Daniel has a lot of rough behavior towards his mother. While working with the mother, she explores some of the difficulties she has with such behavior and remarks she was brought up to be quiet and contained. We did an exercise similar to the one above; it helped her to pretend she was a child, specifically in this case, her son. We wrestled around and spoke loudly, and she realized it was actually fun! The following week, she reported to me that she engaged with Daniel with this more active and physical style and he loved it. In fact, they had such a good connection, they ended up giggling on the floor and Daniel said he wanted to play with his mother like this every day.

EXPLORING FEARS

Fear is an important emotion in the spectrum of human experience and comes up quite frequently with children. Understanding something about fear can help parents, caretakers, and educators intervene more meaningfully with children.

Many of us tend to become fearful of what we do not know, of that which is outside our comfort zone. Yet others meet the unknown with curiosity and enthusiasm. Sometimes a child will respond to a new event with curiosity and at another moment with trepidation. Going to school or to the doctor, getting an injection, performing on stage, or even seeing a dead body, are some common moments in life in which fear is evoked.

Parents can help children by preparing them beforehand. Role-play is extremely useful. Imagine the new classroom together and play out the teacher and other children. Go through all of the school's expectations and have your child play all of the roles in order to get a sense of herself in that new environment. Show her what it will be like when she gets an injection. Give her a quick little pinch on her hand and show her how fast it will be. Have her do it to you. Then, when she gets the shot, have her squeeze your hand at the same time. This has the effect of putting the child's attention on the one who is giving the shot instead of the one who is receiving it. Make a fun noise that goes along with the injection, like "ping."

Together imagine the performance your child fears and role-play it. Have him take the role of the audience too. What does the audience think and feel when it watches him? Are there loving eyes or critical ones? Help him explore and transform critical views and take in loving ones. What is the difference in performing at home or on a stage at school? Such exploration goes a long way to helping a child feel more secure.

When visiting nursing homes and hospitals or attending funerals prepare children by describing the situation. Talk about it, draw pictures about what people might look like, show them with your body, and demonstrate different speech or movement patterns they might encounter. This will support your child in facing new experiences, and do so in a way that allows for imagination, play and the fullness of their feeling nature. I will expand on this in Chapter 7, The Big Questions.

Besides preparing children for the unknown, help a child find an ally or a totem. Ask your child who is their biggest supporter and who makes them feel most at home. It could be you, another family member, a friend or an imaginary friend, a pet or stuffed animal. Help her feel connected to this ally, to even feel the ally inside her body, or see the ally in her mind or hear its voice. You can find a totem by asking your child if there is a special object that makes him feel loved or at home. He can carry this special object in his pocket and touch it or think about it when he needs it. Some years back when my son had a challenging encounter in the playground he decided to take a special necklace of mine and wear it to school the next day. He called it his "bully shield" and wore it for a couple of days. It gave him a certain inner strength and sense of protection at school.

It is important to support children this way when they are facing a change. We often try to provide a sense of familiarity and security for our children, yet the world is a place of constant movement and flux. How we deal with the changes of life teaches our children how to encounter change. Are we able to flow with change and disturbance? Can we find meaning, learning, or adventure in the surprising elements of life? When our plans are thwarted, disappointment is natural. But then what? Can we also be resourceful, notice that another experience is emerging, and adapt to what life presents us? When parents model this fluid view of life, children will pick it up.

FEARS AS POTENTIAL POWERS

Often our fear of the unknown is the fear of a power we have not yet explored or embraced. I already discussed the childhood dream and nightmares as energies that are great powers. Children (and some adults as well) tend to identify as small and powerless. The events and energies that emerge in the childhood dream are frightening because we are not connected enough with them. The same phenomenon happens in waking life. We become fearful of people who display a behavior or energy that is less known to us. A young teen is afraid of her critical teacher. And yet, when we play out the teacher, the girl realizes she, too has lots of criticisms that she normally holds back. In fact, her criticism is an analytical power and ability to use her mind in a new way. At first, this power represents itself as a fear of her teacher. By embracing her own critical and analytical abilities she began to feel more comfortable with her teacher. She also found herself wanting to challenge and deeply engage her teacher around her studies.

Work with your child by naming the energy or experience they fear. Then gently step into the experience and explore it. By playing with it and discovering the energy, we can befriend and transform it into a power.

1. Have your child describe what they fear.
2. Support their fear and be gentle.
3. Then suggest you play a game to help them with their fear. Encourage them to play it out, to be the person, thing or experience that they fear. Do it together.
4. What is the basic energy of the frightening thing? Get beyond the content and just stay with the energetic experience.
5. How can that experience be a basic power that your child might need?

VALUING FEAR

Too often we teach children to "get over" fear. We tend to override our own experience of fear as well. We try to be brave and strong for our kids. However, fear is an important emotion. Often it takes more strength and courage to acknowledge fear. It is an emotion that is way too marginalized in our culture and we do not model it well for our children. Being able to notice fear can be a lifesaver. Fear alerts us to common sense awareness. Kids who marginalize fear do not speak up when they are in potentially dangerous situations. Children who are nurtured to respect fear and see it as a valuable emotion can find the courage to take a stand, or to walk away, and protect themselves against potentially dangerous situations.

Showing fear is also healthy and can deepen relationship. When we show fear, others around us can show up as caretakers, helpers, or comforters. Our fragile moments invite others to be close.

WHY SO SHY? . . . WHY NOT?

In the U.S. many parents and educators have a bias against shyness. "She is less shy," is often spoken as a compliment. Other cultures that are more quiet and internal respect shyness and don't have this kind of bias.

Within the experience of shyness is an inner world that is precious, tender, and needs appreciation. Some kids and grown-ups are more direct and can meet you head-on. Others are reticent, take time, and are more delicate. Different human natures reflect the diversity of the earth. We are electric and sudden like lightening, tender as a new green shoot, ferocious like lions, and timid like deer. We are all that and more and reflect nature in its diverse expressions! Even though we might identify more strongly with one quality, we really are quite complex, and within us dwells the capacity for all of nature's diversity. Each of us has moments when we feel more forward and extroverted or when we might feel shy or more internal.

It can actually be fun to allow yourself to be shy. For some it is a relief to not have to "be on." Shyness gives us the space to drop into a quieter part of ourselves. Young children have more freedom to follow their shyness. When I sit with such a child in my office, I join them in their shyness. I don't ask questions or try to pull them out. Instead, I try and explore their world. I will often play peek-a-boo, hide my head in my arms and then peek out. I might extend only my pinky finger and wave hello, or gingerly let my finger touch their toe and then move away. It is a dance of moving closer and then away, checking each other out, smiling and giggling, letting ourselves be seen and then hiding. Young children do this naturally. But actually, many adults feel this way too, and would act the same way if they were free to follow their impulses.

Nonverbal body language that signals shyness, such as looking away, closing one's eyes, or dropping one's head, or turning the shoulders away can be an attempt to hold onto inner feelings and states of mind. If it spoke, the body might say: "I am trying to hold onto where I am; I am inside my own world, following experiences that might not be as accepted."

I recall working with a man on his shyness and how he was taught that shyness was weakness and that he should look people in the eye. I asked him to show me what he was like when he felt shy. He looked down and was silent; his shoulders slumped towards his chest. I encouraged him to amplify his posture and to go inside of himself even more. He pulled himself up into a ball and took a big breath. "What a relief," he whispered. "I feel at home in here. Sometimes at work I feel this expectation to be very engaged, to make suggestions, and offer solutions. It is a great pressure." I then asked him if he could imagine feeling this sense of home in that work situation, allowing himself to drop out from those expectations. "I would just want to assure everyone that we will find a solution. We might not know what it is in the moment, but we can wait, give time, feel, and imagine the next steps. There is never time and space in my work world. I want us all to have this feeling of ease and trust."

What a nugget of gold that my client discovered in his shyness! Shyness was trying to transform the work environment and the way my client and others related. Certainly, with so many of us feeling pressured by stressful work environments, his process shows a new way to do business and relate to people that could be healthier for all.

For many children, being shy is a natural way to meet someone. The dance of hiding and coming closer respects both the feeling of staying close to oneself and being curious about others. Thus, if you join children in their shy style of contact their experience shifts quickly. The child feels close to you just by the fact that you are open to entering their world.

I recall a six-year-old girl who came into my office hiding behind her mother. I also hid behind my chair. I said "hello" to her from behind my chair; she said "hello" from behind her mother. I peeked out and then quickly retreated, and she did the same. After a while, bit by bit, more and more of our body parts snuck out from behind our respective hiding places. We ran out and then back again. The little girl ran out once and made a stomp. I followed her and came out with a stomp as well. The next time I came out with a little growl. She giggled and then came out with a big roar. Suddenly, we were lions, clawing and roaring. We had a grand time with all of that energy. Initially uncomfortable, the mother began to play with us too and even felt she had never really experienced her own powers quite like this. The girl's eyes lit up when her mother began to act like a lion. It was a touching moment where mother and daughter connected in a way that was new and important to each of them. Big powers are often behind shy behavior, but we must follow the shy road to find them.

EXERCISE: EXPLORING SHYNESS

1. Imagine being shy or remember a time in the past when you felt shy.
2. Play out the scene; go into the body feelings of shyness. Let yourself have the freedom of a child and really take the posture of a shy person. Notice your different body feelings. Allow them instead of pushing yourself to be different.
3. What can you learn about yourself in this experience?
4. Notice how you would like to be related to in this state.
5. This might give you a tip on how to relate to a shy child or adult!

EVERYDAY KNOCK-OUTS: DEALING WITH INNER CRITICISM, LOW MOODS, AND DEPRESSION

All of us from time to time are plagued by inner criticisms, internalized negative voices from people we have known, societal comparisons, and inner perfectionism.

Exploring inner life also means helping kids to navigate the rough terrain of their moods and more difficult feelings. One day my son came home from a basketball clinic. His mood was a little low.

Dawn: How was basketball?
Theo: Sucky.

Dawn: Oh, how so?

Theo: My team was sucky. I was sucky. We lost every game.

He sulked away and slumped down on the couch. My usual approach would be to remind him of his love of the game, to extol the virtues of having fun versus winning and outcome. But something was different this time. His mood was so low, his posture so slumped; he looked as if something was sitting on him. "Aha," I thought to myself, "Time to wrestle with the worthy opponent."

"Theo, are you ready to use all of your super powers to meet your biggest enemy?" He looked up at me for the first time since coming home. "I am going to play the most awful, terrible, and powerful opponent. And you are going to have to use all of your super powers to battle him. Are you ready?"

"Sure," he said. "What do I have to do?"

"Well, I am going to show you a terrible enemy. Now stand up and get ready. When I begin to play this enemy, I want you to use all of your powers against him. I don't know what you will do. We will have to see."

He stood up and faced me. I tried to look menacing and mean, and spoke in a growly and threatening voice. I told him he was the worst basketball player ever, that he was "sucky," awful, and should never ever attempt to play again. I told him he was a loser, and he should just stay in the house and never go to this basketball clinic again. He was taken aback, tears began to well up and then he lunged forward and yelled, "Stop it!"

"I am not going to stop so easily. You are a sucky player," I continued.

"You are mean and I don't like you," he countered. "I am too gonna play basketball, and the point is to have fun." He then charged at me and wrestled the "opponent" to the ground. After he pinned me to the ground and had sufficiently protected himself, he jubilantly got up. We gave each other a high-five and I congratulated him on using his super powers to combat his toughest opponent.

As parents, we suffer when we see our children drop out of activities, give up when things get hard, and retreat into bad moods that seem impossible to penetrate. In the most serious cases, children become depressed if they identify with an inner sense of failure or worthlessness. Boosting our children by valuing them and their abilities is important. In a world where competition and excellence is rewarded many parents counteract the focus on winning by emphasizing the joy of experience. And yet, even with the best of intentions, inner and outer critics can undermine our passions and sap our energy. Sometimes they're so powerful that as parents we find ourselves powerless trying to convince our children otherwise.

Another view is that the child is having a brush with his worthy opponent.[5] How can an opponent be worthy? We should protect our children from opponents! Yes, and no. We can't always protect our children from opponents; the ultimate opponent is the one that gets inside of us, maintaining a life of its own in the way we talk to ourselves and believe in its views. This is the case when children begin to internalize negative self-perceptions, attitudes, and dialogue that they have picked up from society, friends, bullies or family members. An opponent becomes worthy the moment we take the experience as a potential experience to grow from. At that moment, we are no longer the victim, but we are facing a challenge and are ready to learn and experience something new. Heady stuff for children? Not really. Kids are much more fluid to drop into something new and meet a challenge, given the right feeling approach.

With younger children parents can present the encounter with the worthy opponent as a game. Prep your child by telling him he is going to need all of his powers to meet a really nasty creature. Tell him to get ready. Then role-play the negative voice. Exaggerate the voice, facial gestures and posture, and make sure it is different than yours. The child should be clear that the voice you are representing is *not* you as a parent. It is a monster, a demon, his biggest enemy, whatever you want to call it. Then encourage him to use all of his powers to meet the opponent. At some point he might even want to play the nasty figure himself!

Encourage verbal and physical interaction. With small children wrestling is great. Older children like to wrestle too, but might be stronger than you. Protect yourself and create a safe place for physical expression. Hitting pillows or punching bags allow kids to get in touch with their physicality and vibrancy. Verbal interaction helps kids stand up for themselves and practice essential verbal self-defense skills. Make sure to notice and appreciate your child when she fights back; acknowledge the power in her stance, how she stares her opponent down and uses her power to transform herself and her opponent.

APPRECIATING MOODS

Moods often need appreciation and compassion. A mood will persist until we make contact with it. Telling a child to "snap out of it" usually doesn't work, not for adults, nor for children. It's better to create an opening for our children and not make them feel bad for what they are experiencing and feeling.

For older children this often means being a good listener, being engaged, feeling into what they are going through, and trying to understand them. It usually does not mean fixing it. Our tendency as parents is to try and give a solution. It's hard for us not to want to "save" them and fix the problem. However, solutions can sometimes discount the child's experience. We move too quickly with an answer instead of just feeling with our kids and giving them the sense that we are with them. Often just your acknowledgement is the solution. Then they might feel an opening to talk about what's bothering them. In that moment, they might ask for your thoughts. Those invitations are precious. Make sure you look for feedback to see if your answer is really the right direction for them.

Younger children typically do not remain in such moods, but are more fluid in their ability to play and express their experience and then move on to the next thing that interests them. As children age, and self-consciousness sets in, there is more influence from the outer world, and expectations become more internalized. Their challenging moods are often an expression of these experiences and lack of social power. By middle school and into high school, children become more aware of an inner dialogue that is often filled with self-criticism. The mind becomes obsessed with fitting in, measuring up, failing or succeeding, and comparing oneself to others. Additionally, the growing independence of older children mixed with a need for acceptance can create a complex stew for any parent living with a teenager.

THE POWER OF A MOOD

The presence of a mood can easily make us feel like we are walking on eggshells. Many teenagers scare us—although we might not admit it! Some have a chip on their shoulder and are just waiting for a fight or someone to cross their path. The fact is *they are in a fight.* Many have good reason to be angry, on-guard, and confrontational. And, the fight is inside (although ready to erupt outwardly), and the chip on their shoulder is their defense, a strength or protection against an invisible antagonist. Rarely is the chip seen or acknowledged as a strength. Instead, parents, teachers, and even friends either confront the teen about her attitude, or walk on eggshells and avoid her. This obviously becomes a difficult atmosphere to live in.

Most of the time your teen doesn't feel powerful, but rather at the mercy of social situations, parental and societal expectations, school pressures, and a world that she is wanting to enter, and yet is afraid to do so.

Take Charles, a sixteen-year-old, brought in by his parents because of his difficult moods. Charles wouldn't talk to his parents and wasn't doing well in school. When he came into my office, he sat slumped in a chair and looked at the clock as if to let me know that he was definitely there against his will. I could feel the power in his mood and resistance and his inner strength to hold strongly to his convictions. Instead of trying to move him and make him listen to me, I simply told him that I experienced him as extremely powerful. In fact, I said, he was even a little frightening. He smiled despite himself. I continued, "My guess is that people don't really value and see the powers that you have." I had his attention. "I believe you know what is best for you and you have your own ideas." He nodded. "If you feel like it I would love to hear your ideas and how you see things."

He then opened up and shared how he felt about school and his teachers. He complained that he was incredibly bored and that the teachers were hypocrites. A teacher had put him down in front of the class because he challenged her. He felt his parents were too pushy, wanting him to succeed, and that he couldn't talk to them about what was important.

Out of respect for him and his inner sense of power and direction, I asked him if we could explore some of those experiences together because I wanted to encourage him to use his powers. He agreed. I told him that I appreciated that he challenged his teacher and asked him to actually go further and challenge all authority and bring out his vision of what school should be like. He had a lot to say! He felt school didn't really engage kids and only emphasized tests. He felt teachers didn't understand and appreciate the importance of relationships. He felt teachers talked down to him as if kids didn't know anything. He felt school was just too much pressure and not enough fun. As he spoke he was vibrant and passionate. Gone was the low mood, the provocative chip. He was an activist, an educational reformer, and had many ideas. I praised him for his views and his ability to articulate them. And then I challenged him. I asked him how he might use that power with the teacher he had challenged, who had put him down. He acknowledged that he was probably too rough on her in his challenge, that he could have been kinder. And, he said that he would have told her that it also wasn't cool for her to put him down, especially in front of the class.

SPEAKING THE UNSPEAKABLE

Moods lack language. They are deep feelings that we don't know how to put into words. The feelings in a mood are the usual ones: anger, jealousy, hurt, self-criticism, need for love, need for appreciation, hopelessness, and inferiority. But because of beliefs against expressing them, they get stuck, somatized, and trapped inside.

Once we value them, as with Charles above, we are able to express what's at the core of the mood. Another way to loosen up a mood is to "speak the unspeakable" for your child. Give voice to the feelings of hopelessness, fear, or rage. Many teens can look rather low and depressed, but beneath that demeanor is rage. The scent of that rage keeps everyone at arm's length. However, the rage is never voiced. The child tries to control it and no one ever invites it to come forward. Such a child will roll his eyes, look at others with disdain, slump, and shrug. Speaking the unspeakable might mean to read into what the child feels and ask if you might speak for him. Then get on his side and really show anger, speak the words that he is unable to: "I am so furious! No one understands me! I feel confined in this family. No one appreciates me!" Then you might add, "This is how I imagine you might feel. I don't blame you one bit. In fact, I want to hear more about it."

Parents can also share their own unspeakable experiences. "I get jealous too sometimes. I look at my sister and wish I had her athletic abilities." Or, "I remember a time when I hated going to school. I felt no one liked me and I didn't know how to reach out to others. I felt I wasn't as good and would compare myself." These comments open the door for children to feel understood and have a language for their feelings. Our ability to share also "normalizes" what they are feeling and creates an atmosphere where they feel less stigmatized and more at ease to explore their feelings.

Obviously, moods that remain intact and impenetrable over time do indicate the need for outside help. Depression among youth is serious as is unchecked anger over time. Depressed children often struggle with the sense of not feeling valuable, of not belonging, and that their deepest nature is not being appreciated. Many feel deeply misunderstood, or that no one cares or loves them. Some of our children have been so hurt, abused and put down, that it is almost a miracle that they are still standing.

Depression and anger can be close cousins, in which anger is often the road out of feeling depressed. Many of our kids are depressed as a result of feeling downed, whether that is internally or from an external source. The big downing power sits on top of them. In my practice, many so-called depressed teens love to pummel my punching bag and finally react to the forces that down them. The expression of the anger underneath is freeing and puts them in contact with a power that can react, has impact, and takes them away from being the victim. With younger children, like the example with my son in the beginning of this section, the use of play and engaging super-powers is helpful. The key to unfolding these moods and helping kids to move through them is to support them in speaking the unspeakable. Often it is not enough to just reassure them of their virtues and to tell them everything will be okay. Inner criticism and outer circumstances that dampen their spirit and produce seemingly impenetrable moods need engagement.

Parents might also consider that low moods can be an attempt to go deep inside. So much of our world is overly extroverted and fed by constant stimulation. It doesn't nourish inner states of mind. With the rise of technology and electronics, quiet and stillness can masquerade as depression. Depression could be an attempt to bring us inside and to have more contact with our inner selves.

TIPS FOR NURTURING THE INNER LIFE OF CHILDREN

- Nurture curiosity and discovery. Follow the openness that is within children.
- Be a parent that nurtures your own inner life and personal development.
- Support different realities. Remember dreaming and imagination.

- Help to give words to feelings and experiences and also notice and support your child to create new language for his/her experiences.
- Model emotional intelligence by being open in yourself to the whole realm of emotional experience.
- Listen to what is underneath anger and frustration.
- Explore fear and see it as a potential power.
- Get to know the world of shyness instead of pushing your child out of it.
- Unfold moods and inner criticism.
- Further a child's own leadership and independence.
- Encourage body awareness.
- Make space for the big questions. Ask children what they think about their lives, the creation of the universe, why they were born, etc.
- "We are the world." Model that with your child by seeing the "other" in ourselves.
- Give the freedom to experiment and make choices as well as mistakes.
- Support kids in their own emotional experience even though it might be different than yours.
- Encourage kids to have their own opinions—especially in relationship to you!
- Acknowledge *your* learning when your child is your teacher.
- Show flexibility when you find yourself changed.
- Model amazement and mystery.
- Play and dream and encourage a "second attention."
- Emphasize meaning and learning, instead of success and failure, or right and wrong.
- Discover the unknown powers in your child's dreams.
- In general, play with dreams, act them out and have fun.
- Role-play and act out experiences that seem less known to your child. Often they will have a solution.

- Death can be a place for learning; give kids an opportunity to develop and express their own worldview of life and death. Pace your child and his or her interest. You needn't bring it up; death comes up in life naturally, and children bring it up themselves. (See more in Chapter 7.)
- Help children to find their own inner experience of you as a parent.

power at play

Power, Autonomy, and Relationship

I am going to use my polar-pac power.
It freezes out bullies so they don't get me.
—Theo, age 8

I have special powers that no one knows about. They get
transferred to me when I am asleep.
—Martine, age 9

My practice is full of people of all ages who do not identify with their tremendous gifts and powers. As adults, our lack of awareness of our power and how we use it has a significant effect on our interactions with children. Many of us have been hurt by those in positions of power, in family life, schools, in religious organizations, community groups, or by societal institutions.

When I teach and facilitate workshops for adults on the theme of conflict or parenting, I frequently ask the participants if anyone can recall a positive experience they had as a child when dealing with an authority. It is incredibly rare that someone shares an experience that was fruitful. Then I ask people to remember how their family of origin dealt with conflict and disagreement. Again it is surprisingly seldom that someone can relate an experience from their family of origin in which conflict resulted in a positive outcome: people feeling closer, respecting each other more, or sharing more open communication. Instead, the typical responses I hear are that one or more family members:

- Shout each other down in the middle of a conflict.
- Withdraw from the conflict or the relationship.
- Lay down the law and everyone else must go along.
- Appear afraid of one parent or the other.
- Use addictive substances to cope with the conflict.
- Resort to violence in the face of conflict.
- Withdraw love.
- Mimick, tease, or put-down others.
- Have the conflict behind closed doors.

With few positive experiences of power and conflict, it is no wonder parents are so challenged by power issues with their children. Though most parents strive to do better with their children than their parents did with them their personal history affects their parenting in ways of which they are not aware.

For example, my client is a mother who was raised in a traditional family structure in which the father was authoritative and gave orders that had to be obeyed. Children were to be seen and not heard. Her mother went along with it. Everyone feared the father. As a result, my client who now has her own children promised herself that she would never be the strict, authoritarian parent that her father was. Some would call her parenting style very permissive; her kids have lots of freedom.

Not surprisingly, she has lots of conflict with her husband over their parenting styles. He feels she is too lax, and that he is the only one that says "no." When he does say no, she is critical of him. She finds him too harsh and says he reminds her of her father. Yet she is also exhausted by the children and unable to stand for her own needs. Paradoxically, she is as powerless as she was as a girl. She is unable to be firm in relationship to the kids and make boundaries based on her own needs because she is still fighting the hurt she experienced with her father. Of course she doesn't want to be like her father, but she has marginalized her own power and ability to be firm, out of fear that she will be like him.

Our own unresolved personal history haunts us like a ghost, tainting what we model and teach children about power. Therefore, it is helpful to explore our own history.

EXPLORING OUR OWN RELATIONSHIP TO POWER

Our own childhood history with our parents and other authority figures can inform us in how we use power in parenting or educating children. I invite the reader to reflect on the following questions in order to learn about some of your early experiences of power.

- How were children treated in your family of origin or in the family structure you grew up in? How much power did the kids have?
- Did you feel powerful as a child? If so, how?
- Did you feel powerless as a child? If so, how, and how did you get that message?
- How would you have liked to have been supported in relationship to your own power, when you were a child?

SOCIAL POWER AND CHILDREN[1]

In most cultures kids have no social rank. They have no power in the consensus reality world. They are dependent upon parents and social systems. They can't vote, their views are not sought out or appreciated, and they are generally not included in adult conversation. Most kids want to get older because they feel how little power their age offers them.

Adults create the schedule kids must follow. They have to march to our beat. Even the smallest activities of our everyday lives are punctuated by power. For instance, think about walking to the store with your five-year-old. You have only an hour to get there and back, and have other things to do as well. You're walking quickly and efficiently. But your child is dawdling, looking at the flowers, and singing a little song. You tell her to hurry up and keep pace. She tries to go faster, but then gets distracted by an insect. You have to keep nagging her to walk faster and your tone gets more and more irritated. She starts to sulk and now you are angry. She starts to cry and now doesn't want to walk at all. You know this scene. It happens all the time.

This little vignette reminds us how children must constantly adapt themselves to our rhythm. Parents might complain about power struggles, tantrums, and children who don't listen. But put yourself in their shoes; they rarely lead the way but are usually expected to follow. Children need to feel powerful; we all need to. Remember the first time you lived on your own? Remember the feeling of no one telling you when to eat, when to sleep, how long you could watch TV, whether or not you could go out, with whom you could hang out, when you had to wake up, go to school, etc. What a freedom to follow your own inner body rhythms!

I am not saying children shouldn't have to follow rules or that children don't need firm boundaries and guidance, but I do want us to reflect on how we use power and how little social power children have.

Children need to feel their own powers; to only follow others creates resentment and doesn't allow your child to learn how to take the lead. Try experimenting with small activities that empower your child and let her lead. If you do have the time on that walk, why not adjust yourself and follow your child's rhythm? There are many things parents have to be firm about including nutrition, safety, and homework, to name a few. But there are many places in life where *we* can adjust. Is that phone call really necessary? Is it really that important to do that errand right now? Or can we pause and take a more rambling route to the store? I often suspect that we are addicted to a fast pace of life and it can do us good to yield to the leadership of a little person and let her show us a new way. Imagine saying to your child that you have to go to the store but that you want her to lead the way. As you walk you follow her and notice what she notices. You join the fantasy and dreaming world that is happening before you. Suddenly, behind the bus stop is a dragon, and instead of insisting your child move on, you become another dragon and join her. The walk is now a great adventure and you have not only tapped into her fantasy world and had fun, but you also have empowered your child.

PSYCHOLOGICAL OR SPIRITUAL RANK[2]

Social rank describes power that is created by the dominant cultural values in society. People belonging to certain groups have social rank due to such characteristics as their age, gender, race, religion, sexual orientation, education, and health. Kids are low on the totem pole in terms of the powers that society bestows upon them.

And yet, kids are tremendously powerful. An infant who is up crying at night demanding that her needs be filled is incredibly powerful. This so-called helpless creature has the power to create sleepless nights and put everyone in a bad mood! The way that children, particularly younger children, insist on their own needs makes them very powerful. Every parent knows how young children's needs run the show. You are about to leave the house, you're in a hurry and, suddenly, the baby poops all over the place. Now you are terribly delayed cleaning up, changing clothes, and tending to the baby's needs. As the child gets older and can control his needs or gets chastised for having needs, he loses this sense of power.

However, kids are still powerful in their relationship to us—they can defy us, talk back to us, and withhold love and relationship. They can hold opinions about us that hurt us or that we disagree with. Just as adults can use emotional means to exert power, so can children.

Psychological rank refers to an inner freedom and ability to feel at home in our own skin. It can be cultivated by self-knowledge and personal development and perhaps some of us inherently possess such emotional ease and sense of self. Psychological rank is what gives us the ability to be fluid in relationship with others. It is the knowledge of our feelings and inner diversity. It is a wisdom that even children at a young age display. As we get older sometimes we have to re-discover or re-develop this inner wisdom. Children who have the ability to stand up for others and resolve conflict amongst peers possess a lot of psychological rank.

Spiritual rank is the feeling of being supported by something greater in life. You feel centered and moved by something greater than yourself. Some people have this experience through God, nature, or an inner center. As children, many of us felt great strength in standing for our beliefs even when the outer world or parents put us down. Many people who were terribly hurt in childhood were somehow able to maintain some inner sense of well-being and survival, and will tell you that a guardian angel, a pet, a place in nature, or something special pulled them through.

Take a boy from a large family whose family is just getting by and the parents are too busy to notice and appreciate the amazing talents of their son. This thirteen-year-old is astonishing in how he supports himself to do his schoolwork. He dreams of starting a community center where kids whose parents work and have no time can come and get support for their aspirations. He is being the parent that he wishes he had. He is guided by something on the inside that supports him; he has spiritual rank.

Spiritual rank gives the child or teenager the ability to stand for basic truths even when it goes against parents and society at large. Some kids can see right through their parents; they see their flaws and personal challenges. They see where they are different and they have a very detached and clear picture of their family scene. This view gives them a special power.

A sixteen-year-old girl I worked with many years ago was terribly abused by her minister father. No one believed her. She took him to court. Her sense of justice propelled her. Despite the pain of having to stand against her father, she was empowered to fight for the freedom of both her and her younger sister.

As parents, caregivers, and educators, we can appreciate power struggles by encouraging children to find their own powers and to use them responsibly. We can discuss how power emerges in kids and how we can support them, as well as, learn useful ways to interact for the benefit of all. As parents we can also learn from the powers our children do have, and be inspired by their uncanny psychological and spiritual rank. When kids feel powerful, there is less of a struggle for power.

POWER OF OUR NATURE

The feeling of power is intimately connected with a child's sense of inner value. We feel valuable when our basic nature is noticed and nurtured. One of the most amazing experiences of parenting is discovering the unique personality of our children. Children feel valued and powerful when we value their essential nature. Of course, this is quite easy to say, but much harder to do in practice.

As a highly extroverted person, can we support a very introverted child and see her gifts instead of pushing her to engage? If we have a very energetic child can we support her high energy instead of dampening it? If we are very practical are we able to value a child who is more dreamy and fantasy full? If we have been raised in the school of tough-knocks, can we nourish our child's exquisite sensitivity? Can we value interests that our children have that we might not share? When we nurture these fundamental attributes in our children, we are building healthy self-esteem and encouraging children to feel powerful in who they are.

It is important to support our child's unique nature, especially when those qualities are outside the norm. This comes up often in regard to gender. Can we support boys who are sensitive and emotional? Can we support girls to engage as physically or athletically as boys? In a relatively progressive local elementary school, in a kickball game dominated by boys, I witnessed a few girls watching on the sidelines. Later the girls shared that they wanted to play but felt like they couldn't. An invisible line was drawn that is hard to cross.

In addition to being directly loving and supporting of our child's nature, adults can also model behavior that expresses their own individuality. Children learn how to value themselves by seeing parents who dare to be proud of their own unique nature.

Nature is also expressed in the body. Children need support to be at home in their bodies. Different body types have different talents and gifts. Each of us has our own inner experience of what our body feels like and how it moves through space. We have different ways of expressing ourselves in how we dress and look. Can we help our children to expand our conventional and media-centered view of beauty? Recently, I was in a middle school and saw a fabulous poster. There were two posters, one with a group of middle-school-aged boys and the other with girls. Each child was a different size, shape, color, and in different stages of puberty. The kids sported different hairstyles, clothing, and attitudes. In big block letters the poster asked, "*What is normal anyway?*" What a relief to see a poster celebrating different physiques and asserting them all as normal!

DREAMING POWER: THE CALL OF CHILDHOOD DREAMS

In Chapter 1, I discussed how a significant childhood dream reveals mythical and unique powers to the dreamer. Such dreams occur just as we start to see ourselves as separate from our parents, the seed of our own identity. Powerful childhood dreams remind the child that he is much more than his small self. These dreams are callings that alert us to our earliest and more extraordinary powers.

Although children are socially dependent—a view reinforced by society—dreamland does not let us get away with this perception. In dreamland children *are* the sunlight, the witch, and the tiger. In dreamland, children possess enormous powers. Of course, like all of us, the child identifies with his little self in the dream. He does not think he possesses the power of the figures roaming around his dreamscape. That is why dreams of great power are also nightmares: because the child still feels himself to be the 'little self' in the dream and not any of the mighty and powerful creatures. The dream experience wants to destroy our small view of ourselves. Such early dreams hold significance throughout our lives.[3] It is not only the small child who does not identify with her powers, it is also the aging adult who is challenged to embrace her greater self and accompanying powers.

A woman I work with dreamt as a child that she was running through the woods and suddenly a mysterious light shone through the forest. She was mesmerized and terrified because she had no idea where it came from. She couldn't take her eyes off the light. Even though she felt it was burning her eyes, she was unable to look away.

This woman is extremely rational and linear. She has a strong aversion to religion and anything spiritual or mysterious. The mysterious glow revealed something mystical and irrational, an experience she marginalizes in life. Her analytical ability and need to understand things is crucial to her, but the dream was threatening this. The mysterious light would 'burn her eyes out' or challenge her way of seeing the world. The dream showed up first when she was seven, yet as a woman in her thirties, she is still challenged by it. Less known to her is a mysterious, intuitive power, perhaps even a psychic ability or shamanic way of perceiving the world.

HELPING CHILDREN CONNECT WITH THE POWER OF THEIR DREAMS

We all know the experience of a nightmare, when a child awakens us at night with a scary dream. Most parents comfort their children and tell them "it is *only* a dream," and in doing so, inadvertently dismiss the potential power their child might discover.

We can help our kids identify with these powers by playing with dreams. Kids who can discover their essential powers at younger ages feel more confident as young people. Obviously you might be too tired to try the following in the middle of the night. So, comfort your child but tell her that you have a special way to help those dreams not be so scary, and that you will play together the next day.

1. Tell your child you are going to play a fun dream game that will help make her dreams less scary. Bring a playful attitude and have fun!
2. Listen to the dream and notice the dream figure that is most frightening, strange, or awesome.
3. Ask your child if she can describe or show you what the figure does. Find the energy that this figure has. Be gentle at first, because she might still be fearful. Follow her lead.
4. Explore this dream by getting to know this dream figure. You might act out the dream figure, draw it, move like it, speak with its voice, make music to express it, etc. You might also use puppets, stuffed animals, or dolls to re-create this figure. (If the child is afraid to act out the dream figure, it is less threatening to draw it or act it out with puppets, or you can do it yourself.)
5. As you play, notice the core energetic quality of this figure. For example, once you start to play it out, a scary criminal may display confidence; a monster that eats people might be brave or determined; the experience of being trapped in the earth might contain a feeling of quiet and stillness that is actually relieving. Find the quality or energy within the dream figure and explore it more fully.
6. You might do a role-play where one of you is the scared child and the other is the powerful figure. Play and let them interact together. Switch roles and have fun. Let your fantasy unfold and create new scenes and stories together. Bring it into movement and encourage the child to be the monster that eats you up!
7. Support, encourage, and celebrate the new power your child is discovering. Remind them that they can even use that power in their dreams next time around.

One of my son's earliest recurring nightmares was a dog that would chase him and bite him. We would play with that dream using a dog puppet that would bite other puppets. Imagining our hands were like big dog-jaws, we would clamp down on each other's arms. I recall one particular time when we played with the dream together.

"Got you!" he squealed in delight.

"No, you don't!" I shrieked back.

He then came after me, not letting me get away. "I got you! Grooow-wl! You can't get away."

Then I said, "Yes, you certainly do have me. I can't get away. You are quite powerful. You can really get things and grab onto things when you need them."

He beamed with happiness. Suddenly, a little boy, rendered powerless in the night, was a powerful and amazing creature radiating a special kind of confidence.

After playing with the dream, I reinforced the experience by encouraging him to inhabit this new quality in his daily life. "You are powerful. You can get what you want. Go for it." Some months later, my son reported to me that the dog dream came, but this time, when the dog came after him, he put his fist in the dog's mouth. This stopped the dog and those scary dog dreams. He had picked up that power and I could see it in his behavior. He felt more confident at school, was able to go for friendships that he was interested in, and really "bit into things."

SUPER HEROES: SUPER POWERS

Kids love to play superheroes, cops and robbers, and act out fights between "bad guys" and "good guys." The fantasy games are ways for kids to explore power. Many parents and educators are fearful that these kinds of games proliferate violence, and indeed, some of them are over-the-top and can de-sensitize children to violent behavior. There is important discussion in regard to violent video games and media and the effects on children. However, giving aggressive fantasies safe expression can help kids connect with their own power and work out conflict.

Gerard Jones, in *Killing Monsters: Why Children Need Fantasy, Super Heroes and Make Believe Violence*[4], shows how children gravitate to many of the super hero and violent fantasy games as a way to feel more powerful. In the format of "play" kids get to act out and review some of their own life experiences. They get to kill the bad guy, be the hero, stalk powerful creatures, and develop special powers. And, they get to explore the energy of the "bad guy." This is a power.

I remember a mom brought her seven-year-old to see me because of his obsession with what she called, "super-hero-violent-play." She felt he was too aggressive and that the play encouraged it. Charlie and I began to play together and he was immediately drawn to the samurai sword in my room (a dull blade souvenir-type sword, but very realistic and cool looking).

"I am going to cut off some heads," said Charlie, strutting around my office.

"Yeah, let's find some juicy heads to slice off," I said, joining in his fantasy world.

"Okay, you can be my assistant," Charlie offered.

"With pleasure," I responded. "What is your name swordsman?"

"I am Crayton," he said.

"Crayton, where do you come from, and what is our mission?" I asked.

"I am from another planet, and our mission is to chop off some heads," he replied.

"Show me how we will do that, Sir Crayton," I asked.

"Well we press this button on our belt and become invisible. Then when we are right in front of someone we will become visible and swing our swords and chop off their head." Crayton swung his sword to demonstrate.

"What a great swing you have, Sir Crayton. I love how you use your sword and the head just falls off. Can I try too?"

We got deeper into the game as we made ourselves invisible and met different people and then swung our swords and chopped off their heads. We did it many times, delighting in that powerful swing of the sword.

After a while, I asked, "Why is it important that we cut off the heads?"

"Well," Crayton explained, "we have to cut off the heads so they can't tell us what to do anymore."

"Yeah, we want to make the rules. We get tired of people always telling us what to do." I said.

"Yeah," Crayton chimed in.

We continued playing and as we did, I asked him what kinds of rules he was most tired of. He began to tell me what kinds of rules he found unfair. He had a lot of good ideas about his family and school life and new rules he'd like to make. Afterwards we introduced Mom to Crayton and shared with her some of the new rules and ideas that Charlie had. Mom actually enjoyed hearing Charlie's rules and saw that she needed to include him more in making rules and decisions in their daily life.

Children are drawn to super heroes and super powers in an attempt to connect with their power and talents. When adults listen deeply to children, they may be able to notice and bring awareness to the powers their children show them. For instance, a ten-year-old girl told me she had special powers and could see through people. Her parents were worried because she often spoke like this and they wondered about her mental health. I told the girl I believed she had special powers and I would like to get to know them. "Really?" she asked me in disbelief. I assured her that I did indeed want to know. She said that she felt she always had special powers but no one had ever believed her. I asked her to look at me and see through me. She was shy at first but then looked and said that she saw the color purple. She said she saw a long purple robe like a wizard would wear. I felt seen by her. I don't identify as a wizard, but I felt as if she saw something in me that does support experiences that people have that are "other worldly" and less conventional. She then shared with me all kinds of things that she saw in people, and her parents admitted that she was extremely insightful, sometimes eerily so. This was a power that needed support. From the perspective of the parents, however, it seemed unusual and eccentric. Some of our powers are unusual and unique. If this child had lived in another culture, her more mediumistic or shamanic talents might have been more readily appreciated.

Parents can support children by relating to the super heroes and powers that emerge in the daily play of children. Play with power. Enter the world of bad and good guys, super heroes and bullies. Feel the power that children demonstrate and reflect it back to them. "Yes, you are amazingly strong! You have incredible powers."

Ask the super hero how to deal with a problem that you know they are occupied with. "How would Spiderman get along with a kid at school who always took his lunch? I will be the kid taking the lunch and you be Spiderman." Bring out the wisdom, confidence, and strength that children are trying to connect to in their play.

VIOLENCE AND ALIENATION

There is a lot of research around children who become violent as a result of alienation.[5] Children who become violent feel incredibly powerless. Violence comes from hopelessness; it is a last resort and reveals serious problems. Check your child around how they feel relative to others socially. Are they being hurt, bullied, or ostracized? How do they get along with being different? Then take steps to support them by making outer changes, for example, changing schools, seeing a counselor, and helping them interact with others. In such situations, kids often have not cultivated the language to express themselves, nor do they have an open ear of someone who will listen. Sit with these kids, listen to their heartbreak, and draw them out. Help kids to express feelings, stand up to others, and love their differences.[6]

THE POWER OF FEELINGS

There is tremendous power in feelings. Too often kids and adults have been put down for their feelings, and, as a result, don't have the inner support to see the power in their emotional lives. For example, people often feel that they don't want to show hurt. They see it as a sign of weakness; being affected by someone and feeling hurt reveals powerlessness. Being strong is translated into self-sufficiency and being unaffected by others. I think this is a cultural problem not only for kids but for adults as well. As a result, when we mask our hurt and do not embrace our emotional needs, we become defensive and tough. However, defensiveness is not true power. In fact, tough and defensive behavior can be a form of self-hatred. We dislike our needs and vulnerabilities. We can't stand for our feelings for fear of the self-loathing that might follow. When we do this, we have turned against ourselves. We have rejected essential parts of ourselves. The reality is, expressing hurt and showing vulnerability can soften and deepen relationship. It can also stop hurtful interaction, retaliation, and revenge. In the animal world, when an animal shows its belly, the aggressor moves off.

It takes power to stand up for feelings, not back off and hate ourselves for what we feel. If a child says she is hurt, and kids make fun of her for being hurt, she shows self-esteem by standing for her feelings, and saying, "Why would you want to hurt me? Are you trying to be better than me?" Or, "There is something wrong with you guys that you don't stop when someone is hurting." This is emotional self-defense, and she can be proud of her authentic self-expression.

It is important to support your child's feelings and to help him stand up for them. For example, if accused of being sensitive, he can say, "Of course, I am sensitive. That is a good thing. You are incredibly insensitive and I don't want to be around you." Or, "It doesn't make you strong to hurt others, it makes you mean."

The ability to stand for feelings and express them is a psychological power. I have been in many conflict situations and I can tell you that the thing that changes hearts and minds is the expression of human feeling, particularly sensitivity, pain, and hurt. Strength in terms of dominance, self-protection, and force rarely moves hearts and does not create better relationships between people.

Take a teenage boy who was being hassled at school for being weird. Kids felt he was weird because he was quiet, didn't socialize, went directly home after school and didn't go out on weekends. What the kids didn't know was that his single mother had cancer and he was her primary caretaker. He felt he didn't know how to talk about his feelings in regard to his mother. He loved her dearly and wanted to care for her. He also felt burdened. He wanted to have fun with others and make friends, but was often feeling down and terrified that his mother would die. Finally, he was able to share his feelings with a few kids. The stoic strong boy cried a river of tears. After a year of self-denial and hating himself for his feelings, while keeping up a strong façade, this boy risked finding power in his feeling life. The teens around him were moved and listened intently. They felt terrible about how they had isolated and teased him. Instead, they began to reach out to him and his mom; some offered to cook meals for them, and his home soon became a place where other kids came to hang out, keeping him company while he cared for his mother. The expression of genuine feeling became absolutely transformative.

FEELINGS OR PRINCIPLES?

Parents too often rely on principles instead of feelings when we relate to our children. We don't realize how much power there is in simply telling our children how we genuinely feel. Principles that kids don't understand or might even disagree with, just feel like power from above. Power from above might get temporary results, but doesn't improve relationship and understanding. Kids will go along with power from above, but they do it out of fear and coercion. Later they will fight you by withdrawing, rebelling, being moody or lying.

For example, if I say, "Mama is so tired, I really need you to let me lie quietly here," spoken with genuine feeling and need, it can be very effective, and even a two-year-old can understand it. Compare this to, "Be quiet now, because I said so," or, "Be quiet, or I won't play with you later." We need to let kids in on how we feel. If they can feel us, they will then respond to us in kind. This also teaches children empathy, and to do things out of kindness and care, not just because they should.

When we let kids know how we feel, we model for them how to be proud of their feelings and express them. You don't have to tell your kids every little thing, but kids notice how we feel even if we don't say it. We can say to them, "I had a hard day at work. I feel really frustrated. My boss didn't appreciate me." When we model this for children, they can also come home from school and tell us they felt put down by a friend, or not valued by a teacher, instead of just being in a bad mood, throwing their backpack on the floor, and snapping at everyone. Sharing our feelings teaches them expression and compassion towards others.

For example, take a divorced father who is having trouble with his eleven-year-old daughter. She says she doesn't want to live with him. He tells her she has to, and when she gets angry, he sends her to her room. He is actually hurt, but he marginalizes his feeling. Instead, he stands on principle: the daughter shouldn't talk to him like that. She has to live with him and get along with it.

This father needed to learn to say he was heartbroken. He wanted his daughter to love him and *want* to be with him, and he wished she would. He didn't know how to express and show his hurt and, instead, reacted with anger and force. This relationship turned around when he could talk about his broken heart and his need for her love. He shared that he was learning about that and often didn't know what to do to make the relationship better. He then apologized for reacting with anger and force.

The girl was moved by his expression of feeling. His way of being strict and not really expressing his feelings was what was disturbing to her.

THE POWER OF THOUGHT AND DREAM-LIKE IMAGINATION

Kids need to know the power of their own thinking. We can support kids to think for themselves and to value their own thinking at a very young age. As toddlers, children are exploring the world and they ask us to define things and why things happen. It is exciting to witness how those young minds work and try to comprehend the world around them. However, such moments also present a grand opportunity for us to draw out our child's thinking. Even though they ask questions, they often have their own ideas, ideas that they might not be aware of and that are more connected to a dreaming or imaginary world.

Young children are closely connected to a dreaming, imaginative, or playful world, a world that seems more magical and has a wisdom all of its own. When a child asks you why the moon changes shape every night, you *can* give them the scientific answer that we all agree on. In addition, how about asking what they think? Their answers might surprise or inspire you. "The moon changes shape because it wants to show us that we can get big and small," described one little girl. That certainly gave me something to ponder; the moon attempts to reflect our differences back to us. What a wise child, a teacher, or sage!

When we ask kids the big questions in life, we bring out their views, value their imagination, and nurture their powers. Enjoy asking your children questions that deal with the mysterious nature of life. This gives power to a reality that many of us disavow as we get older, but seek out in our dreams as we age and come closer to death.

You might even consult your child. Their ideas can be really fun and imaginative, and they can come up with things you have never thought of. Tell them a problem and ask them how they see it, what would they do. You might not take their advice, but just that you ask their opinion values them and their thinking. It also includes them in your world.

Kids learn fairness when we consult them. We give the message that we want to hear them and that their voice is important. We instill in them the feeling that they will be heard and treated fairly. It neutralizes power dynamics. As children get older, if they do not feel supported in their own thinking, they are more at risk to be swayed by the thinking of peers.

THE POWER OF OPINION AND DISAGREEMENT

We discover our own ideas when we disagree with others. Someone else's view allows us to wake up to what we think. Whether in a book, TV show, or talking to a friend, we often only discover what we think when we first hear what others think. Likewise, when our child disagrees with us, we can appreciate that they are trying to find their own view.

Yet many parents enforce compliance or punish children for disagreeing or talking back. This silences disagreement, and along with it, silences a big part of your relationship. If kids can't voice their views they can't talk to you. If your word is the final word, they may go along with you outwardly, but they will not submit inwardly. Your relationship will suffer in terms of trust and diminish their feeling that they can talk to you.

Helping our kids to disagree with us is crucial. If kids can't stand up to us, how can we expect them to stand up to bullies or peer pressure? They learn this at home.

Parents, who hammer home their view and repeat reasons why their view is best without letting their child voice his view, inadvertently teach their child to devalue their own thinking. Children get hopeless when they can't get their point across, or when their parents always have the better argument. Parents can still have great arguments and be open to hearing their child's viewpoint. In fact, seek their view. Notice how they might defer or dismiss, swallow their words, or be fearful to speak, and encourage them. Helping our children to disagree with us or voice a contrary opinion helps them develop self-esteem, believe in their own thoughts and creativity, and learn how to have good relationships with authority figures.

I worked with a mother and father who were having trouble communicating with their teenage daughter. The parents claimed they were very open and wanted to listen to what their daughter had to say. With the parents dominating most of the conversation, I asked the daughter what she thought. Before she could even complete a sentence, the parents were countering her view and reinforcing their own. The girl then became hopeless and gave up. The parents were caring people but were unaware of how they didn't leave room for the daughter to have an opinion.

I helped the parents to support their daughter to express her viewpoint, regardless if they agreed with it. Could they understand it, try and feel into why she thought the way she did, and appreciate her ability to have a view that was different than their own? The parents listened to her with this new perspective and were able to understand their daughter more deeply. The girl also felt relieved that for the first time she could speak without feeling like she was on trial or had to make the perfect argument.

A child who can bring her view forth to an authority figure gets an incredible boost in esteem and confidence. I remember when my son was in first grade he came home from school one day and was really upset; he had been part of a group of boys at recess who were chasing another boy. The principal said that the next day all of the boys had to stay in at recess. My son was upset and in tears. He struggled to express all of what he felt, but he finally said, "I didn't get a turn to speak. Ms. Mason talked to all the boys, but not me."

He didn't get a turn. He was trying to say that he didn't get a chance to tell his side of the story. He felt it was unfair. I don't think he even had the language then to say "my side," or even knew the word "fairness." I supported him then to tell me the story, to "have his turn," to tell his side. It turned out that he was trying to protect the boy who was being chased and to tell the other boys not to chase him. For a six-year-old this was hard to verbalize. I needed to be quite patient and help him to tell me this story.

The next day driving to school, I asked if he needed help to go talk to his principal. He said, "No, it's between me and Mason." I had a little chuckle over his phrasing and felt good that he wanted to follow up with her. As I was leaving the school, I happened to bump into the principal. I told her that Theo had thought he didn't get a chance to give his side of the story. She actually agreed and said she felt bad about it and wanted to talk with him. Great principal.

That afternoon I picked him up, and he was elated. The first thing he said was "Mama, I talked to Ms. Mason!" He felt so proud of himself and also happily exclaimed that he had been allowed to go out at recess. I was delighted that he could have such a positive experience with an outer authority figure and feel his sense of power; not only could he express his view, but he could even make an impact.

LYING AND SNEAKING AS A WAY TO DISAGREE

As parents, we teach our kids not to lie and it's easy to feel hurt and insulted when they do. We take it as an affront and feel they have done something morally wrong. However, we need to give more thought to the experience of lying. What is happening when kids lie?

Lying can be an expression of powerlessness. Having no power and no voice cultivates a climate of lying. When children or adults feel weak or unable to stand up for their viewpoint or behavior, they lie.

An atmosphere of obedience, where children must submit to authority without a discussion and clear understanding of where authority comes from, creates rebellion, secrets, and lying.

It is a fine line we walk as parents. We are authorities. We are responsible for our children, at least as responsible as any human being can be "over" another. We do guide our children, make decisions on behalf of their well-being, and lead the way. And yet, how we do this is crucial to how children will relate to us and to authority figures in general.

When my son was about seven, he called on a neighbor boy to play but the boy was not allowed to come out until he had finished his chores. Two hours later, Theo wanted to call on the boy again. I told him he couldn't do that because the boy's mom said he would come out when he was ready, and we didn't want to disturb them. Theo wouldn't have it. He then concocted a story and told me that he really hadn't called on the boy the first time. I asked him if he was telling me the truth and he insisted it was true: he hadn't gone to the boy's house. I knew he was lying and suggested that maybe he was lying because he didn't agree with my viewpoint. He then admitted it was a lie. But here comes the great teaching: my job was not only to get him to tell the truth, but also to encourage him to have his own opinion, and to use his power in relation to authority. So, I also had to support him to disagree with me directly, not just lie to me.

Theo thought for a moment, working on his point of view, and then told me that he felt it was okay to call on the boy again, since enough time had passed. I complimented him for expressing his view, but I said it was important to me that he also understood my position. I explained to him that people feel disturbed if you bother them too much, and I was nervous the neighbors would find him intrusive and disrespectful of their needs, and as a result wouldn't want their son to play with him. It was hard for Theo to understand. But then he suggested that perhaps he should call on his friend and also apologize for disturbing them. I agreed it was a possibility, but that it would be a risk. He still might disturb the family.

I thought we had a good discussion and I noticed I felt changed. I felt he had more of an understanding of my view and had even incorporated it into his plan to approach the neighbor. He went over to the neighbor's house and came back and reported that his friend wasn't home. He told me he spoke to the boy's father and apologized for disturbing him. His friend's dad was nice and understanding and it turned out to be a good experience all around.

I let my mind be changed by a seven-year-old. Some might see this as being inconsistent, that "no" means "no." I believe in being fluid; that demonstrating an ability to be changed by others and to be genuinely impacted by our children models relationships based on mutual respect and learning, not just on power.

Simply condemning lying without understanding its deeper structure around power creates more clever and deceptive forms of lying as children grow up. Furthermore, kids who can disagree with their parents are able to stand up to bullies and other people in their lives who threaten them.

Bess was a sixteen-year-old girl who snuck out at night to see her boyfriend. Her parents caught her and were very distressed. She sat in my office smug and non-communicative, while her mother screamed at her for lying. Her mother began to disparage her boyfriend as well as her character. Bess turned to me and said, "See why I don't tell her anything?" Bess was looking for support; she wanted me to be on her side because she felt weak. The deeper relationship issue was that she felt put down by her mother and felt unable to talk to her about the things that were on her mind. It is a typical teenage problem.

Parents naturally have strong feelings in terms of how much freedom they allow and what they feel is safe for their child. At the same time, teenagers need and want to feel their independence. This is a clash that creates a terrible tension in many families. The key is to have a good enough relationship with your teenager that allows for discussion of these things. Without a good relationship where teens feel free to express themselves we can only expect lying and deception. You needn't agree with your teen but your ability to listen and discuss issues furthers the deeper process underneath the behavior. Remember, if you can listen and appreciate her view, she will also value yours.

I encouraged Bess to tell her mother why she didn't want to talk to her. At first, Bess shrugged and said, "Who cares."

"It sounds like you have given up on someone caring," I said.

"You don't think I care?" her mother shouted.

"I don't know, you're always yelling at me," mumbled Bess.

Her mother shot back, "You just don't listen to me. You don't know about the world. I know what it's like out there." Bess slumped down more in her chair and rolled her eyes. When those eyeballs roll, it can be so annoying to the parent for whom they are meant. But those eyes were rolling because Mom just told Bess that Bess didn't know about the world. In so doing, Mom might have felt she was trying to protect Bess; instead she downed Bess's unique experience of the world. Mom was unaware of how she disregarded Bess and her views. Bess felt too weak to disagree and thus, got hopeless.

I suggested to Bess that her own experience of the world was valid as well as her Mom's. I encouraged her mother to share her experience without putting Bess down. I suggested that maybe Mom had some rough times and wanted to share her experiences and didn't mean to come across disrespectfully. Perhaps she was fearful for her daughter.

Mom then began to cry and shared a story of being raped as a teenager. Bess had never heard this story and was visibly moved. She came closer to her mother and her eyes welled up with tears. "That is why I want to protect you. I don't want you to go through what I went through, ever."

"I'm sorry Mom," Bess said.

"Maybe I am too hard on you. I am just so scared," her mother said.

"You are Mom. You are too hard on me. I need to have my own experiences. You can't protect me, not always."

Mom nodded in agreement. There was suddenly an understanding between them. A door had opened in their communication.

When communication is open, and kids can disagree, they needn't lie as much. This means they can disagree without put-downs or ramification, without you withholding love, being terribly disappointed, or be in a lingering mood. And it must be said that lying hurts others. It breeds mistrust and can destroy relationships. Parents must also talk about the hurt, sense of betrayal, and lack of trust they feel with their children. However, this must be done genuinely and not from the perspective of a moral higher ground. We must get to the root of lying and encourage our children to speak their minds even in the face of disagreement or conflict. That is a challenge for all of us!

NOT LISTENING

Parents, caregivers, and educators frequently complain about children who don't listen. Each situation is unique, but not listening is frequently a way for children (actually for all of us), to not only block out what others say, but to hold onto our own views or experiences. It is also a way for us to say "no," particularly in cases where this might be difficult. There is a sense of power in not listening. However, not listening also creates relationship problems, so exploring the process of not listening and helping children to express power in better ways is more effective.

We might consider how we expect children to drop everything they are doing and listen to us. They should immediately stop what they are engaged with and do as we ask. When you think about it, in most situations we would find this quite disrespectful; we would want to finish what we are doing on the computer, or stop our reading at the end of a paragraph or chapter, or finish any number of tasks at hand. We often do not give our children this same respect. Instead I have heard parents say, "Oh, he just has a hard time with transitions."

Children are engaged and creative. They have pride in what they do and also need the respect to complete their tasks or to find a good place where they can stop. This is one reason why they do not listen and obey. Parents can help by giving them ample warning time and even ask them how much time they need.

With teenagers, this dynamic is a little more complicated. A father complains that his teen is dismissive to his ideas and complains, "She doesn't listen." In his voice, I can hear his hurt. This is a typical pattern with teenagers; the young person dismisses others in order to find and elevate her own views. Fighting against authorities and parents is one way to find one's own views and feel strength and independence. The parent would be well served here to help bring out the views of his teen. This father needed to find out more about what his daughter was thinking instead of only focusing on how she didn't listen to him.

Even if the parent disagrees, the teen's ability to state her views and have her own opinions relative to a parent cannot be emphasized enough. It is a developmental process that supports self-esteem and gives teens the confidence to get along in the world. Enjoy the ideas, find out why she thinks the things she does, share your opinions not as *the* way, but *a* way. So many teens and parents complain about not being able to talk with each other. Teens say parents don't understand and just disagree with their ideas. Parents say teens are disrespectful and rebellious.

To further this kind of interaction, the next step would be to engage authentically in how your teen's behavior makes you feel. Remember the father who was hurt? Parents do get hurt, and teens need to know the effect of their interactions and that they can have an impact on parents. Too often, when parents get hurt, instead of showing hurt, they get angry, indignant and begin to take revenge by withdrawing love, making rules, or being punitive. It is a great inner challenge for many parents to show hurt. By engaging on this level you teach your teens an emotional intelligence; you show them how to express hurt and how to interact around feelings. Too often parents don't realize that when we try and get above our hurt and then turn sarcastic, punitive or angry, that this is the behavior our teen reflects back to us and to others.

In the above case, after the father had listened to his daughter, I encouraged him to also show her how hurt he felt when she didn't listen to him. He expressed it so genuinely, without putting her down, and really showed his emotion. He apologized for not valuing her views and stated that the way she spoke to him, or didn't listen, really hurt him. She softened and apologized to him, and then told him how deeply she loved him. It was quite touching to witness.

It is important to remember that if we don't value the viewpoints of our young people and make room for disagreement, their expression will happen in more covert ways. Some things might be so hidden that we may not even know about it such as lying, cutting school, or using drugs. Disagreement and saying "no" can be expressed indirectly in subtle signals such as not calling home, turning their back on you, going up into their room, or playing loud music. These forms of resistance become a way of feeling powerful and saying "no" when the teen feels she cannot do it directly.

With that said, we must remember that kids still need to do many things that we won't agree with. They need to feel different and have their own experiences. However, if your child feels your love and interest in her views and feels free to voice her opinions even when they go against yours, then you have cultivated a good relationship, a relationship in which your teen will value your opinion as well.

FINDING THE SUBTEXT OF POWER STRUGGLES

Power struggles can get out of hand when we miss the subtext and get stuck in the content. The content of the fight is not the most essential piece of communication. The subtext is about the child's growing autonomy and power.

It's important to value the subtext and to address it. When my son was about five he was playing on our block and many neighbors were outside. I told him it was time to come in. He didn't want to. I said that dinner was ready. He then said, "You are not the boss of my body." The mothers around me sort of looked at each other knowingly, bracing for how I was going to handle his resistance. One mother said under her breath, "Oh yeah, that's what you think." I said to my son, "You are absolutely right; I am not the boss of your body. No one is. You really are, and I am glad that you know that about yourself." Theo beamed, and I continued, "I am also really, really hungry, and dinner is on the table and waiting for us. How about if we go in?" We then walked towards the house together holding hands. The other mothers saw a power struggle and their body language let me know they were expecting a fight. However, I reacted to the subtext. I really am not the boss of my son's body and I am glad he knows that. This is the "battle" he needed to win and winning this battle allowed him to accompany me to dinner without complaint.

In the midst of power struggles, try and step out of the content, feel into the subtext, and address it. For example, "I feel your strength right now. Wow, you are really independent! I like how you think." Or, "I like that you can go against me and people in authority. I like that you question and don't just go along with things." Such statements relate to the deeper message your child is communicating. In fact, when you relate to the subtext, the feeling or energy in the background that your child is trying to convey becomes the central focus and often the content is even forgotten. The child feels supported and validated for her experience in the moment, be that her independent thinking, power, or courage.

DE-ESCALATING TANTRUMS

With young children who refuse to listen, dig their heels in, or won't be budged, a helpful way to address the subtext is to join their communication style.

If your little boy is singing and trying to tune you out, try singing along and tell him what you want him to do: "It is time to go now, we must clean up. I know you want to play, I know you want to play, ladidaa, it is fun to play and also clean up, ladidaa ... " Interacting in this way makes life more fun. Your child feels validated because you joined his style; you are not against him, so he is also free to clean up and needn't fight it.

If your child is jumping and stomping and won't go to bed, you can playfully stomp too, and say what you want in the rhythm of the stomp: "The mama bear needs help to get her babies to sleep, can you help round them up? Let's bring them upstairs to bed now."

For those terrifically dramatic moments when the child is having a full-blown tantrum, I have had success by playfully joining the tantrum. Take over the energy of the tantrum and do it better than the child. Find something in the moment that you feel strongly about and insist on it in a child-like way. Stomp your feet, make a child voice and say, "But I really want to go out and have a coffee with my friends. I want to have a turn. Pleeeeeease, we have to go now. We have to, we must!" Take it to the limit. It is often quite the show-stopper and your little one will stare at you, stop, or burst into giggles. I acknowledge it can take a lot of energy, but it is worth it in terms of fun and laughter. It is also a relief to de-escalate those meltdowns in a way that leaves everyone feeling well. Children are predominantly identified with being needy and wanting their own way. As a result, parents often marginalize their own needs. When parents take over the insistent one or the needy one in the relationship dynamic, surprising interactions can occur. The child might actually take over the parent role, "Calm down Mama, it's okay," or they may see your position and want to help you fill your need.

Another possibility is to act out the two roles in conflict. This is helpful to do with your partner. One of you has the tantrum: "No, I don't want to take a nap! I won't! I won't!" The other person can step into the parental role: "You need to take a nap because you need your sleep. Sleep is healthy. When you wake up you will feel better."

Young children enjoy watching their parents act out what they are doing. They even stop the tantrum to watch. They are seeing a dramatic moment in their lives being played out before them. They might even correct you and direct the show. Encourage them to direct both roles. Ask them for advice on how to solve that conflict. Some children will so enjoy watching their parents have a tantrum they will ask you to do this again and again. They want to see us in our wholeness, not just as parents, but as children, too. And they also get to see themselves in their wholeness; they are not only the demanding child, but are also the rational and caring parent.

CHILDREN'S INNER AUTHORITY

Authority is more easily seen in others outside of ourselves than experienced within. For instance, it's easier for kids to see all those around them as having more power than they do. This leads to power struggles with parents, teachers, and other authority figures. One way to support the inner development of your child's power is to help them to connect with their own internal authority.

When my son was in second grade, the teacher said he wasn't focusing as well as he could and was a little wild at times. I thought the best way to help the teacher was to help Theo get in touch with his "inner teacher." I did a very simple exercise with Theo. I asked him if the "teacher" had to live somewhere in his body where would it be. He said it would be in his foot and stomped his foot on the ground. We then played around together stomping our feet and saying, "Stop!" It was fun, and he enjoyed feeling the power of his inner teacher. The stomp (like using the word "Stop") carried a kind of abrupt energy that he needed at times to curtail his wild impulses when they weren't helpful. He actually needed to learn how to focus his energy and not be driven by it. The next day we shared our exercise with his teacher, and all agreed that if Theo was too wild or not focusing, she could whisper to him, "Remember your stomp." The teacher loved the idea, and that afternoon reported that in the morning she whispered it to him and it helped immediately. That problem quickly resolved as he got in touch with his inner teacher who could help him with self-control.

It's a natural need and development for kids to pick up their inner authority. Whenever I work with families, the kids can't wait to play the parents. They want to be the authorities, and parents often cringe when the kids reflect or exaggerate their worst authoritarian traits. Using the power that kids see in parents and teachers is enormously helpful. I remember one parent who came in feeling at a loss around her kids putting off homework and just playing video games. She had a hard time holding a line. I asked the kids to play out the role of the parents and they took on the task easily. They even made a schedule of when homework should be done and if it wasn't done, no video games. By creating the schedule themselves, they felt empowered as the "parents."

Sometimes older children feel the teacher or parent inside of them but are hesitant to bring it forward with their peers. When a teen feels pressured to go along with something she doesn't feel good about, she might use her parents' disapproval as an excuse. However, deep down she is relieved that her parents forbid the activity because she lacks the inner power to go against the grain. Some kids even approach their parents with the slight hint of hope in their voice and ask, "I can't do this, right?"

Sometimes we have to help our kids interact with outer powers that aren't kind. Some situations even call on us to intervene and protect our children if it is too great a power for them to interact with. Yet, even if you must defend your child, you can still do so in a way that is empowering, by helping him to pick up the power of the "disturber."

Picking up the power of the disturber is like the martial art practice of Aikido in which you use the power of your opponent to empower yourself. Have your child play out the mean or scary person, and as you do, notice the energetic quality of that figure. Don't be too focused on what the figure says, which is often just mean and hurtful, but find and explore a quality or energy that your child might find useful.

I remember working with a fourteen-year-old boy whose father was mean and emotionally abusive. Clearly, the boy does not want to become an abusive person. When we played out the father energetically we discovered that the father had a certainty about him. His father would be absolutely certain in how he interacted with the boy. He was unmoving. How could the boy use this quality? I asked him what his deepest beliefs about life were. Was there something he felt with absolute certainty? He said he believed in a world where people were kind with each other and parents showed love to their kids. We worked together on his ability to stand for what he believed in, even in relationship to his father. We then had a session together with the father and he insisted that his father change and stop hurting him. He told his father he needed kindness and love and if the father couldn't do that then he wasn't the right father for him. That father had a wake up call and began to cry about how he was never loved by his father and he didn't even know how to show love anymore. The boy showed him how to do it, how to say, "I love you," and not take things out on him.

POWER AS DIVERSITY

I join the parental wish that my child experience as little pain as possible and that he feel included and at ease in the world. We watch like hawks as our kids go off to school; we want them to feel well socially, to be accepted by the world around them. We fear the middle and high school years in which many of us experienced social isolation and loneliness and hope our children fare better.

As children develop a sense of themselves, they also want to fit in. Oftentimes fitting in means that kids will hide or deny parts of themselves for fear of being different, not acceptable, or worse, bullied. We need to create a new paradigm that underscores the message, "Power is in our differences." Cultivate regard for being different, model it in your own life, and help your child stand up for his unique nature. The deepest power we have is in our capacity to feel at home in our own skin. Even if your child is alone, or has been hurt or rejected, her ability to feel a deep connection to herself is her most essential power. Such children grow up knowing the difficulty of being on the outside, but also feel the strength in the resiliency of their own spirit. This is immense inner power that offers immunity against self-hatred and an inoculation against depression from being downed.

Those moments in time when kids might be pressed to stand up for their differences become life-changing experiences. Kids remember those into adulthood. They become mythical stories that can inspire future work, relationships, creativity, or life purpose.

Keep in mind that cultures and families that value difference create a safe place for everyone.

TIPS FOR EXPLORING POWER AND SUPPORTING YOUR CHILD

- Be aware of your own personal history in regard to power and how this affects your own parenting.
- Remember that kids have little social power and that they are learning about power through your relationship to them.
- Help your children connect to hidden or unknown powers that are present in dreams and dream-like experiences.
- Encourage child-play in regard to superheroes. Explore super-powers that can emerge in fantasy.
- Elevate your child's feeling life and see the power in their expressiveness.
- Support your child to think independently and ask about their viewpoint.
- Encourage and teach your child how to disagree with you.
- Show your child how he impacts you, how his feelings and behavior affect you. Relate to him genuinely through feelings and not principles.
- Consider that when your child does not listen to you, she might be unable to stand up for her own direction.
- Find the subtext in power struggles.

- Join the communication style of your child as a way to meet his energy and unfold tantrums.
- Explore why children are lying: it often happens when kids feel weak and un-free to express their views in relationship to you. Encourage open communication in which your kids feel free to express their viewpoint.
- Support your children to find their own inner authority. Help them to explore the inner "teacher," "parent," "police officer," etc.
- Treat your child with the same respect you expect from her.
- Encourage the often hidden powers that are within diversity and difference and help your child stand for his uniqueness.

your child in the world

Diversity, History, and Social Reality

*I am related to everyone because I have
everyone's DNA inside of me.*
—Aisha, age 12

Parents are the child's first guides to life outside the family sphere. We introduce our children to the world often choosing carefully what we deem appropriate. We filter what the world offers and impress upon our children the values and perceptions that we carry. Yet the world also imparts life lessons and sometimes thwarts even our best-laid plans. Children absorb quite a bit, grapple with their experiences in the world, and eventually develop their own opinions no matter how much we try to shape them.

Many parents give quite a bit of thought to how they will or will not expose their children to social issues, history, and the great diversity of people, cultures, and countries that make up our world. Other parents don't think much about it. Personally, I find this topic fascinating to think about and consider as a parent. Why and how do I present and filter some experiences and not others? How do I introduce and frame history? How do I interact with my child and his relationship to the world? In this chapter, I offer the reader some of my musings and experiences.

TEACHING HISTORY

Much of history is so painful that many of us don't see the value of teaching it to young children. Others feel more motivated by pride, social justice, or a sense of lineage, and want to make sure their kids know their history and become socially aware. Many families don't have a choice whether or not to introduce their children to social issues because they live with discrimination as a social reality. I found myself at an interesting crossroads when my son was very young. Though I wanted to expose him to the diversity of the world, I was hesitant to discuss history and its relationship to oppression and discrimination.

Teaching about oppression has its challenges; one does not want to inadvertently reinforce values of discrimination or add to the unconscious baggage of a victim identity. Teaching about our very complicated world reveals divisions between people that young children do not yet perceive.

I remember an instance when an African American friend of mine wanted to see if my light-skinned son perceived racial difference. My son was about three or four and this man held his arm next to Theo's and asked him what the difference was between the two arms. My son said, "Your arm is bigger." My friend was fascinated that my son said nothing about skin color. Size was what he perceived, the difference between a child and an adult was more in his consciousness.

Speaking about slavery and its painful and repugnant history introduces ideas that are abhorrent and challenging to a young, open mind. The idea that a human being can "own" another is almost impossible to comprehend. Planting that idea in the mind of a young child, even as historical fact, introduces a form of difference-making that was heretofore not present. Suddenly, in the midst of ordinary playground conflict, name-calling is connected with skin color and its ugly history without really understanding the deep social ramifications. Hence, it is important to introduce the histories of oppression when a child has the maturity to comprehend the social gravity of that knowledge. (It would be artificial for me to offer an appropriate age to introduce such information because it depends upon the social realities a given child faces, as well as his or her individual nature.)

There are also the subtle feelings that a child has when he learns he belongs to a disenfranchised or oppressed sub-group. To learn that your family has its roots in slavery, or your ancestors were murdered in the holocaust, or your indigenous culture had been destroyed, has an effect on the consciousness of a young child. It could inadvertently reinforce a sense of victimhood and unintentionally foster feelings of alienation or not belonging to the world. Difference is then understood in terms of good people and bad people, victims and oppressors, bolstering a very polarized view of our world.

I believe that perceiving difference is innate and is a quality to nourish in children. When the child is mature enough, the painful facts of history, the struggles and victories, must be introduced and framed in a way that the child can comprehend and relate to in her own life.

A child who has her roots in an oppressed group can begin to appreciate the struggle of her social and ancestral identity. She can feel pride in overcoming tremendous opposition and be inspired to create a different world. A child who has an identity with a majority or mainstream group can also learn to appreciate difference and become aware of the painful and historical struggles of people who are different from his social or ancestral group. He can also be taught to identify his own points of difference and explore where he might be misunderstood or condemned by others so he can learn to feel empathy as well as connect with his ability to stand up for himself and others.

Exposing children to difference is a social and political act. A child who is comfortable with a diversity of people is a child who is a global citizen, someone who values the basic human rights of all people. Children who are exposed to differences and who are encouraged in their own individuality feel less of a need to bully or put down others. Such children greet the world with interest and curiosity instead of fear or contempt.

RE-CREATING HISTORY[1]

How we teach the history of oppression is a matter of timing, maturity, and individual circumstance. History needn't be static. In fact, history is an invitation for engagement and transformation. Though the cruel facts of war, genocide, and oppression cannot be denied or rewritten, the facts of history wait for us to interact with them. The ghosts of history haunt us in the present day and offer an opportunity to more deeply understand ourselves.

Take Thanksgiving as an example. One year, when Thanksgiving was approaching—an American holiday steeped in the traditions of family gatherings and sharing food—I decided to broach the subject of the holiday's history with my son. Like most non-indigenous Americans I was taught that Thanksgiving celebrated the joint harvest of the Indians and Pilgrims. As I got older I learned about the unspoken story of Thanksgiving including the cruel Indian wars and genocide that took place during the European invasion of the United States.

What was the curriculum in my son's grade school? How would they teach about Thanksgiving, I wondered? In our Portland, Oregon public school, teachers were clearly in conflict about this holiday. I approached my son's first grade teacher to see which history she would teach the children. She told me there would be no mention of it, just a friendly goodbye and "have-a-nice-Thanksgiving" the Wednesday before.

How could I explain Thanksgiving to a six-year-old? A week before Thanksgiving we were walking in the woods and had the following conversation:

Dawn: You know Thanksgiving is next week. We will get together with family and friends and have a big dinner and think about everything we are thankful for in our lives.

Theo: Yeah, I can't wait to see my cousins!

Dawn: I want to tell you where Thanksgiving came from. A long-time ago in our country there were people from Europe, called Pilgrims, who came to the United States. The native people, or the Indians, were already living here. The Pilgrims and the Indians lived very differently. The Indians lived in teepees, tents that were circular and made of animal skins; the Pilgrims lived in houses that were square-shaped made of stone and wood. They wore different kinds of clothes and ate different foods. They also looked different. People from Europe were lighter skinned and Indians were darker skinned. They spoke different languages and had different ideas about life. When people meet others who are different and unfamiliar, they sometimes get scared; they might compare themselves and feel they are better and that their way of being is better. Many Pilgrims felt this way about the Indians. They weren't curious about the Indians and didn't try to live together, but instead they wanted to conquer them and take their land. There were many terrible wars and many people died.

Theo: That's not fair.

Dawn: No, it is not fair at all. So many Indian people were killed. And still the Indian people in our country suffer quite a lot because they used to have lots of land and they had their own way of living and the Pilgrims hurt them terribly. But you know what? We can do it differently today. Let's act out the story and see how we can do it better.

With the trees and bushes around us, in the quiet of nature on a warm day in November, we acted out the story of Pilgrims and Indians meeting. The "Pilgrim" said, "Your houses and clothes are weird. This is our land and it is meant for us. We are going to take it." The Indian said, "No, you can't do that. We will fight you off. This land belongs to the Creator and we have been here for many years." We went back and forth playing out these two roles.

Then Theo intervened in the story. Exasperated, he spoke to the Pilgrims: "How would you like it if someone took your land? You have to learn how to share. This is not your land. Just because these people are different than you doesn't mean you can take their land. You should try and learn about who the Indians are!"

We then had an inspiring discussion about differences and sharing between people. We learned about being curious about people and customs that seem foreign to us. We were re-creating history by making the kind of world we wished to live in. My son didn't just learn the facts of history, he also learned that he needn't repeat them, but could intervene.

We also discussed the holiday of Thanksgiving as an opportunity to celebrate the *dream* of sharing and living as a community of peoples. However, this dream is incomplete without the knowledge of the entire story between First Nations peoples and Europeans, and needs to be understood in a present-day context. This history is present whenever we feel unable to value someone who is different and instead try to dominate them with our ways. This message can be easily conveyed to children in order to deepen the meaning of the Thanksgiving holiday; we can talk to our kids about how they interact with others who are different. Additionally, the background dream of Thanksgiving can be valued with children by nurturing the feeling of gratitude and reaching out to those who are in need. This myth of Thanksgiving cannot die in the United States because it is a dream still waiting to happen. We are still wanting and needing to bring our diverse country to one big Thanksgiving table, and be grateful for all of the gifts we each bring.[2]

Young children are curious, creative, and sensitive to injustice. These qualities invite us to engage with our children in the living history of our lives and can inspire us to right injustice. The Thanksgiving story above offers a taste of how you might explore historical facts and roles with children.

CONFRONTING DISCRIMINATION

Many children don't have the luxury to avoid discrimination and oppression. Being part of a group that has been socially hurt and disenfranchised, or that is different than the norm, can stir up confrontation. It is challenging to prepare children for the potential discrimination they might face, while at the same time avoiding instilling a feeling of victimhood, low self-esteem, or suspicion and defensiveness.

One Monday morning, when my son was in second grade, he went to school and had only been there five minutes when I got a call from the secretary: "Theo says he feels sick and wants to go home. Please pick him up." I went to pick him up, but he had no fever or any other ostensible symptoms. I asked him what he felt in his body and he said, "My feet are going in a different direction than the rest of my body." It was quite mysterious, but I understood that he was saying that most of his body was in school, but that for some unknown reason, his feet were leading him home.

We got home, and he went directly to his bookshelf and pulled out his Todd Parr books, *It's Okay to be Different* and *The Family Book*.[3] "Mama, I like these books because they are about families like ours." Then out tumbles a story that on Friday afternoon at recess, a boy had teased him for having two moms. He said he felt so hurt but was also embarrassed because there were a lot of other kids around. No one could say anything. Apparently, he had forgotten all about it on Friday when he came home from school, but the memory came back in full force upon entering school on Monday morning.

At the age of seven, he had experienced the world enough to know that most children had a mother and a father. He also knew children who were being raised by one parent, divorced families with many parents, as well as some same-sex parent families. He knew he was unique and more than a few times, he had to tell classmates that yes, he did indeed have two moms. However, this was the first time he had been teased. In preparation for entering school, I had mentioned to him that sometimes children might tease other children for being different and that it is important to learn how to stand up for yourself and interact in such situations.

Together that morning we discussed what had happened. First we spoke about the shock of the situation and that it had happened in front of others. No one said anything to defend him and he was speechless as well. So we acted out different responses, role-played various situations, and had some fun with it. Theo could find his voice and a powerful body stance to go with it. He admired a necklace I was wearing which he said looked like a "bully shield." Indeed, it looked like a shield, a round, curved black and silver piece of glass. I offered it to him so he could remember his own powers.

The next day he came home from school and excitedly shared the following story. "I went up to Zach Francis in the playground and I said, 'Zach Francis, on Friday at recess you really hurt my feelings when you made fun of my family. It really hurt my heart, and I want you to apologize.' Then Zach apologized, Mama, and we just played."

I was so proud of him that on his own initiative he had this interaction. He was beaming. I had also been in contact with teachers about how they might be of support and do an educational piece. I suggested to Theo that we might take those Todd Parr books to school and read them together to the class. "Great idea, Mom! I will take them and read them to the kids." I thought he might have wanted support and my presence to read those books, but it was all his. He wanted to do it, to read them aloud to his class. The teacher was fabulous and was able to facilitate a meaningful discussion around the book. When the page came up in one of the books that showed a two-mom family, one of the children yelled out excitedly, "Theo, that is like your family!"

This story is small, yet it is huge in its effects. Not only was Theo proud of himself, and it's a moment that will remain significant to him as he grows up, but also, such life stories become inspirational teachings for others. The next day with a client of mine, a pregnant lesbian woman who fears how the world might greet her child, I shared my son's recent experience. She was hungry for stories that gave models for what her child might encounter and deeply valued this sharing.

VICTIM, OPPRESSOR, WITNESS, AND FACILITATOR

Any slice of social history reveals four main roles that are present: the victim, oppressor, witness, and the facilitator, or someone who can help people work out differences or conflict. Some children will hear history and identify with one of these roles based on their own ethnic, racial, religious, or social background. One of the biggest teachings we can offer our children is to compassionately show them how these four roles are alive in them in any given moment.

Too often, as parents, we do not see the wholeness of our children. Numerous times I have worked with families who only see how their child has been hurt. They are unable to notice how their child might be offensive or provocative with others. Other parents only see their children as instigators and cannot see how their own child is hurting.

The least embodied role in our history, and in our everyday conflicts, is the facilitator role. Victims and oppressors abound and the public plays witness. Rarely does a facilitator come forward, someone who is able to listen deeply, encourage interaction between polarities, and lead through encouraging better relationship and community building. Both adults and children could step into the facilitator role more often. One of my personal goals in the work I do with children is to empower them in their ability to lead and facilitate difference and conflict.

When President Obama was in Ghana in the summer of 2009, he visited the Cape Coast Castle, a weathered fort through which captured

Africans were sent to the "New World" and enslaved. In an interview with Anderson Cooper of CNN, President Obama described how he wanted his daughters to learn about the complicated history of slavery; he didn't want his girls to identify only with either the victim or the oppressor, but wanted his girls to be aware that they could also be in the "oppressor" role at times, relative to those who are different than them. Here is that piece of the interview:[4]

Cooper: How do you explain it to Sasha and Malia?

Obama: Well you try and explain that people were willing to degrade others because they appeared differently. You try and actually get them to engage in the imaginative act of what it would be like if they were snatched away from mom and dad and sent to some place that they had never seen before. But you know, part of what we also try to do with kids is to get them to imagine themselves on the other side as being the slave merchant, and that slave merchant might have loved their children and gone to that place of worship right above the dungeon, and get them to make sure that they are constantly asking themselves questions about whether they are treating people fairly and whether they are examining their own behavior and how it affects others.

Cooper: Do you think what happened here still has resonance in America? That the slave experience still is something that should be talked about and should be remembered and should be present in everyday life?

Obama: I think the experience of slavery is like the experience of the Holocaust. It is something that shouldn't be forgotten about. I think it is important in that the way we think about it and the way it is taught is not one in which there is simply a victim and a victimizer, and that is the end of the story.

I think the way it has to be thought about, the reason it is relevant, is because whether it's what is happening in Darfur or what is happening in the Congo or what is happening in too many places around the world, you know the capacity for cruelty still exists, the capacity for discrimination still exists, the capacity to think about people who are different not just on the basis of race, but on the basis of religion or the basis of sexual orientation or gender still exists, so trying to use these kinds of extraordinary moments to widen the lens and make sure that we are all reflecting on how we are treating each other, I think is something that I want my kids to think about and I want every child to think about.

PARENTING ON THE FRINGE

Many families identify as being on the margin relative to the mainstream culture in which they live. Social issues that other parents can put off explaining stare them right in the face daily. How can we teach our children about the world and their place in it without creating an antagonistic view of the world? How can we prepare our children for what they might encounter without hypnotizing them into holding a defensive stance towards the world? And finally, how can we also help them discover what might be empowering and special about being on the fringe—what is the value for their own lives and for the world at large? Can they find the contribution that such a fate inspires?

Many people believe that "fitting in" protects children from adversity and that living in a home that mirrors the mainstream culture around them will allow them to succeed while those who don't will suffer in life. This belief originates in the desire to protect our children and not cause them undue pain. We might think that if we can pave an easier road in life our children will thrive. While I can appreciate the sentiment, I also believe there is a wealth and depth of experience to gain when we encounter challenges in life. Kids who have to confront the difficulties of being an outsider can also be supported to mine the potential richness of that experience. Too often we focus only on what is lost, but not enough on what can be learned and gained.

Adults often reflect back on their childhood experiences and realize that the times they were marginalized or discriminated against shaped them in positive ways. Despite pain and loneliness, many will say they learned about compassion. Others learned how to appreciate difference. Some found unknown strength and courage in the face of an incredible challenge. And others learned about perseverance and found something within that could never be put down. Obviously, this is not the case for all; others do get injured and never find their way through. Yet it is often the case that adults who suffered discrimination find themselves called to do the work they do based on these early experiences. These are the people who are now giving back to their communities as social workers, health practitioners, community leaders, teachers, conflict workers, leadership consultants, business leaders, politicians, community volunteers, non-profit leaders, and engaged parents.

We needn't wait until we are adults to get this insight. Children can also be taught to find the purpose in the struggles they go through. A parent who is able to help her child understand what she is going through, help her to meet and confront those challenges, and then frame the experience in the context of being a conscious and contributing world citizen, instills a sense of pride and purpose in her child.

Take, for instance, the story of Farid. Farid came to me because his high school work had plummeted and he seemed moody and upset. In our session, Farid told me that he had been excited to move to the U.S. from Saudi Arabia, but things had not worked out the way he had hoped. Kids avoided him; it was hard to make friends, and he felt isolated. He would overhear negative comments about Muslims and Arabs and he began to keep more and more to himself.

He shared with me how humiliated he felt one day in the cafeteria. He sat alone at a table and noticed as a group of girls stared at him and giggled. We guessed what those girls might have been saying. In his imagination Farid discovered that they were curious about him. Although they acted rudely, Farid felt that deep down they were interested in his difference. He imagined they were filled with stories and stereotypes about Arab people. Farid's mood lifted making this discovery and together we explored how he might interact with this situation. He was faced with his biggest challenge—how to approach girls!

We role-played the situation as a practice. Farid walked over to the cafeteria table and stated the obvious: "Hi," he said, "So, my name is Farid, and I have a sense you don't know much about people from Saudi Arabia. I struggle a lot in school because people tend to avoid me. They have lots of stereotypes about Arabs. So, let's talk about where I come from. Feel free to ask me questions and I'll tell you about where I come from."

This was a big step for Farid, but his next step was to talk about his path in the world. What does it mean for him to be an Arab teenager in the United States during these times? We reflected on this and he got very quiet. Then he said, "I am a messenger of peace. I want kids in America to know that we are basically just like them. We want the same things in life. We want friends and to have a place in the world."

This touched not only me, but Farid as well. His problem in school was connected to a life purpose, a calling. He realized that to be a messenger for peace and to take that seriously would give purpose and meaning to his life. Farid broke down walls at his school and approached that daunting cafeteria table. As a result, he became more socially involved in school, and his grades improved. Farid and I also spoke with his parents about how they could support him in his calling to be a messenger of peace. I know he is someone who has made and will make a significant contribution as an adult. Kids like Farid are cultural transformers and filled with the knowledge and sense of a larger task.

Parents can support their children by preparing them for what they *might* face without arming them against the world. Pace your child. Ask kids if they feel comfortable at school. Ask if they feel different and if that difference is celebrated; or do they feel ashamed and need protection? Initial questions should be light and inquiring. If nothing is happening— wonderful! Answers to such general questions will give you the direction you need to follow.

If children do feel shame or are in need of protection, help them connect positively to their difference, and support them to feel proud of who they are; let them know everyone is different, even if it isn't always obvious. If children feel defensive invite them to talk about a situation in which they have needed protection or one in which they fear they might need protection. Play the situation out. Model how your child might defend himself. Role-play different interactions until your child feels more at ease.

Share your own stories about where you have felt different as a child or as an adult. Tell kids about the times when you were able to stand up for yourself and the times you felt you couldn't. Share with them where you got stuck and ask for their advice. What could you have done differently? Your experiences will create a deeper relationship between the two of you and help them not to feel as isolated. Most kids love to hear your stories from childhood. Chances are that the places you felt stuck in your own childhood could be the same issues your child is faced with now. It is an opening where you can both learn together.

Finally, discuss different social action projects that would support your child and educate others. Some possibilities include: creating school forums where diversity issues are discussed, attending inter-faith services, reading a book to a class, or encouraging classmates to share food, art, music, stories or something unique from their family or ethnic culture. The list is endless and is a wonderful way to engage your child's creativity and allow them to make a significant impact.

WE ARE ALL DIFFERENT: EXPLORING THE "DISTURBING" CHILD

Regardless of the social groups children belong to, there will always be someone who appears different relative to them. Kids often complain about the kids who are disturbances or seem "weird." For example, my son reported in first grade that a boy kept slamming into him. He didn't like it and had told the teacher so the boy would stop. I learned that the boy was from Russia and did not speak English very well. After talking to my son, we discovered that Anton was not really trying to hurt him, but wanted to play and didn't know how to express himself verbally. Anton was a big kid and didn't realize his own physical strength. His lack of English and his way of slamming into kids to make contact left him excluded and disliked by the other children. Helping my son understand Anton and discussing how he might feel and communicate if he didn't speak English was very helpful. We even spoke with the teacher about how we could support Anton to express himself in a way that wasn't hurting others.

BEING AN ALLY

We all need allies and friends who can be there for us when we most need them. Children need encouragement to ask for support when they need it. Many kids don't know how to ask for help and just go silent, wanting the difficulties to go away. Or, children don't yet have the language to express how they feel. It is rare for a child to say to another, "Hey sometimes it is hard for me being only one of a few Asian kids in school. Do you notice how kids sometimes make jokes about my eyes? It hurts me. It would be great if I had your support and help in these situations." By far the biggest majority in schools are not the bullies nor their targets, but the bystanders. We have an enormous silent majority that could be potentially quite powerful.

Some kids are natural allies; they jump into the mix and speak from their heart. However, many are afraid of being a target themselves or fear being ostracized. But I think both children and adults just haven't found their voice. They fear their own strength, power, and self-expression. Kids who learn about the power of their own expression at home are the ones who most easily take up the role of ally for others.

In addition, adults have their own baggage about exclusion, bullying, and marginalization. One father I worked with insisted that his son drop his friendship with another boy because this boy had no friends. The father said this boy was weak and that his son needed to associate with strong and popular kids, otherwise he would also be seen as weak and undesirable. This father was running from his own personal history of rejection. By forcing his son to drop this friend, he was teaching his son to reject his own need for friendship and to perpetuate a popularity culture that ends up hurting everyone.

In order to be an ally, we have to model this for our kids—we need to stand up for those who are not able, to speak up for the richness of diversity in our world, and give our children the language to express themselves. Take Natalie, for example, a ten-year-old girl who is one of the few African Americans in her grade. She has not faced any direct teasing in regard to race and seems to have many friends. In her school we are doing a program for girls and we are doing an exercise around appearance. I notice that she is quite sad, and she shares with me that she feels ugly. Her hair is not "right," she says, "I don't have good hair." One of her friends, a white girl, approaches us seeing that her friend is sad. She reaches out to Natalie and asks why she is sad. Natalie can hardly speak through her tears, but manages to share the sense of inner criticism that she suffers from in regard to her hair. Zoe is quite surprised, but also serious, taking in the words and feeling that Natalie is sharing. With the sincerity and naïveté of a ten-year-old, Zoe blurts out that she loves her hair and all of the beautiful styles that Natalie wears. Natalie is in disbelief. "Really?" she says meekly. "I feel so alone. There are hardly any African American kids here." "I really love your hair," states Zoe. "In fact,

I really just love everything about you and I am so sorry you are so sad." Zoe takes Natalie in her arms and the two girls give each other a big hug.

Zoe and Natalie had been friends for a while, but had never spoken about race. It was not an issue in their friendship. However, it was obviously something that Natalie had thought about and reflected on relative to her reality in school and in her community. Zoe had an insight into Natalie's life experience that she hadn't known about before. Zoe's response was beautiful and deepened the bond between the girls, breaking down barriers and inspiring Zoe to be an ally.

After the girls hugged, I asked Zoe if there was anything about herself that she felt was more unusual that she might be embarrassed or shy about. I did this because too often we see difference one-dimensionally. We are all different, and the more we know this, the more the world becomes a home for all. Well, hair must have been the big thing that day, because Zoe said she couldn't stand her straight hair sometimes. She felt it was boring and wished she could do more things with it. The roles switched, and Natalie then stroked Zoe's head and said she loved her hair and would show her how to make braids.

There are so many taboos that leave our children isolated and create family secrets that are hard for kids to carry. Having a parent in prison is a common experience for many children. Many kids don't know how to speak about it. They might lie about it because they have been told to or just feel too uncomfortable. Some fear if other kids knew, their parents would forbid contact. It is an extremely complex issue, and there is not one solution for all situations; everyone has their own story. However, we must remember not to identify people one-dimensionally, labeling them as "bad" and throwing them away. For example, take a child whose father is in jail. Yes, her Dad has problems with drugs, but we don't want to discount his whole being. He loves his daughter; he has talents, ideals, and longings, and life has been hard and he is hurting. Being able to speak openly about the nuances of people can be very healing for a child and bring her into contact with her community. And yes, there are horrible situations—people in prison for more heinous crimes. Children of these parents need to also know *they* are not their parents. We cannot put them in a "community jail" by isolating them. These kids also need friends and allies.

Many children are deeply sensitive and become natural allies. They are drawn to stand by others and truly desire a world of inclusion. Some children, especially with age, forge friendships based on their differences. Kids find those special friends with whom they can confide in and feel supported by. I was recently moved by a conversation with the mother of one of my son's friends. Our boys have known each other since birth, they go to different schools, and yet they have maintained their friendship. This mom told me that her son shared the following sentiment. "My friendship with Theo is important even though we don't see each other so much. I feel we will always have a bond and can support each other because I am mixed race and he has two moms." This young boy is already astute about the world, what it means to be on the margin, and how allies are important.

PARENTAL ALLIES

Being an ally and feeling that we have friends and allies in this world who can stand up for us are crucial to our well-being. As children mature and become independent, friendships become more and more central. Some friendships can become quite intense, and at times, kids may need help from parents to manage that intensity. For example, children who contemplate suicide might share these feelings with a close friend. That friend then carries a big burden; secrecy has been promised, and yet, it is a secret that is too big to hold. As parents we need to be aware of the weight our kids carry. Being an ally does not mean that a child has to carry this weight alone; as parents we can be allies to our children. Obviously, for our kids to feel comfortable in sharing with us we must have a good relationship and open communication. As parents we might reflect on the kind of relationship we would have needed in order to confide in our parents. What would we have needed to be able to talk openly about issues of suicide, teen pregnancy, birth control, addiction, or abuse?

Parents can help prepare their children by talking about the important issues that their kids might face as they discover the world around them. I have worked with many adults who reveal stories about their childhood in which they felt alone, frightened, or paralyzed to understand and navigate some of the life experiences they were faced with. Unfortunately, many children endure terrible physical, verbal, and sexual abuse. Some of these kids will share their hardship with others. Some children are too frightened, embarrassed, and ashamed to speak. However, their friends pick up the signals. They notice that some homes simply don't feel right. Kids can sense the fear, the harshness, or an impending danger. They are confused by and cringe with unwanted sexual advances or innuendos. These are difficult themes to address, but it is important to bring up these subjects with children with the right timing and sensitivity to their age and life experience.

A good opening with the youngest of children could be the simple question: "Do you notice that different friends' houses feel different than ours?" This question is good to help kids gain awareness of the world outside of their home, whether to notice a potentially dangerous situation or just a situation that is different and challenges their view of the world. Such a conversation can help kids learn about different family constellations, economic diversity, ethnic and religious differences, as well as the different atmospheres that families create. This is incredibly useful in allowing kids to feel comfortable in situations that are less familiar.

You can help kids to notice danger by helping them trust their feelings in different environments. "Did that home feel relaxing, uncomfortable, fun, scary, tense, or angry?" Ask your child what made him feel that way. All it takes is one child—your child—to be able to value his feelings and notice if something harmful is happening.

BRIDGE BUILDING

Children of mixed race and mixed ethnic and religious backgrounds often find themselves faced with special challenges. In the United States, children born of parents who are of different races and religions are soaring in numbers. As our world becomes more global, countries that had been more homogeneous are also finding that love has no boundaries. Depending on life circumstances some children will feel quite comfortable with their mixed race identities, so much so, that it is a non-issue. Thank goodness this subgroup is becoming more prevalent in our society, offering role models of public figures that are too numerous to name! This has certainly had a positive effect on many children growing up in these times, and yet, for many, identity challenges still remain. Particularly around race, many children find themselves rejected by both racial groups and feel insufficient in both. Unfortunately, many of our schools, communities, and social groups are still divided by race, some also by religion and ethnic background.

People tend to congregate around shared values and backgrounds and are drawn together more by similarities, rather than differences. Children reflect this and are similarly inclined to stay within their comfort zones. There is nothing wrong with that; it is exquisitely human. However, that pack mentality camouflages difference. We might all be the same color, religion, or class background, however we are each incredibly unique. If you hang out long enough with one social group you can begin to feel both the security and confinement of social rules that keep the group homogeneous and together. You can also sense the individual desire to break through group norms and do something different.

By virtue of not belonging to only one racial group, mixed race children often become bridge builders. Unable to fit in to one racial group can cause dejection, great insecurity, and pain. And yet, for many people it can become freeing. Take fourteen-year-old Andre, who has an African American mother and a white father. He feels he just doesn't know where to place himself. In the cafeteria, kids are racially divided in friendship groups. There is some crossover in sports, but socially he feels there is a big separation. He often ends up eating alone or he sits with the black kids, but feels isolated. In our work together, we played out the role of not belonging and gave it a voice. "You don't belong. You are not part of us. You aren't really black; you don't talk like us or feel like us. You aren't really white 'cause your skin is brown." As we role-played this rejecting voice I encouraged him for the moment to really take distance and thereby "reject" the others, not just be a victim of rejection, but to actually *be the rejecter*.

"I don't want to be part of your group. In fact, you guys are so limited. Your world is so small. I find it boring to be with you, you are all the same," spoke Andre. He then continued and spoke to the white group, "You just assume that your way of doing things is the best. You never even think to ask about how other people see the world." He then turned to address the black group, "You all act so tough, and you have stupid ideas about race when you tell me I am not black enough. What is black anyway?!" his voice rising with emotion.

Andre had just voiced feelings he had never really expressed before. Shaken by the power of his own words, he realized he really didn't want to fit in. He liked who he was. He wanted people to see him as an individual and to stop trying to pin him down to one racial group. "I am so much more than being black or white! And so are they!" With this statement, Andre made a big discovery. He also had been looking at kids too one-dimensionally in terms of race. At the end of our session Andre felt empowered to reach out to kids who interested him instead of focusing on fitting in to either group.

Mixed race children who break out of group norms are truly heroic and are often bridge builders, helping to educate those around them. They defy being identified one-dimensionally and often take the road less travelled. Their fate gives them a special understanding of different worlds and many are extraordinary in their ability to hold an inner diversity that allows them to be open to all.

BEING THE "ONLY ONE"

Many families who find they are "the only ones" face all kinds of special challenges. It is hard to be the only child or family of your racial, ethnic, or religious group. Similarly, it is hard to be the only one who is gay, transgendered, or is faced with physical, cognitive, or emotional challenges. To a person representing such difference, not only can people be rejecting but they can also be "pedestalizing," putting the person up on a pedestal, idealizing their uniqueness. This often creates relationships based on guilt, where people try to do the right thing or attempt to elevate their own status by associating with someone on the margins. However, such a relationship is impersonal and not based on the merits and qualities of the individual person. Whatever the reason, children and parents alike suffer from this form of tokenism. They feel embraced because of the social group they represent but not for who they really are.

Parents are acutely aware, albeit sometimes unconsciously, of the effects these expectations place on their children and on their parenting. There is an enormous pressure to be *the one* that the community accepts. Without exposure to enough diversity, society sees them as representatives of their whole sub-group and not as unique individuals. An African American mom, whose son goes to a predominantly white school, shared with me the difficulty her son was having in school. I noticed how strict and critical she was with him. I told her that I really liked her son and that I found him friendly, smart, and talented. Our conversation deepened and she realized that she was being so hard on him because she was afraid that he would be judged. As a black child, he had to be extra-special and "well-behaved." She had to work overtime to dispel the judgments of a white world that sees black kids as bad. Though her intentions were to protect her son, in her strictness she inadvertently internalized the "white community" judging her son. She was saddened to realize this and felt she could ease up on him a bit.

Kids of gay parents may feel this burden as well. Much of the world assumes that if you are a child raised by gay parents you will inherently have problems. This becomes a weight on the child who feels if he has troubles it will reflect badly on his family. This can create a cloud of secrecy around the family. Additionally, the desire to be validated as "normal" may result in parents being overly optimistic, not noticing, or dismissing problems that arise in order to be "like everyone else." This unconscious pressure might make it hard for children to bring up difficulties they are having.

Over time these kinds of burdens can become too much for kids. They want to break out and be free. They stop being the "good one," get into trouble, and may even put themselves in dangerous situations. Parents need to be aware of how these dynamics influence their parenting. They can help their children by supporting them in their wholeness, not just as representatives of the marginalized group they belong to. They can become empowered to approach and creatively deal with their life circumstances. And finally, as a world community, we can help such families lighten the burden by challenging ourselves in our diversity consciousness.

GENDER

I came of age during the women's movement. When I was pregnant and found out I was carrying a boy, I felt a surge of excitement. Now I was going to also be part of a men's movement! Over the years, many things have changed for girls and women and yet we can't deny there is still a ways to go. Women throughout the world still earn less money than men, are not represented equally in politics, boardrooms, or other fields of power, and are overwhelmingly the victims of rape and violence. Sexism focuses on the inequalities of women, yet we need to realize that

sexism hurts boys and men as well. Over and over I see men in my practice who are hurt by or judged against cultural definitions of masculinity.
A central way men suffer from sexism is in their negative relationship to
feelings and emotion. Of course, women, too marginalize their emotions.
However, culture gives women more permission to feel and express feelings
such as fear, sadness, vulnerability, dependency, and love.

It takes social cues and development for children to perceive gender
difference. Without being introduced to someone with a gender reference
(such as using the word "he" or "she") or seeing the person's actual naked
body, a young child will not easily be able to distinguish gender. I found
myself struggling to convey to my son the subtle differences in determining
gender, particularly in pre-pubescent children. I felt uncomfortable saying
that boys had short hair and wore pants or played rough and tumble
games. Gender markers like hair length, clothing, and play preferences
are culturally based and therefore, biased. It was true, we knew more boys
with short hair who wore pants and certain colors. However, we also knew
boys who had long hair, wore pink, and liked rough and tumble games.

When we formulate gender difference we are in danger of reinforcing
gender stereotypes. How would you or did you describe to your child
the difference between boys and girls? And if you could find a difference,
could you not also think of a child of the other gender who displayed
those same characteristics?

The fact is, that with time, kids do pick up the social cues that enable
them to assign gender, and most, form relationships based on that gender
identity. I remember being on the playground one day, and a child with
long blond hair, dressed in pink, came flying by on a skateboard. The
kids informed me that this person was a boy and acknowledged that
he "looked liked a girl." They had learned the cues, but they knew this
person was a boy. With my son, I tried in the simplest of terms to explain
the challenge I faced. I told him that it was difficult to say if someone
was a boy or a girl, and also a man or a woman at times. I said it seemed

that boys had mostly short hair, and girls had longer hair, but that actually both boys and girls could have any hair length. I did the same with clothes, behavior, and play preference. I shared that it was often hard to tell someone's gender unless you knew that person. And furthermore, that it was okay to not know. In fact, it was not even that important.

I think not knowing is perfect. Many people get uncomfortable if they cannot determine gender. I think this discomfort reveals more about the one who is uncomfortable and our culture. Having a recognizable gender identity gives people the feeling of security, of a world with clear expectations. Gender uncertainty opens up a world of *human* experience, not male experience or female experience. It means as humans we are unlimited in our capacity and interest in being whole, not being split in a gender category that defines us.[5]

I am repeatedly taken aback by unconscious gender-oriented comments some parents make about their children. "He's a real boy," or "She's a girly girl" equate stereotypical gender behavior with the child's gender identity. Though these comments seem innocent enough, children pick it up and can feel pressured, judged, or hurt.

One day in the playground, a dad with twin boys described his kindergarteners to me. "Will is a real boy's boy," he said watching him throw a stick. "I have to keep my eye on him." Will's brother Dean was sitting nearby under a tree and looked up at his father. Dean had overheard the comment. What did he really hear? He heard that to be a boy, he had to do what his brother did. I responded, "Your other son is just as much a boy as the one who throws sticks."

Another Mom proudly describes her daughter as a tomboy. I am glad she is proud but I wonder what we convey to athletic girls when we describe them as tomboys? Instead of assuming that her physical abilities belong to her nature, she defined those abilities as a male trait. This can make some girls feel hesitant to engage physically, since it implies they are not quite 'real' girls.

I know many people will see this as silly and that I am denying the reality of hormones and gender difference. I know many parents who have raised their children gender-neutral only to discover that their sons are more rough, physical, and less nurturing, and that their daughters are more relational, quieter, and less physical.

I do believe that hormones affect behavior, and yet, hormones affect us all differently. To cite physiological proof that most children match the behavioral expectations for their cultural gender identity ostracizes the many children who do not fit those ideas. It also instills gender behavior and makes it all the more difficult for children to explore experiences that are identified with the opposite gender.

I was doing a conflict resolution program for second graders and we were discussing some of the problems that had come up for the children. Paula courageously stood up and said, "I want to play kickball and the boys think girls shouldn't play kickball." I found it fascinating that in 2010, in Portland, Oregon, this message was still prevalent.

I then asked the girls if there was anyone else who sometimes wanted to play kickball. The girls fell silent and looked at each other. They were scared to answer, scared to be the only one. I broke the ice and said, "Well, I am a woman, and I love playing kickball and other sports." The female teacher and student teacher also raised their hands. Immediately about three quarters of the girls' hands shot up.

I then asked the boys, "Who thinks girls should not play sports?" A handful of boys raised their hands. I asked them why and they said they did not know. One boy then shared that girls could easily get hurt. The teacher piped in and said that boys can also get hurt and reminded them of how many scraped knees she had bandaged. A few boys then said they think girls should play kickball. We continued the conversation listening to the different opinions. At the end of our conversation the class had decided that girls should be included in kickball games.

The most illuminating answer came from the majority of the boys who said they had no idea why girls shouldn't join them. The boys didn't know how they had picked up that message. These unspoken messages around gender are powerful. As soon as a child goes to school, their gender identity becomes paramount. After a few years of grade school, kids mostly separate into gender groups in their play. And yet, there will always be the few children who will want to, and do, cross the gender line. These kids often become targets for bullying. With freedom and encouragement, I believe more children would cross that line. More children would express curiosity about activities and play that they identify with the other gender.

Hang out in the schoolyard and you will get a real earful of gender-related insults.

- You look like a boy with that haircut.
- Your shirt looks like a girl's shirt.
- You throw like a girl.
- You scream like a girl.
- She's sort of like a boy.

These comments are meant to unconsciously uphold gender roles. Children are actively involved in this, supported by what they pick up in the culture around them. I remember when my son was a toddler, he liked the color pink and went to kindergarten with a pink Scooby Doo lunchbox. By the end of the school year that lunch box was off limits. He never said that pink was for girls. But he clearly asserted that he didn't like pink.

As parents we can support our "whole" child. Instead of only parenting to their strengths, which might be reinforced by cultural gender bias, we might notice less dominant qualities in our children. With attention and encouragement such qualities may blossom and offer more dimensions to our children. Obviously, the main goal is to deeply follow the interests and dreams of your child and to follow their feedback. Enjoy the boy who is excited by physical activity, who is assertive and into superheroes, or the girl who likes pink, princesses, and dress-up. But also enjoy the son who is full of fantasy, loves dress up, and enjoys more relational games. Delight in the daughter who is physical and athletic and disinterested in talking circles and beading. These are human behaviors and preferences; identifying these as gender traits hurts us all.

Engage your children in discussions around gender. Don't just be passive when watching media. Bring in your own viewpoint. "I don't like that movie because it teaches kids that girls can't be strong." Or, "I think the man in that movie should say how he feels." Ask your children what they think and enjoy the discussion. Find out what they feel. When they make observations around gender, question them, bring in your own experiences, and talk about history. My son could hardly believe that when I was in grade school we played "girls basketball," a very different kind of game with different rules and lots of limitations so girls wouldn't be so physical. He listened intently to my struggles of being a female who loved basketball and had so few options.

GENDER, SEXUALITY, AND BULLYING

On April 15, 2009, in Massachusetts, a boy by the name of Carl Walker-Hoover, an eleven-year-old, hung himself after being taunted all school year. The kids called him gay. He played football. He couldn't do a push-up. He had a smile that lit up the room and he hugged his teachers.

Kids who are perceived to be gay are tormented. It is still the worst insult to be called "gay" in school. It is a heart-breaking story to see Carl's shining smile across the television screen, to imagine what he endured, and to feel the agony of a mother who loved him and tried to stop it.

Carl's story reveals how gender experiences are equated with sexual orientation even before a child has any sexual experience or any conscious sexual attractions. Carl was bullied because he hugged his teachers and stuck up for an overweight girl who was being teased. Carl's behavior wasn't male or female, gay or straight. It was human.

The association that many make between conventional gender attributes and sexuality is limiting and misguided. A child who displays characteristics that have been more traditionally associated with the opposite gender does not mean they are gay. Attraction and sexual interest have nothing to do with specific behaviors or activities. There are gay football players, police officers, and soldiers; men who are tough, assertive, and resolute. And there are straight men who are sensitive and caring, who work as decorators, dancers, and social workers. There are lesbians who are dancers, strippers, and models, as well as straight women who drive trucks, lift weights, and go to war.

It is a matter of great social urgency that our boys can be loving, sensitive, and expressive and that this behavior is also seen as masculine, or better yet, human. Without including these feeling skills in the development of boys, we teach boys to disavow their own feelings and that it is okay to hurt others. We teach that being one-sided and resolute is better than being flexible and seeing things from someone else's perspective. We teach that everyone should be the same. These same qualities are pre-cursers to war. We need sensitivity and care for others in all genders and sexual orientations. We need each of us to develop our full potential—our full humanity that is unlimited by gender and beyond the labels of sexual attraction.

RAISING SOCIALLY CONSCIOUS KIDS

What does it mean to raise a socially conscious child? We all have our own viewpoints, and each of those views must be included to answer this question.

My view is that children need to be exposed to as much outer diversity as possible, at least as information and discussion. However, it is perhaps more essential that children are encouraged to explore and acknowledge their own inner diversity. Our ability to appreciate and nurture the parts of ourselves that seem different and unique or stand out gives us greater appreciation for others in addition to enriching our own lives.

Being socially aware means that we don't only polarize the world into good and bad or victim and oppressor, but that we can see the potential of both sides in ourselves. Kids (people) who have been hurt often unconsciously hurt others. We need to be aware of these tendencies—even children can see this. They know that when they have been hurt they want to go and hurt the other child. They know the tendency in themselves to want popularity and as a result might suppress aspects of themselves that are different.

We must engage the bystanders who are often too frightened to intervene in bullying situations. These children are the majority in all schools, and they need our attention. Our children need our support to find their own deep powers and inner courage to stand up and be allies.

We need to raise our children to know, explore, and celebrate the richness of their personal circumstance. Race, ethnicity, gender, religion, economic background, sexual orientation, different abilities, health challenges, etc., socially define who we are. At the same time, we need to see beyond these social identifiers and see the individual as a unique being. We need to question stereotypes and explore where they come from. Parents can do all this with their child. Each day, life teaches us and opens up discussion to inner and outer worlds. It is an opportunity for parents to raise a global citizen, a gift to the world.

bullies, victims, and bystanders
Prevention and Empowerment

*I feel terrible about hurting people. I didn't really know how much
I was also hurting myself.*
—Andre, age 16

Bullying is an enormous topic, central to any critical discussion
on parenting. Both adults and kids need a deeper understanding, as well as effective tools, to deal with bullying. Studies show
that parental involvement is crucial in reducing bullying.[1] In fact it
is often the case that bullying behavior stems from the bully feeling
misunderstood and unable to talk to anyone. Thus, we need to know
our children: whether they are the victims or the bullies and whether
they are feeling hurt, angry, isolated, or powerful. For example, one
mother I worked with only sees her child as a victim. The school
sends reports about his aggressive behavior and yet she defends him.
Undoubtedly, he is hurt and feels victimized, but she doesn't want to
see how he also bullies others. In this chapter I address the dynamics of bullying, offer parenting suggestions, and detail concrete skills
how parents and children can navigate this complex and challenging
terrain.

PARENTING AND BULLY PREVENTION

Bullying, aggression, hazing, and the culture of cruelty among young people have often been understood as rites of passage. We speak about "surviving" middle school. We read the classic *Lord of the Flies* and take for granted that our children will run into cliques, gangs, and peer pressure.[2] As parents, we want to protect our children from these dynamics. We hope they will be strong, confident, perhaps popular, and not be touched by the cruelty of their social surroundings. We place a lot of hope and expectation on school systems to be a safe place, to prevent and deal with bullying. However, we as parents are just as responsible. We need to navigate these waters with our children, in schools, and in our own homes. To begin our discussion, parents might reflect on the following questions:

- How do we use our power in relationship to our children?
- Do we use it to uplift our children and bring out their deepest nature, or do we use it in a way that dampens their individuality and demands conformity?
- Is our word the final word or might we be flexible and listen to the viewpoint of our children?
- Do we respect our child's unique thought process, feeling life, and innate differences?
- Do we feel our children are well behaved because they do as they are told and do not dare to express their viewpoint?
- Do we model curiosity with regard to people who are different or do we meet difference with mistrust, fear, and criticism?

If our children are not encouraged to have their own views and even disagree with us, we cannot expect them to stand up to peers and bullies. It is an enormous act of courage and confidence, and requires an inner belief in oneself to go against the crowd. Think of your own childhood and the situations you went along with because you couldn't say, "No." Think of the times you heard jokes or put-downs or witnessed cruel behavior and how you were fearful to stand up to it. And yet, we ask this and want this from our own kids. We want them to be safe and courageous in standing up to peers; to be the child who says, "You can't drive this car because you are drunk. We have to find another ride home." Kids cultivate this kind of relationship power in their homes with us.

In order for your children to have the capacity to make such courageous statements as the one above, you will need to encourage your children to express their own opinions. Do not condemn, make fun of, or disavow your child's views, even if they go against your own. You might not agree with your child's opinion, but create a space for them to express it. Listen respectfully to your child's thoughts; admire his courage in expressing himself. Supporting your child to think independently builds healthy self-esteem. It is okay to disagree and just enjoy the practice of disagreement. Two, three, or four viewpoints can all exist at once! Notice how your kids might withdraw and be shy to express their opinions—particularly when your view is strong—and then encourage them to have their own view, to even refute yours. Parents tend to demand obedience and may develop a heavy-handed authoritarian stance towards their children. But, remember that we can't expect kids to stand up for themselves and challenge others when they are unable to challenge us.

BACK TALK

Many parents fear that their child will be "fresh" or "talk back." When children interact with us in a way that feels mean or hurtful we must react, but humanly and genuinely. This teaches our children relationship skills, particularly empathy, and instills an emotional intelligence in your child. Too often in these heated moments we react with power by putting kids down in kind, punishing them, and insisting on our way. This rarely turns out well; the child storms into her room, seething, and feels misunderstood. The parent feels hurt in the background but acts angrily, asserting her powerful stance in the foreground.

What we have missed in this interaction is a precious opportunity for growth. As parents, we need to show our children our hurt: "That hurts me. It's shocking when you say those words. I can hardly respond. It's mean." If we can have our wits about us and be aware of our parental power, we might continue by saying, "I must have really hurt you, which is why you are speaking to me like that. What did I not notice that hurt you? Have I not heard or noticed you?" These kinds of interactions are more fulfilling; instead of just condemning your child for disrespectful outbursts, we open up the possibility for greater understanding and deeper relationship.

CRITICISM

In my many years of practice I see how injured many people are by criticism. Criticism often begins in our earliest family experiences and then becomes internalized. Critical parents should not be surprised when they find their own kids being intolerant of others. However, what might be less visible is how your child has internalized criticism to such an extent that he either has little self-esteem or pushes himself relentlessly to succeed. Parents who berate their children and use put-downs will find this behavior mirrored in the interactions their children have with others. For many, criticism is a learned communication style. Its roots may lie in a need for perfectionism, feelings of jealousy, or low self-esteem and inadequacy that result in a need to be better than others. However, often criticism comes from a one-dimensional view of the world that sees anyone who is different as inferior. These views breed bullying behavior.

WE ARE ALL UNIQUE!

One central reason that children are bullied is because they are perceived as being different. Thus, raising kids to appreciate and explore differences goes a long way to creating a bully-free culture, as discussed in the previous chapter. I know many of us attempt to be open to difference, but how we marginalize differences in ourselves and others is extremely subtle. Study yourself and how you react to new situations and people that seem unusual or foreign to you. Are you fearful, critical, or curious? Do you inquire, disavow, or ignore? Our children observe how we meet difference in our lives and our actions speak louder than our words.

Our kids notice how we meet and interact with people who are of different races, ethnicities, religions, and sexual orientations. They watch how we interact with cultural customs that are different than our own and how we relate to others' style and dress. They notice how we value and elevate certain kinds of communication styles and neglect others. For example, parents who are very rational might be unaware of how they de-value emotional expression. Other families who value direct and extroverted conversation might not notice how they lack understanding of families who are more internal and quiet.

Kids who do not meet difference with curiosity tend to make the following kinds of comments to others:

"What kind of outfit is that?" (said with derision)
"That food looks disgusting; are you *really* gonna eat that?"
"That kid is really weird."
"He is so gay."
"She acts like a boy."
"You like *that music*?"

Such comments might seem innocent and indeed they are common amongst youth. We hardly notice them until they escalate into more direct insults or verbal abuse. However, these are the pre-cursers to bullying, and these slight quips make school intolerable for many of our youth. At the very least, they force our kids to create a tough shell, and cut off their sensitivity to themselves, others, and the world.

Take the seemingly innocent interaction that I recently over-heard. An eleven-year-old boy comments that he doesn't want to share a locker with a classmate because there is a funny smell in his locker. He whispers to a friend, "It's because he's Korean. He eats weird food." Yes, Korean food is different than the food this boy is accustomed to; however, his curiosity is missing. Difference is perceived as something to protect against. Distance turns into isolation, an in-group forms, and a target is created. The "different" child is excluded, sometimes without knowing why. When we see others as different, it creates distance and therefore a certain kind of freedom to be inhumane. As parents, we have the opportunity to intervene and model how to meet diversity; it is a political, social, and humane act that creates an environment that feels welcoming to all.

Much of the growing up process is learning to adapt to the outside world; kids want to fit in and be like everyone else to seek a feeling of security. And yet, we are all different. Our ability to model difference at home, by accepting differences between family members, differences in opinions, different creative ideas and inclinations, different personality traits and characteristics, helps kids to support their own unique nature.

Since bullying usually targets those who appear different, parents and families who belong to more marginalized groups, or are a minority relative to a majority community, need to feel proud in their own skin. Modeling pride and individuality will help the child to do it too. This confidence makes it harder for bullies to really attack and have an impact.

Obviously this is not easy. The effects of internalized oppression due to societal attitudes towards race, gender, sexual orientation, ethnicity, religion, and class backgrounds run deep in each of us. It is a journey to learn how to free ourselves from oppression if the world outside is downing us. Those of us who belong to mainstream culture can help marginalized families and children by educating our children about diversity. Kids with heterosexual parents will help to create a better school environment if their parents educate them about different family structures. Kids who come from middle and upper income families need to know about families who struggle with finances and putting food on the table. Kids need to know about different ethnic, racial, and religious groups. Every home is not like the one we are raised in.

GENDER AND BULLYING

When we speak of diversity, particularly the diversity of behavior, it is important to speak about gender. Many bullies choose targets that do not conform to stereotypical gender roles. Our culture is obsessed with gender identification and as children age the social cues of what it means to be male or female proliferate. Boys who are sensitive, not athletic, or who like flashy clothes tend to get the lion's share of bullying in the schoolyard. Girls who are more physical, athletic, intellectual, or not interested in clothes can also experience greater isolation and be tormented.

As adults, we need to model all behavior and expression as *human*. Boys don't have the market on being rough and tough, and girls don't have one for sensitivity and style. These qualities are found in people: male, female, straight or gay. This basic education is imperative, especially considering the escalation of suicides as a result of bullying based on the diversity of gender expression, perceived sexual orientation, and of course, children who do courageously come out as gay.

BULLYING OR JUST KIDDING

Many of us grow up in cultures and families where teasing is part of the communication style. It is supposed to be fun and for many it is. However, for many it isn't. Those family members are then deemed too sensitive and become marginalized. I have two views. Yes, we can kid around and tease and it can be fun. But when such banter is not received that way, the teasing needs to stop. It is the more human and empathic route to notice your teasing isn't being received well. Instead we tend to blame the target of our teasing and say things like, "You can't take a joke," or, "You're too sensitive." Many of these so-called jokes are actually digs or things that are not said to us directly. We then wonder what the other really thinks about us.

Teasing is a form of indirect communication that is hurtful. And because it is indirect, when called on it, it can be denied. Kids say horrendous things to each other and then say, "Just kidding." Often children go along with the teasing culture because they are too shy to object. They feel they will be more ostracized and hence, silently suffer.

When kids see this behavior at home, they take it to school. This is why kids are often surprised that they have hurt anyone. They think their behavior is normal or innocent. But they need to see how teasing can be hurtful even though it is not intended. In fact, many adults will share with me how they went along with an atmosphere of teasing in their childhood home and how they just didn't notice how much it had hurt them.

Some children will tease each other because they don't know how to relate. If basic relationship skills are not taught or modeled at home, children don't know how to ask another child to play; they don't know how to begin a conversation or talk about how they feel. We need to reach out to those children and help them to learn how to converse and verbalize their need for friendship.

Respect your child when she says teasing hurts. Even if you think it was a small thing and not meant to be hurtful. Stop and apologize. You might also reflect on why you were teasing. Was there something you were unable to say directly? Were you trying to make contact with your child and you didn't know how else to do it? Enjoy kidding around when there is laughter and fun. But notice the times when there are forced smiles and withdrawal. When the recipient of the teasing says, "Stop, I don't like that," and the teasing continues, it is bullying behavior.

SIBLINGS

Children who bully others are often bullied at home. Kids who bully others have often been put down by parents, other adults or authority figures, or children at school or in their neighborhood. It is extremely common that kids who bully others outside the home are being bullied in their home. As parents we often accept a certain kind of banter between our kids as "normal." We say, "Kids will be kids," and feel hopeless. We are unprepared for the role of conflict facilitator between children. It is challenging and at times overwhelming to deal with the dynamics of bickering, jealousy, fighting, and name-calling that happens between siblings. Parents are already so over-worked that our own need for self-care and respite might make us negligent or unaware of the potential bullying dynamics between our children.

Younger children are often enamored of their older siblings. They learn about the world through the influence of their older brother or sister. As a result of their admiration or infatuation, they might tolerate the abuse and bullying by their older sibling. Younger siblings are often torn between winning the favors and privileges bestowed on them by their older brother or sister, and the humiliation and hurt they have to endure as targets of bullying. It's the price they pay to be included.

Sometimes, older children take the rap for their younger siblings; as parents we tend to see the older child as carrying the responsibility. Younger children can be invasive and annoying to their older siblings who need to learn how to set clear boundaries with kindness.

For example, six-year-old Alex is a really physical child, and his nine-year-old brother Dominic prefers quiet and independent activities. Alex frequently barges into Dominic's space knocking things down and demanding attention. Dominic eventually gets furious, pushes Alex off of him, and Alex gets hurts. As this situation continues to escalate over time, Dominic begins to physically threaten Alex and calls him hurtful names. This family came to me because Alex got sent home from school for punching another child.

The parents were not fully aware of the situation between their sons. Alex needed to learn how to approach Dominic more respectfully, for example, "Dominic, I really want to play with you. You look like you are doing some interesting things in your room. Can you show me what you are doing?" And Dominic needed to learn how to say, "Alex I really want to work on this model alone. I'm sorry. Maybe we can do something else together later." These are simple and obvious statements that many kids do not know how to verbalize.

The work with Alex revealed that he was angry at school that day because his brother had called him stupid and had threatened to lock him in a closet if he took one step in his room. The child Alex had punched was smaller and was pestering Alex to look at some of his Pokemon cards. Here the roles switched: Alex was unable to defend himself against Dominic and used his anger instead to hurt another child who was smaller and wanted his attention. Alex repeated the behavior he learned at home.

Bullying behavior at home can sometimes reflect bullying at school. Older siblings who are bullied at school can become abusive towards younger ones at home. Unable to defend themselves at school, they express their hurt and anger towards their more vulnerable sibling. It can become a vicious cycle if then the younger sibling goes back to school and bullies others. As parents we need to be more aware of these relationships and give children language to explore and express their feelings.

It takes a little more patience and time to sit with your kids and explore the dynamics between them. Too often, in our efforts to find out whose story is "right," we get exasperated and just simply order them to stop bickering. Slowing things down and exploring the dynamics between the siblings and helping them voice their feelings is a better long-term solution. Children learn more about relationships and will use those skills in their other interactions. Parents also learn more about the relationships between their children as well as potentially uncovering disturbing incidents at school that might call for their intervention.

PARENTAL INVOLVEMENT

If your child was being bullied do you think she would tell you? The better the relationship you have with your child, the more comfortable she will feel. If she feels you can be an ally and help her, she will also have an incentive to consult you. If she feels criticized or put down by you, chances are she would not tell you for fear you would agree with her tormentor. If your child feels that you would involve yourself in a way that would embarrass him, he would rather keep a secret. And, children who have been threatened with future abuse may also keep silent.

We can prepare our children by talking about bullying behavior and what they might confront. Tell your children that some kids fear difference and will put down those who stand out. Ask them why they think kids bully and offer ideas of your own. Tell children that some bullies threaten others with further harassment, and that the worst thing she can do is to keep it a secret. Tell your child that you are an ally and discuss measures you would take if your child were in such a situation. Assure your child that you would take them out of school if need be. Talk about different strategies and practice them.

Many kids fear they will be called a snitch and become more isolated. Discuss with them some of the stories in the news around bullying behavior. There are numerous cases in the news of children who have been severely bullied, some of whom have committed suicide. Later it was revealed how persecuted the student was and how they had feared being a snitch. Have a discussion with your child and ask questions such as: Would they risk telling you or a school authority? What would they need from you to feel safe to potentially share such information? Take time to explore what these safety guidelines are. Often kids may not be forthright or initially know what they need from you to feel safe.

FAMILY LIFE CHECK LIST

Here is a short checklist of important feeling attitudes and skills that you can cultivate and model in your home life with your children.

- Model how to express anger and frustration. Family members who take anger out on others in the family who do not react, create a home life that mirrors a climate of bullying.
- Teach how to have a constructive conflict (see Chapter 6: Growing through Conflict).
- Teach and model how to stand up for oneself, to find one's inner authority, and to conflict with authority.
- Stand up for feelings, all feelings, including hurt, shyness, and sensitivity.
- Model curiosity in your approach to those who are different. Introduce differences of culture, religion, race, sexuality, family constellations, health, and financial situations. Explore diversity as an inner experience.
- Teach seeing the "other" as a part of each of us. We can all potentially be the "other" or the "outsider."
- See the wholeness of your child and all their sides: the one who is powerful, who can hurt others, and who can make an impact; the one who feels sensitive and weak; and the one who has answers, wisdom, and resolution as well.
- Teach children to notice fear. Most of us override our fear. We freeze and go into shock. Help children notice when they are afraid and teach them the signals that indicate when others are afraid. Noticing fear can keep you out of potentially dangerous areas. Noticing fear in others can help you intervene in a conflict. Model this by noticing if and when your child fears you. Help her express her feelings.
- Teach defense and street smarts.

STRATEGIES TO SUPPORT OUR KIDS

Dealing with bullying behavior requires different interactions depending on the situation and the nature of your child. Here are some tips that could be helpful.

Standing up for differences. School social life emphasizes conformity; kids create their own safety net by establishing norms related to "cool" behavior, fashion, music, and interests and yet we all know that we are extremely diverse. Many kids will then create a culture around their differences as a way to find support. However, over and over, kids who are bullied often stand out in some way relative to whatever culture, clique, or in-group is valued.

Help your child to see his own uniqueness and value difference in your family. This is a big step in the process of planting the seeds of self-esteem in your child. Have a family discussion around how each member is different and talk about all of your unique gifts and talents. Each person might share one thing about themselves and then a quality you see in each other.

Go further and role-play different scenarios in which your child, or others, are teased and bullied for being different. Help your child to be proud and stand up for differences. Support them to use their voice, to look someone in the eye, and to take a posture of power. I often ask kids to find the most powerful place in their body. Where in your body is your power-spot? Have them feel that place and ask them what it feels like. For example, does it feel strong, solid, warm, cool, or electric? Encourage your child to connect with that experience and feel it in his entire body. Then have your child stand and walk around with that body feeling. You will notice that a different personality might emerge in your child, someone who is identified with his special body powers. When your child has this sense of himself, he is then more able to verbalize and stand up for things that are important.

Take, for example, a fourteen-year-old girl who once told me that her place of power was in her heart. We imagined the warmth of her heart going into her whole body and she felt the steady pulsing of her heart. "It felt warm," she said, and it had a "constant beat that never stopped." She explained, "It feels like love, and that is the most important thing. It doesn't stop no matter what." I then encouraged her to walk and hold her body as if she really were that special warm love that was always there. This gave her a different confidence in herself and she stood taller and had a kind and loving radiance about her.

I then role-played the bully she had been having trouble with. "You are fat and ugly," the bully said. Instead of shrinking away as she usually did, she walked right up to the bully. "I'm a great person who you will never be able to really appreciate. I am kind and value all kinds of people. I can even see that you bully me in order to be loved by others." Her statement totally disarmed me as the bully and she stood beaming in her ability to champion her own unique nature.

Seeing into the bully. Bullies can be disarmed when others see into their deeper motives which are often unbeknownst to them. Many bullies hurt others because they have been hurt. When they hurt us, it is difficult to see them as the victim. And yet, this is sometimes just the view that can turn things around. "You must be hurting me because others have hurt you. I wish *they* would stop hurting you and that you would stop hurting me."

One boy stopped another boy from bullying him by saying, "You really like me, but hitting me is not the way to be my friend. Just tell me you like me and want to play." Pretty sophisticated? Yes, but absolutely in the realm of children's abilities.

A teenage girl who was teased by a group of girls at school turned to the group and said, "You are all doing this to me and going along with it because you are afraid if you don't others will turn on you. I would hope you could be more courageous. It is hurtful and I don't want any of you to go through it." Our kids are insightful and they gain power by telling it like it is.

Standing for sensitivity. Our kids learn to toughen up quite considerably as they age—as we have as well. For many of us, it isn't until we are adults that we realize we had to create such a tough exterior in order to protect ourselves and survive our childhoods. Many parents grieve as they watch a certain sweetness vanish in their children when they are confronted by a hard and cold world. However, too often we inadvertently help that shell to harden. We might be hard on our kids by being critical and insensitive and unaware of how to support their deepest natures. Additionally, we want our kids to protect themselves; we don't want them to get run over by others.

Paradoxically, the biggest protection is to stand for our sensitivity—and to do it with power, strength, and conviction. Kids who are perceived as weak and sensitive often find themselves as prey. They make easy targets and usually do not know how to defend themselves. However, true defense is not to harden. Too often kids toughen up by turning off their feelings, internally downing some of their best qualities, and acting "tough." It is rare to see a child proudly standing for his sensitivity. "Yes, I am sensitive. I like that part of myself." "It hurts when you say those things. Stop. You wouldn't like being teased like that." To say these things with absolute inner authority is powerful.

I remember working with a group of teenagers, many of them with gang affiliations. At one point in our work, a sixteen-year-old stood up in front of his peers and declared, "I don't like all the talk behind people's backs. It hurts me and it hurts us all. I want it to stop. If anyone has something to say to me, say it to my face. It really hurts." Tears came down his face and the room fell silent. Others were visibly moved to see this very popular boy speak like this. This is the power of standing for feeling, sensitivity, and humane dialogue. Our kids can do this. These situations become life-long memories of courage; they build character and create experiences of inspiration that they can always fall back on.

Using physical defense. Being physical with bullies is a complicated strategy in our culture. Most schools will suspend students who fight, even in self-defense. Therefore, the advice I offer in this section comes with my recommendation that you consider it with great caution and an awareness of the possible consequences for your child.

There are times when your child may want to and need to defend herself physically. Even if she never engages physically, it is great for your child to feel and know her own physical strength. One of the most favored accessories in my office is my punching bag and gloves. The big bag is disguised as a couch with a piece of material covering it, nestled on the floor against the wall. In my toy chest, kids find the gloves and my couch becomes a formidable opponent or a vehicle that allows the child to feel her strength. And adults enjoy it as much as kids!

We all love to feel our physical powers. The experience brings us a confidence and energy that is beyond fighting. In fact, the energy itself is often a kind of self-defense. One becomes energized in a way that changes the way we walk, present ourselves, and interact with others. Additionally, some kids join martial arts, boxing, or self-defense classes.

It is empowering to be able to physically defend oneself. It is not the first choice of action by any means, but when one is physically attacked, self-defense can be essential. Of course, one can—and should—walk away or flee from dangerous situations. It is also helpful to employ other forms of defense that are not physical; there are many different de-escalation methods, conflict resolution tools, and other verbal interventions (many mentioned in this book). However, those special times when one must fight need to be included in our strategy.

Some physical interactions can quickly be stopped, especially with younger children. Younger kids may charge towards another child, and their contact tends to be quick, often in response to some frustration. Usually the beating is not prolonged. In such circumstances teach your child to physically defend themselves without hitting back. Teach your child to take a strong postural stance, make an X with his arms in front of his body and to say "No," or, "Stop it," very firmly. You can show your child how to grab the wrists of a child, who is hitting them, to again verbally say, "No," and to then firmly let the wrists go.

In those extremely challenging moments, when our kids are attacked, it is helpful that they feel able to physically defend themselves. I do not advocate that any child starts any kind of physical conflict with anyone, and yet, there is a time and a place for self-defense. For many children, their ability to defend themselves is a matter of life and death, and for others, even if they are injured in the fight, they may feel good about being able to at least hold some ground.

Using the energy of the bully. Children who are fearful of bullies, or who have been hurt and tormented by them, can benefit by exploring the energy of the bully inside of themselves, and then use that "bully energy" for their own defense. Kids often love to play the bully or the "bad guy." They enjoy it because it allows them to connect with forbidden or unfamiliar energies, and to be able to explore those in a safe environment. I do not want children to become bullies by hurting others; however, I do want them to have an opportunity to play out the disturbing energy or quality at the core of the bullying behavior and use that energy or quality for their own growth.

For example, Kyle, a soft-spoken nine-year-old, was being teased in school. He described to me how some of the boys in his class called him names and took his things. I asked him to show me how they did this. At first he was quite hesitant, so, we used my puppets. He took my alligator puppet with big teeth to show the bullying behavior, and I used my snail puppet to play him. The alligator told the snail in a much louder voice than Kyle usually used, that he was stupid and began to push my snail puppet. I gave some resistance as the snail, and the puppets began to wrestle each other. We ended up giggling and having fun. We experimented with having really loud voices. We yelled, "Stop!" "Don't come near me!"

and, "Don't you ever call me stupid!" This was an energy that Kyle needed in order to protect himself. His soft-spoken gentleness was beautiful, but he also needed to be able to stand up for himself and use his voice.

Kyle and I were stealing the energy of the bully. Children love that concept. I tell kids we are going to steal or take the powers of the bully. It doesn't mean we are going to be mean and abusive like the bully, but it does mean that we are going to find some kind of energy in the bully that we can use for the child's advantage. When I work with girls, I am often amazed at the different energy they step into when I ask them to play the "boy" who is bullying them. One of the first things to notice is how they use their body in space. They sprawl out when they sit and take up more space and they walk and stand as if they own the world. By connecting them with this energy they discover a confidence in themselves that allows them to respond to the bully and walk more confidently in the world.

Being unpredictable, stepping out of the interaction, and using humor. Bullies expect people to fear them and to not react. They thrive on the support of the group. Using humor, and saying or doing something that is unpredictable can be very effective in stopping the bully. In order to do this your child must also have a certain confidence and belief in himself. He must appreciate his unique nature and ability to step out of the expected reactions. It is something you can practice with your child. One of you can play the bully while the other steps back from the scene, loosens up, and picks up something ridiculous or irrational. Here are some examples:

Bully: You are so weird, weirdo, ugly....

Target: You don't know the half of it! I can be awful, just devastating, terrifying. It is unbelievable how horrible I can be!

Bully: Oh, look at her, oh my God, where do you buy *your* clothes?

Target: You know, I really love that shirt you're wearing—where did you get it? You look so cool. How did you get to be that cool?

Bully: Go back to where you came from you %$*&#!

Target: I was just thinking of your grandmother. She must have had a difficult time when she came to this country. Have you ever asked her?

Bully: (approaches threateningly)

Target: Oh wait just one minute before you make me drop my books. I know that is great fun, but I just wanted to know what your purpose is in life; why do you think you were born?

In the examples above, one response demonstrates how we can agree with the bully and take the comments further in a way that empowers the target; by identifying with the attack, the child can then embellish it and turn it around into a power. Other responses attempt to dig deeper and comment on the bully's behavior, but in a surprising way. They force the bully to reflect on his actions. Some responses can more directly challenge the bully by looking beyond the bullying behavior. For example, "I actually almost like you. Somewhere I know you are a kind person, you're just shy about that part of yourself."

Adults may find these responses useful in the challenging interactions that life presents. When you drop out of the expected reaction and drop deeply into yourself, surprising observations or feelings can arise. What makes these responses so effective is that they let the bully know that you are not playing their game. You are not impacted and are connected to something else inside of yourself. This allows you the freedom to respond in a way that can be shocking, penetrating, and even humorous.

Getting help. Many kids fear getting help. They don't want to rat on friends or be seen as weak. They also fear retaliation and further isolation. Prepare and speak to your children before bullying even happens. Ask hypothetically what they would do if they were bullied. Would they tell you? Would they be afraid to speak openly? Assure them that you could help. Share with them what you would do. Encourage them to tell you, even if the bully has threatened to hurt you or other children. Let them know that you have strategies to deal with even the worst situation and that you are stronger together. Bullies count on their targets to be secretive and this keeps the cycle of abuse going. If worse comes to worse, assure your child that you would take them out of that school. No child should have to endure such abuse and be fearful of going to school.

WORKING WITH THE BULLY

Although some children might demonstrate bullying behavior more than others, it is important not to stigmatize the bully. It is equally important to know that we are all in some way both bullies and victims. In some minor way, each of us can display bullying behavior. When we ignore feedback from others, insist on our way, use power with little awareness, gossip about others instead of having direct conversations, or marginalize others because of their differences, we inadvertently step into the bully-zone. Obviously, such behaviors are all relative. However, it is important to know and to acknowledge that we all can be the bully, victim, bystander, or facilitator in different situations. Knowing this helps us to not stigmatize children who demonstrate bullying behavior and to not freak out when our own child exhibits behavior that upsets us. We can inadvertently contribute to the cycle of bullying by isolating and scapegoating the bully and not seeing their greater wholeness and humanity. This makes it much more difficult for the child to understand and learn from her behavior.

Children who are stigmatized as bullies become more isolated and hence, more troubled. Detention and punishment usually do not penetrate the core disturbance that motivates a bully. Many children who bully have been bullied or feel powerless in some area in their lives. As parents and educators we can help to uncover these stories, and help the bully react in the situations where she is feeling powerless.

Another kind of bully needs help to explore his own sense of power. Although bullies seem powerful, and many of them are socially popular, they somehow don't deeply feel it. All of their power is dependent upon the fear or admiration they arouse in others. Without this outer recognition, they have no sense of self, no enduring and independent self-esteem. These kids need help to reflect on who they are separate from the fear or admiration they arouse in others.

It is often challenging for parents to notice behaviors and attitudes that children learn from us at home. For example, some parents can be extremely critical and ride their children. Often times the parent is unaware of the critical culture that has been developed at home. The child takes this critical attitude out into the world. She is overly critical of others, often humiliating her victims. This is how the child feels in the family.

Children who put down others for being different are often terrified of their own unique natures. Parents, caretakers, and educators can help such a child discover and explore her own differences. Such kids need a broader introduction to the world and themselves and they need the love and acceptance from adults for their uniqueness.

Another kind of bully hates weakness. They pride themselves on being tough and strong and often despise their emotions, which they perceive as weak. When they beat up on someone who they perceive as weaker, they are really beating up a part of themselves. This kind of bully suffers from an inner dialogue that doesn't allow for feelings of vulnerability, love, or needing help. Often they have grown up in homes that mirror these values. Such children need support to explore and embrace these disavowed inner experiences.

REACHING OUT TO THE BULLY

Though keeping a distance from the bully is a helpful strategy for the child or children being bullied, from a community viewpoint, however, isolation contributes to more bullying and school violence. Too often bullies remain isolated; they feel stigmatized and become even more alienated.[3] These bullies internalize the world's contempt into a powerful self-hatred.

Isolation is not just a social consequence of bullying, but is also an experience or feeling the bully has. These kids often feel hopeless, misunderstood, and shut down. They have often been criticized and controlled, and their emotional life has been put down. Some bullies are driven by the need to be the best, and have an intense sense of perfectionism. When they don't meet these inner and outer standards, they feel a deep sense of shame and anxiety, followed quickly by self-criticism or hatred.

In the dynamic between the roles of bully and victim, the role of the protector is missing. When I work with children who bully, often a story emerges in which they were the victim. Someone has hurt them, or ignored, criticized, or humiliated them. What stands out in the story is that a protector was missing. The child could not defend himself, and no other adult was able to as well. Some were unable to stop serious abuse and others did not have the language to verbally defend themselves. In such instances, the child who bullies needed to use his power to defend himself in the situation where he was powerless.

We must reach out to kids who bully others. They need help not isolation. There are different reasons for bullying behavior. Here are a few ideas parents can reflect on to try and understand their own children and those around them.

- Many kids who bully do not feel powerful. Even though they appear quite powerful and might even be popular, they use dominance as a way to feel on top. Because their power depends upon others boosting them up, they are actually weak and not in contact with a deep sense of inner power and esteem.
- Some kids will say they are just having fun and horsing around. They need to learn that their fun is someone else's pain. In such cases the

bully models an insensitive culture they internalized. By demeaning and downing the victim, they do the same to their own sensitivity.

- Many kids do not like qualities they perceive as "weakness," like sensitivities, inabilities, neediness, or hurt. They put down others who display these characteristics and are unaware how they also put themselves down for the same thing. These children need support to embrace these qualities in themselves.

- Some kids feel secure by being part of a homogeneous culture. They feel threatened by their own tendencies that make them stand out and ostracize other children who dare to be different. These children need to be exposed to more of the world; they need help to open up to their own unique natures.

- Kids who have been hurt get strength by switching roles and dominating others. Many bullies have been hurt or have been in situations in which they were unable to defend themselves. They find their power and strength by experiencing the more dominant role.

- Kids who bully believe they get status from power and aggression. It is like the world we live in: downing and conquering others gets prestige. This is a world problem that we can change in our families by showing ways to gain status without dominating others.

- Some kids don't pick up outside feedback. They push forward when people say no; they boss others who clearly don't want to go along; they override the feeling reactions of their victims. Young children do this quite innocently and need help to notice others and pick up the feedback around them.

- Bullying behavior is sometimes motivated by vengeance. Kids who have been extremely hurt feel they have nothing to lose and will lash out and hurt others. Explore the experience of revenge and the hurt that precipitated it. Understand that when we want to hurt the other as they have hurt us, we are longing for the other to awaken to the pain they have caused, and to feel remorse and apologize.

AN INVOLVED CITIZENRY:
EMPOWERING OUR CHILDREN AS ALLIES

Bystanders are the majority and yet most of them (us) are silent. Here are some of the common reasons why kids don't intervene:

- They fear they will be treated similarly to the victim.
- They fear retaliation or revenge at a later date.
- They fear they will lose friends.
- They fear they will lose status.
- They fear they will be called a snitch.
- They do not have experience or knowledge of themselves as a person who can speak out on important issues.
- They fear or do not know their own power.
- They hope someone else will intervene.
- They don't want to stand out and bring attention to themselves.

Parents, caretakers, and educators can help by engaging the bystanders. Begin by asking them what they fear and create an open atmosphere where they can discuss the topic. Ask kids what kind of a world they want to live in, what kind of a school they want to attend. Ask them to imagine a situation in which they are being bullied with many kids standing around. How would they want those bystanders to react? Gather their answers and support them in taking action. Encourage friendship groups, siblings, and classrooms to agree to be active bystanders. Put their principles into action. Practice by playing out different situations and encourage bystander participation.

These discussions are extremely helpful for creating a safer, healthier school and home environment. They also engage our children and give them a sense of what it means to be a responsible, kind, and involved citizen. Children long to take responsibility and feel their own power. Over and over again, I have heard the stories and felt the pride, from both adults and children, who weren't just passive bystanders. I have also heard the regret and helplessness from those who were too fearful, or did not have the skills or sensitivity, to engage and make an impact in their lives and in the lives of those around them. We can change the culture of bullying and not simply accept it as a rite of passage.

growing through conflict

A Toolbox for Parents and Kids

No one listens to me!
—Everyone

Kids first learn how to deal with conflict and disagreement in their family of origin or with their primary caretakers. The fact is, many of us have not had positive experiences of resolving conflict fruitfully. As a result, we avoid conflict, have little tolerance for tension, avoid bringing up issues, drown ourselves with drugs or alcohol, or become volatile and abusive when a conflict arises. Kids need to know and be shown that conflict is a normal part of life, that it can enrich relationship, and that it offers valuable learning opportunities.

To begin, I would like to invite you to reflect on your own relationship to conflict and disagreement. Here are some questions to consider:

- How was conflict dealt with in your home when you were a child? What did you learn about dealing with difference and disagreement as a result?
- Did you ever see a conflict dealt with in a fruitful way? If so, what were the qualities and characteristics of the interaction that made it rewarding?

135

- How comfortable are you in bringing up differences or relationship difficulties?
- How do you deal with conflict and difference of opinion with others?
- How able do you feel to take your own position and express yourself?
- How open are you to taking the other person's side? Are you able to see the validity of their position?
- How comfortable do you feel with strong emotion?

How you answer these questions might shed light on your relationship to conflict and your style of parenting. Your answers also reveal what your children are learning about dealing with conflict. How we get along with disagreement and difference in family life is reflected in the atmosphere of our homes. Some family atmospheres seem very orderly and obedient and yet there is a feeling of fear in the background that prevails. Other homes feel warm and inviting and many views are welcomed. Some family atmospheres are quiet and can feel tranquil or they might feel stifling and oppressive. Families that are loud and volatile can either feel free or abusive. And some family atmospheres can feel free and fun, but they might also be experienced as dismissive or negligent. A family atmosphere that feels open and comfortable to all, where the diversity of each member's viewpoint is valued, is one in which most people feel well. Such an atmosphere can easily weather conflict while supporting family relationships.

THE OTHER IS YOU

Slogans like, "We are the world" emphasize our interconnectedness and urge us to see common ground in the midst of conflict. Many parents reinforce this view by encouraging our children to put themselves in someone else's shoes. It is easy to say in theory. But in practice, it means to understand that we are *the other*, that there is something to learn from those who disturb us. How is this possible when the other feels so extremely different, threatening, or even dangerous?

My son came home from school the first day of second grade and said the following: "Everyone is a bully at school," he said.

"Oh, that must be really hard," I said. "But you know what? Everyone can be a bully. You too. And me!"

He looked at me with big eyes. "Really?" he asked. "Yes," I said, "Sometimes, I can be pushy and so can you. You can push others and not notice what they are feeling and sometimes you think your way is the only way and others must follow. Isn't that a kind of bullying behavior?" I asked. He thought for a moment. "You're right," he said.

This is so crucial. There are not just bad kids or good kids. On one level, we like some kids better than others. Some kids behave more kindly to others, while some kids are more aggressive, and in some cases, can be cruel. But it is important to not cement kids into the roles of bully and victim, because then we don't see ourselves. When we "other-ize" a certain kind of behavior, we marginalize it. For my son, there were a couple of things for him to learn by seeing the bully in himself. First, to see his own power, which can be used as a self-defense relative to the bully, so he's not only in the role of victim. Additionally, picking up the "other" as a part of himself means noticing where he also unconsciously bullies people by overriding their feedback.[1]

When I work with kids and in schools, I do not want the "sensitive" child to be scapegoated. I want all the children to be aware of their sensitivity. We almost always can find the other in us; we are all somehow sensitive, shy, or afraid to be left out. Modeling and teaching this viewpoint supports children to learn about their own marginalized experiences and it also gives them a sense of being deeply connected to others.

This view can be crucial when working with the family system. Too often, families scapegoat one if its members: one person will get strongly identified with one role in the family system. Parents further this by describing their children in terms of the roles they play: "Felix is the sensitive one and Isabelle is the adventurer." While it is true that kids (and parents) are more comfortable in one role than another, by only identifying them with their one role, we miss their wholeness, and we also miss the chance for others in the family to pick up and learn about that role.

Instead of focusing on Felix as the sensitive one who needs others to treat him sensitively, it would be beneficial for the family as a whole to talk about sensitivity. We are *all* sensitive. Let's talk about *our* sensitivity. Some might not feel sensitive or don't identify with being sensitive, but maybe it happens in more subtle ways. We could help other family members notice disavowed sensitivity in their nonverbal or double signals.[2] For instance, when Felix said he didn't want to play with Isabelle, she turned away slightly and put her head down. She felt hurt, but didn't notice it. That is sensitivity. This helps the whole family realize their wholeness and that each one is also the other.

Helping our kids understand that they are also the other supports them to develop compassion towards others. Take a group of kids in your neighborhood playing ball in the street. A new kid on the block stands on the outside watching. No one invites her to play. The kids don't remember when they were the new kid. It might even be happening to them now, in school, or in other groups. They are that new girl, but don't identify with that experience in the moment. You can remind them by asking: Can you imagine feeling like that? How would you like others to relate to you if you were new? Just asking those questions will awaken your child and encourage him to reach out to the new child.

PLAYING WITH ROLES

Role-playing is a very powerful tool for all of us, but particularly for children. It is quite natural for children to spontaneously role-play and enjoy exploring new behaviors, voices, postures, and feelings. They easily take on the role of the superhero, bad guy, baby, or mother, and in so doing, experience more of their totality.

When we have trouble understanding or relating to the other, it can be incredibly helpful and fun to role-play the situation. By playing the other we get deeply under "their" skin. Role-playing allows us to discover aspects of ourselves as well as understand the other person more deeply. It also helps us broaden our inner life by giving us a chance to learn more about who we are. As a result, we also gain more freedom in our relationships and greater ability to work out conflict. We are more able to step into the other person's shoes, to understand them, and to connect to different experiences in ourselves.

Take eleven-year-old Emily who dreads when her younger sister's friend Krista comes over. Krista typically rushes into Emily's room and rummages through her stuff. Predictably, Emily gets angry at Krista and her sister; the big blow up ends in slammed doors and tears. So one day in my office together, I asked Emily if she could imagine being Krista. "Let's be her together," I suggested. Joining children in playing the role helps to support them to express a less familiar way of being and give voice to it. "Let's see, we are seven years old and we see Emily's room and we just run right into it." We both ran across my office to the area we had designated as "Emily's room" and excitedly looked at all the delights in the room. As Emily role-played Krista, I noticed her exuberance. She was smiling and enjoying herself. I pointed this out, and Emily had the insight that Krista doesn't mean to annoy her; she just really likes her and is curious about her.

I then asked Emily, based on her experience playing Krista, what she felt Krista would need from her. Emily said, "She would want me to show her something really cool." We then discussed how she could actually invite Krista and her sister into her room and show them one thing. She would then ask them politely to leave. Stepping into the role of the annoying younger child helped Emily understand Krista and resolve this on-going conflict.

Sometimes kids, like adults, reach edges or blocks to roles that seem foreign to them and difficult to comprehend.[3] We can help them get over the edge by playing out these new roles or behaviors, and thus helping them to expand their universe.

One day I was walking with Owen in his old school. He was very nervous and was trying to avoid seeing a girl who had chased him in the playground and tried to kiss him. He was hiding under his jacket as we walked through the school. My son was with us as well, so I suggested we do a little role-play. My son played the little girl who was trying to kiss Owen and I played Owen. When the kissing girl approached, I told the girl very firmly that I didn't like kissing and to please stop chasing me right now. Owen had never done this before. He didn't know how to be firm and draw a line with another person. This relieved him greatly.

This is also something you can do as parents—play out different behaviors for your kids using role-play. They will enjoy watching you and will learn different ways of interacting. Sometimes they will want to participate. Have fun experimenting with different roles. They will also enjoy directing the action. And remember in conflict situations, role-playing the "other" and stepping into their shoes is a big key to resolving conflict as demonstrated in the exercise below.

EXERCISE: ROLE-PLAY AND DISCOVERING THE "OTHER"

1. Talk with your child about an experience where she was disturbed by someone or afraid of something.
2. Make roles and act them out. Let your child be the director. Enjoy switching roles and exploring new interactions.
3. Model new behavior.
4. Try to find a useful energy in the "other." For example, although you don't want your child to be a bully, explore if there is a "useful" energy in the bully that your child might need. It could be, perhaps, the bully's confidence that your child might need, a particular strength, or protective power.

TIPS FOR NAVIGATING CONFLICT

The following are several points to consider when navigating the rough waters of conflict with kids.

Be open to conflict and difference. This is more than an idea or a belief, but rather a feeling attitude you communicate to your child. Being open translates into an atmosphere in which your kids feel they can approach you with different views. If children feel you respect their differences, they will also learn to respect yours, as well as others. Being open means modeling curiosity and interest. It means creating an atmosphere free of fear by giving your child the feeling that you will find a solution together.

You may say, "I have a really strong viewpoint on this, but it is important to me to know what you think even if it is different than my view. I am curious about how you feel and how you think about things."

Remember the whole relationship. Too often when we differ or are in a conflict, we forget the deeper relationship connection we have with the other. Tempers flare, we feel hurt and angry, and only consider our own position. Remember and convey to your child the deeper love and connection that you have and that this feeling can hold throughout any conflict between you. Remember it is not "what" you are fighting about, but the relationship between you and your child and what you can learn together that is most important.

You may say, "I know things are really hot in this moment, and we totally disagree. But I just want you to know that even in conflict I always feel our love and connection. My goal is to get closer to you and learn something."

Emphasize learning versus right and wrong. When learning from conflict is our goal, then everyone profits. The concept of right and wrong is a limited viewpoint, which doesn't appreciate that many views can exist simultaneously. The one who is "wrong" usually just ends up feeling bad or inferior and even vengeful at a later date. Resorting to punishment without learning teaches fear, encourages lying, and fosters resentment.

Remember the rank and power of age. Kids have less social rank than parents. They depend on us and need us. We provide for them, guide them, and make decisions for them. How we use our parental power is crucial to our ability to deal with conflict. Being aware of rank means noticing we feel more at ease expressing our views and opinions and that our child feels less able to assert his own because of our strength. Encourage your child to bring his views forward even if he disagrees with you; make it safe for him to do so without putting him down, mocking his viewpoint, holding it against him, or threatening punishment.

Be aware of how power is used. Being a parent is difficult and often our feelings get hurt as well. Sometimes we use our power instead of expressing our feelings. For example, a parent who feels hurt by her child might send her to her room instead of expressing hurt. A parent who is embarrassed by something her child has done might criticize her or shame her instead of exploring her own embarrassment and communicating that to her child. Our own frustrations in life often leave children unprotected from our worst moods, as we unconsciously feel free to take it out on them. (For more on this topic see Chapter 3, Power at Play.)

Pick up the subtext. Let's say your child asserts himself and you disagree and perhaps even feel he is not being truthful. The subtext of the communication, however, is often more important than the content. What is the underlying message or the deeper feeling the child is trying to communicate?

For example, if a child says something extremely provocative, instead of just giving a counter-opinion, you might notice what else is being communicated. You might notice the intensity or passion in your daughter's statement, or her ability to think out of the box, or the inner strength it takes to go against you or authority in general. Try to not only respond to the content, instead focus in on the subtext.

For instance you might say, "Wow, you have strong opinions. Great to hear them; I love your passion." Or, "Yes, I like that you can go against authorities and against me," or, "I like how you think outside the box. I can sort of see what you mean." These are all comments that pick up the deeper communication between the two of you. Too often, we get stuck on the content and argue about its merits ad-infinitum! By responding to the subtext, your child will feel seen and the conflict will de-escalate. In fact, the content of the discussion often fades into the background and a new understanding emerges.

Listen deeply and join your child's emotional state. Deep listening means that you remain open to receiving what your child is expressing without preconceived ideas. Listen to the emotional state of your child and the feelings she struggles to express. Join your child by validating her feelings and connect with her in her experience. A comment like, "I see you feel angry," is different from feeling her anger and joining her emotionally. It doesn't mean you feel angry too. It means you feel with her and know what it's like to be angry, frustrated, or disappointed. I know many parents who validate feelings but remain emotionally distant or unaffected. Kids feel this and check out because they experience you as not really understanding them.

Be gentle and giving of your time when listening to feelings that are not easy to express. Feel and see into what can almost not be said. Can you listen to the agony behind anger? Feel the sense of fear behind being different, the relief at finally being able to speak, and the hurt behind toughness.

Model openness by exploring and seeing the potential truth in accusations. Most of us quickly defend ourselves when we're accused of something. This ends the conversation and creates a cycle of blame and defense. Accusations are never altogether right, nor are they altogether wrong. There is usually a small grain of truth in the accusation, of which we are unaware. That is the main reason we defend ourselves.

A child who yells at her mother, "You never listen to me!" probably has a point. The mother defends herself and explains all of the ways that she does listen to her daughter. Her intention is to listen. However, the interaction gets stuck if the mother stays unaware of how she may not be listening. In this situation, it would help, if the mother took a breath, stepped back, and considered what her daughter has said. She might reflect on how she may not be listening, consider what she isn't hearing or noticing in her child. When she discovers this, she can then tell her child, "Yes, it is true. I am not hearing something and I would like to try. I think I am not hearing how upset you are, and I just try and give solutions without really feeling for you. I realize that I want to fix things for you but don't feel what you are going through." If the mother does not know what she is missing, she might ask her daughter. "You are probably right; what am I not hearing? I would like to listen better." Such conversation deepens communication and stops the escalation of accusations and disconnection.

Be aware of double signals or unintended communication.[4] Imagine this scenario: You are playing a game with your child. As you play the game, you notice that your attention is wandering. You're distracted and thinking about some work you have to do. Your child notices and says, "Come on; it's your turn. Pay attention!" You insist that you are playing and become attentive again. Your intended communication is to play the game, but your child has picked up your double signal, the communication you don't intend.

A lot of conflict and misunderstanding occurs because of mixed communication signals. We all know the experience of listening to what someone says, but the way they say it to us makes us feel just awful. We find ourselves unable to listen to the content, and instead, just hear the bossy, hostile, or aggressive tone.

We all respond to unintended communication whether we are aware of it or not. We notice when someone turns away from us or gives us a look that hurts our feelings. Chances are the person did not intend to turn away or hurt our feelings. They weren't aware of their unintended signals. When we notice and bring unintended communication into relationships we clear up conflict and deepen our contact. However, it isn't easy because we're also against it—that is why it is unintended. So, we must be compassionate and gentle when we notice communication signals that are not intended, by giving ourselves and the other person time and support to reflect on the deeper experiences that are more challenging to express.

Let's revisit the above example. Like many parents, the mom is trying to play with her child and gets back on task when her child notices she is not attentive. If she were open to all of her signals, she might have said, "You know dear, I love to play with you, but right now, I am also distracted. I am thinking about a work situation. That is why I am not paying attention. I am sorry for that. I am wondering how to solve that problem. Do you have any ideas?" Such a conversation addresses many things: it validates the child's perception that the mom really isn't fully present; it supports the child to believe in herself and what she notices in others. It also supports the mom to bring her whole self into relationship with her child, even things that she might disavow. This teaches and encourages a child to not just go along with expectations, but to follow her inner experience. And finally, it involves the child in her mom's dilemma, and as a result, values the child's wisdom and input as part of the solution.

Noticing your own unintended communication as well as that of others is a powerful tool in resolving conflict. It takes awareness and courage to bring in these experiences, but the result can be quite transformative!

Make room for all viewpoints. We all need to be heard. As adults we know how awful it is to be shut down. Children feel the same way. A parent who cuts off communication escalates conflict. This may not happen in an overt way, but emerges covertly through lying, mistrust, or indirect communication. Most critically, it hurts the relationship between you and your child and creates distance. Remember your children also learn relationship skills from you. If viewpoints are forbidden, a child grows up potentially fearful and not confident to express his own views or ends up dominating others whom he perceives as having an inferior viewpoint. Furthermore, we inadvertently teach children the tyranny of one view and do not nurture the ability to hold a plurality of viewpoints.

Children need help bringing out their views. Remember your rank and power. Kids get afraid to say what they might really think or they might not yet have language to express themselves clearly. Help them by taking their side.

For example, you might say, "It is hard to say when your feelings are hurt. Maybe I can do it for you." Then try and speak for your child, "Dad you hurt me. I am really sad. It hurts so much that I don't even have the words to say it." Or, "I see you are upset with me and it is hard to say so. I support you to speak up. I think you are unhappy with something I did. I can try and imagine and speak for you; help me if I am saying something that isn't right." Then try and feel into what your child might be upset with you about, "Mom, I am upset about how you spoke to me. I felt it was really harsh." After you speak for your child and support her view, she might join you, correct you, or simply watch and direct you. Then you can take your own side and continue the conversation.

With smaller children, it is helpful to use puppets or stuffed animals to express different views. (Some teens might be into it as well, although some might feel it is too babyish. However, adults love to speak through my puppets!) You might present two viewpoints through the puppet play without even noting that one viewpoint is your child's and one is yours. Both views in any conflict are usually within each of us. The fun of it is that you and your child can play both puppets. Puppets usually have more free- dom to express themselves than people. So enjoy the puppets and notice when surprising solutions occur. Even a third puppet can enter the play as a helpful or wise figure. "This crocodile and turtle are doing quite well in their conversation, but maybe they need help from another animal friend. Which animal do you think might help?" See which animal your child chooses and let the outside view offer answers and solutions.

Allow yourself to be moved or changed by your child's point of view. Many parents feel that they need to be consistent and hold a line. This is often a reactionary stance from a parent who feels weak. Some parents do need support to draw a line where necessary. However, this should not be at the expense of hearing your child out. There are times when we deeply listen to our kids and we can genuinely see their side. In these moments, we might feel something soften or change inside of us. Those experiences of deep listening to all sides are crucial for de-escalating conflict. Small flickers of doubt that arise like, "Oh, maybe I didn't really explain that to her," or, "Maybe I wasn't really fair to him in that situation," or, "Perhaps it is true, and I didn't warn her," are all cues that we are not just one-sided in our own viewpoint, but we can see our child's position as well. There are times when we are emotionally moved by our children and we see their position in a whole new light. It is so incredibly important to have the flexibility to express this, to acknowledge our uncertainty, to express that we are touched by what they are saying, and let ourselves be moved by our child's viewpoint.

When my son was five, we were going for a walk as we had done countless times together. In the past, whenever we would approach a crosswalk he would run ahead and stop at the curb and wait for me to cross with him. On this day I looked ahead and I was shocked to see him crossing the street alone! I frantically ran up the sidewalk and was quite upset. I told him how I felt. I was afraid for his safety and I was also upset because we had an agreement that he stopped at crosswalks before crossing. He apologized for crossing, but I was still upset and wanted to understand why he crossed the street. I could see that he was trying to say something or that he had a different thought. As the parent with more power, my job was to help him express himself. Even though I had a bottom line feeling about safety and I did not like what he did, I still wanted to bring out his thinking and respect it. What he said changed me.

He explained to me that this street was quieter than another big street near our house and he felt he was old enough to cross this one by himself. I had to think about that. My baby was indeed getting older. He was feeling more independent and he was trying to convey that to me. I could actually see his point. It was true, he was bigger, and he was able to cross that street alone. My view of the situation was changing. I realized he could differentiate between quiet and busy streets. We then talked about which streets he could cross alone and which ones not. He named all of the right ones. However, I also needed him to know that in the future, he had to check with me first about his new ideas or activities when they involved his safety. He understood that and it was a valuable discussion. I felt elated to be changed by him, to not hold fast to my own view, but to experience his intelligence and value his development.

Explore spontaneous, unusual, or unknown experiences. It's easy to get rigid in a conflict. We stick to our own position and usually repress any other feeling or thought that deviates from our opinion. Yet, most of us have different emotions and feelings that arise when they are in conflict. We may be standing strongly for our side, but also feel tearful or fearful. Sometimes we acquiesce and go along with the other while marginalizing our own leadership or strong opinions. Other times, we act tough, but feel shy and hesitant inside. Expressing disavowed feelings brings life to relationship and takes us to a deeper level.

Sometimes we might not be able to notice other emotions, but we can still use our dream-like awareness to resolve conflict by bringing us into contact with our wholeness. For example, a mother and daughter were arguing and each felt their viewpoint was right. I asked them to each take a step back from the conflict, to close their eyes and open them slowly, as if they were just awakening from sleep.[5] As they opened their eyes I asked them to notice what was catching their eyes. The mother said she saw a feather in my office. She said it was light and airy. She said she didn't feel light and airy at the moment. The daughter said she noticed my puppy dog puppet. For her, the puppy dog was friendly and wanted to be loved. These elements were disavowed experiences that they each needed to bring into their discussion. The mother became more like a feather, lighter and more flexible. Her whole mood softened. And the daughter told her mother that really she just wanted to feel her love. This broke through their conflict. We are not accustomed to noticing and picking up dream-like experiences in our environments. However if we do, they can clear up conflict rapidly and bring another dimension into our relationships.

Explore Lying. In Chapter 3, I address lying in relationship to power dynamics, specifically that lying occurs when we feel too weak or fearful to express our viewpoint. Children are more prone to lying because the power in the relationship is stacked against them. Therefore, it is important to explore the power dynamic and the different viewpoints that are embedded in the experience of lying.

However, sometimes lying is about "dreaming." It is about the part of us that isn't only connected to facts and everyday reality, but more to fantasy, imagination, and what seems almost impossible. Young kids will assert that they are superheroes and many of us will play along and enjoy our little one and admire her super powers. It is the odd parent who would put down this kind of play and admonish the child for lying. Your young child is experimenting with super powers even though the "facts" stand that she is five years old!

This kind of dream-lying also happens as children age. For example, take a nine-year-old girl who is at a new school and comes home and says she has lots of new friends. The parents are excited, but then find out later from the teachers that she is actually quite lonely and hasn't found a way to connect with the other children. There could be many reasons behind why she has not told her parents the truth. She might feel that her parents would be upset and she doesn't want to upset them. She might feel embarrassed about not having friends. Whatever the reason, in her lie, she has friends. Certainly the lie is an indication of a wish, but instead of only staying with the difficulty of having no friends, we might really engage in the fantasy of the lie: "Really, you have lots of friends—wonderful! How did you make those friends? Let's imagine together how you make friends. How does a girl do that when she is at a new school? How does she walk, approach other kids, start a conversation or connect?" These kinds of comments support the child in her dreaming around friendship and will give her tips in how she can actually then make some friends. Understanding the deeper dreaming behind lying directs your attention to the real issues at hand instead of simply chastising your child for lying.

Find your deepest nature in the midst of conflict. Conflict begins with polarization. Each person identifies with a position and usually tries to argue their case and convince the other. That is a good beginning; it gets us engaged and can be an opportunity for deeper contact as we discover more about the other. However, polarization without transformation creates hopelessness and distance.

Within each of us is a part that is much larger than our smaller identities. It is a part of us that is transcendental or connected to our deepest nature.[6] It is the part of us that can hold many divergent viewpoints and stay connected with the deeper meaning of what is trying to be expressed. We all know people who reflect such eldership and who can give people the feeling of love, acceptance, and value. And we can all have access to our deepest self, even in the midst of a conflict.

Try to connect to this deepest part of yourself in the midst of conflict. Each of us will have our own method; some use meditation or visualization techniques, others connect to inner body experiences, or commune with nature or a divinity. This state of mind gives us access to a wise conflict facilitator.[7]

LEARNING THROUGH CONFLICT

The tools above can certainly be a support to exploring and working on conflict. The ability to follow the process of conflict, to employ any number of these tips as needed, is a practice. Keep in mind, that as children grow up they come up against a terrible inner conflict when they begin to realize that their own independent thoughts and feelings can sometimes be different from their parents and create conflict. As parents we are their first loves, their first authority figures, and hopefully their first sense of safety. When they assert their own direction and find that it is different from ours it can threaten their most basic sense of security. Thus, letting a child know that it is okay to give us a little sting, and that it doesn't threaten the basic thread of our relationship, is essential. Conflict can enrich relationship because it allows us to get to know more about each other. We teach our children invaluable skills when we model the ability to travel through and get to know the many stops on the relationship train of life.

# the big questions

Cultivating a Life of Meaning

*Sometimes when my brain goes quiet
a question comes up in my brain:
Why am I alive?*
—Audrey, age 6

Our world is full of diverse spiritual and religious traditions, beliefs and knowledge, which we pass on to our children. By nature, children are curious about the nature of the universe and wonder about things that are typically discussed in religious and mystical traditions. Regardless of your belief or faith, kids are interested in the big spiritual questions of life and death. They not only have questions; they have answers and theories too! Here are some of the big questions children ask:

- Why are we on the planet?
- How did I get born?
- How did I get in your tummy?
- What is death? What happens when we die?
- What is God?
- Is there a creator?
- What is love?
- Who makes my heart beat?

- Why is the sky blue?
- Who lives in the stars?

These questions are inherently spiritual. They emerge out of a curiosity and need to discover the meaning of life. These questions remind us that we were born to ponder the meaning of our existence. Young children are closer to this spiritual task since they aren't as enmeshed in consensus reality as adults are. They are still closely connected to that which creates them. In *The Secret Spiritual World of Children,* Tobin Hart put together a delightful collection of children's experiences and tips for supporting your child's spiritual or inner growth.[1]

Similarly, in Jack Kornfield's collection of stories about spirituality he shares the following beautiful story: A five-year-old boy who tells his parents that he wants to be alone in the room with his new infant sibling. The parents have a baby monitor in the room and overhear their son ask the newborn baby the following: "What's God like, I feel like I am forgetting."[2] Kornfield shares this story to show the wisdom of children and to highlight how close they are to the more ineffable forces of life.

We, too, can engage in this kind of discussion with our children and will find that it is an awesome and intimate experience. Their questions are the beginnings of very profound and beautiful conversations. Feel free to answer these questions, but before you do, ask them what they think. Encourage their inner wisdom to emerge and support their spiritual development and self-reflection. Their answers are often truly amazing and might stop you in your tracks! Here is a gem from my home life:

Theo: What's God Mama?
Dawn: What do you think?
Theo: God is in the love spirit. It is everywhere.

In another exchange, when my son was six, a friend of our family died. Right before she died she had an experience of being a mallard, a duck, free on the water.[3] In this conversation I invited my son's views and I shared my own.

> Theo: Mama when you die I will see you in the shining moon.
>
> Dawn: Yes, I believe you will. In fact I am shining at you right now!
>
> Theo: How does it happen when you die and your body can become something else, like Sara became a mallard?
>
> Dawn: What do you think?
>
> Theo: I don't know.
>
> Dawn: People have different views. I believe in a spirit that somehow never dies and that is why you will be able to see me in the shining moon.

Likewise, instead of waiting for kids to ask these kinds of questions, you might ask your children what they think about the big questions *you* ponder. Your conversations will be fascinating and their answers might inspire you. Having this kind of conversation signals to your child that you are interested in her inner world and deepest thoughts and that you respect her viewpoint.

When I find myself pondering the big questions in life, I like to ask my son what he thinks. I am genuinely interested in how he sees this world. One cozy morning when he was eight we had the following conversation.

> Dawn: Theo, would you still exist if you didn't have a body?
>
> Theo: Yes (smiling and rolling around tickling and wrestling).
>
> Dawn: What would you be?
>
> Theo: (He points to my chest, encouraging me to guess.)
>
> Dawn: A heart?
>
> Theo: No.
>
> Dawn: A spirit?
>
> Theo: No.

Dawn: What then?

Theo: Love. I would be love.

Dawn: Wow. Yeah, I know that about you. How long have you been
         around for?

Theo: About five hundred thousand years.

Such conversations open up new dimensions of perception and enrich your relationship with your child. Allow yourself to engage and delight in the world of wonder with your children. Some questions I have wondered about and love to hear young minds answer, are:

- Do you remember being born?
- Where were you before you were born?
- Why were you born?
- What are you here to do in life?
- Do you remember being in your mother's tummy? What was it like?
- Why do stars shine?
- What is love?
- What happens when we sleep?
- What makes our body move?

Such questions can be easily put to very young children. Older children tend to be more bathed in everyday life and culture. Yet, they too, need support and quiet time to ponder, wonder, and discuss with parents the deeper issues that concern them. Relationship issues are usually top priority, but bigger issues of meaning and purpose can also be introduced.

I was working with a thirteen-year-old boy who came to me to work on fears. I asked about what he was afraid of and he said he was afraid of not getting his work done at school and the consequences of that. He also shared that he was afraid of the ocean. We decided to focus on his more mysterious fear of the ocean. He described the ocean as deep and vast, with no land. I suggested that we become the ocean to explore its nature. He had been sitting on my big green exercise ball and he decided to use it. He put his head behind the ball, looking into it as if it were the ocean. He swayed his head slightly and I encouraged him to feel the movements of the ocean and imagine the feeling of it in his body. He made water sounds into the ball that vibrated on his lips and made his voice deeper. He enjoyed making those sounds and as the voice of the ocean he had a message for his everyday self. His low and otherworldly voice vibrated through the green ball, "You are not so little, but you are so vast. There are lots of little things, but you are really very big." It was very moving to hear a thirteen-year-old boy get in touch with this vast spirit.

His everyday self was concerned about growing taller and about schoolwork. He feared this big oceanic part of himself because he didn't know enough about it. "What is the meaning of his life? What is his task on earth?" We asked the ocean. "To make the world a better place for everybody and to have fun doing it." I was moved to tears to hear a boy his age interested in such depth. I asked him as the ocean what he should do if he does something wrong, like not completing an assignment, or making a mistake. The ocean said to him, "There is no such thing as punishment. People learn from mistakes and move on." He experienced the ocean between his eyes and he felt it as a pressure. In the future, when he feels down in life or caught up in succeeding and failing, this body experience might help to remind him about the vastness of his being and what is really important.

All of us need deep experiences to relativize everyday life. Our culture tends to suffer from a lack of contact with deep and unifying states of consciousness. Society values success and material acquisition, but does not give enough emphasis to a life of meaning. Older children also seek a purpose in life and long for meaning and connection that is beyond outer success. When everyday reality dominates we miss opportunities for meaningful discussion; we neglect to ask and engage with the big questions in life. If we, as parents, make time for such a focus in our own lives—even a few minutes in a life that might be filled with struggle and survival—we teach our children to tap into a deeper sense of self that can help sustain them during hard times.

NATURE AWARENESS

Many of us experience life's mysteries in our marvel and connection with nature. Young children have a natural affinity with nature. They delight in a snowflake, sway like the trees, and stare out into the endless sea. It is almost as if they energetically join with the essence of nature's expression.

I remember one night on the Oregon coast when the waves were loud as we tried to sleep. My three-year-old whispered:

Theo: The ocean is talking.
Dawn: What's the ocean saying?
Theo: Dream. The sky is listening.

Aboriginal and indigenous cultures are more in contact with the experience of nature, the sense of being moved by the moon or the stars or directed by the wind, and the awareness of power spots in nature.[4] With young children you can support this nature awareness by noticing and encouraging it as well as joining in and playing together. As children age and get further away from this natural awareness you can support them to keep contact with how nature affects them. A sixteen-year-old girl told me that when she is struggling with friendship jealousies she imagines herself to be in a field of flowers. The flowers remind her of a part of herself that is light-hearted and not pulled down by relationship turmoil.

We are nature. When I am in the mountains, I feel as if I am a mountain. I can feel the part of me that is millions of years old, a part of me that is somehow timeless and has seen the ebb and flow of life. I feel more at ease and everyday life has less power and influence. Each of us has these experiences. Our ability to engage with our children to have such experiences supports them to have a sense of being connected to the natural world and gives them a more expansive view of life. Asking ourselves and our kids if we can feel the essence of the sea, the mountain, the creek, the trees, or the soil, opens up an awareness of this connection. Can we hear a message from nature? This might seem far-out to many readers, but this view of nature and our intimate connection to it, has not only been intrinsic to indigenous peoples throughout the world, but has been a central guiding source for artists, poets, musicians, philosophers, healers, shamans, sages, and religious leaders throughout time.

When my son was six, we were walking on a windy day. He said, "The wind isn't doing it. I am." It is quite natural for a young child to identify with the powers of nature. They become the wind, the spirit of creation, or the one who makes wind. It is a very radical, but extremely normal state of consciousness, to identify not with the one who is impacted by nature, but rather the essence of nature itself, the creator. These are deep, transpersonal experiences that connect us with nature, the universe, and a consciousness that is beyond our everyday selves.

Children can be exquisitely poetic in how they express their perceptions of nature. I was with a twelve-year-old girl, diagnosed with autism, and we were sitting by a pond. She got very excited watching the ripples in the water; her body was shivering, and she said, "The water is coming together in kisses." She shuttered as if she were being kissed by the water. I said, "Oh yes, I can feel those kisses and you can too. Oh, how beautiful. The water loves you." She smiled and kept pointing out the kisses. These are very special experiences that connect us with the deepest parts of our beings, our essential nature, or the unity experience of creation itself. In this moment, the water was an expression of love, giving kisses to all who might receive them, and letting us know that we are deeply loved. Joining our children in these experiences validates them, creates more intimacy in our relationships, and deepens a child's connection to her essential self.

Most twelve-year-old children have been socialized out of this essential awareness and are more consumed with everyday reality. Many developmentally challenged children seem to carry a special kind of awareness. Less related to the everyday world, they are often more connected with the dreaming environment, closer to nature and their creative minds. I will always remember a moment years back at one of our large international conflict resolution seminars where a group of 250 people were in terrible conflict. The group was polarized into two positions, each side vociferously stating their view. In the middle of the conflict, a teenage girl with Down syndrome happened to stumble into our gathering. She came right into the middle of the two sides and began to hug people. She solved the conflict by reminding everyone about the need for friendship and connection, even in the midst of difficult conflict.

This special awareness is a hallmark for young children and begs for our affirmation. Notice how young children will utter an essential truth that throws everyone off guard. Quite spontaneously children speak the language of sages and wise elders. Nature holds great powers and becomes an access to such wisdom. So, engage with your child as she instinctively delights in the natural world and reveals answers to life's central questions. You might be surprised at what they say just as I was from the following conversation with my son.

Theo: The moon feels so good to me.
Dawn: What kind of feeling is it?
Theo: The moon is carrying love. It pours down into the house and into my heart. That's why I feel so good.

It is especially valuable during these kinds of conversations to help your children to explore their observations. For example, in the conversation above I asked my son, "What kind of a feeling is it?" By asking him this and hearing how he responds, I can make this experience useful to him in everyday life. I can remind him of this moment, especially during times that are difficult for him, by saying, "Yes, remember that the moon is always there, carrying love, and pouring it down on you."

Many children do not have access to nature. However, even children living in urban environments will retreat or gravitate to locations that make them feel well or at home. Or, they will fantasize about a nature spot that they have never been to. There is a fundamental need in each of us to connect to something greater than our small selves. Nature offers that perspective of wonder. And yet, a child with no access to nature can also find this perspective in her urban surroundings. A teenager once told me that her special spot was a small alley between two buildings; she said it made her feel safe and protected. Another teen found a large cement pipe in an abandoned lot that he called his second home. He would sit inside the pipe and sing. The reverberation of his voice transported him to another state of mind giving him a sense of freedom and comfort.

DEATH AS A PART OF LIFE

Many people try to protect children from death. We treat death as if it were something frightening and too intense for children to understand. We also want to protect them from grief and pain and give them the security that we, as their parents, will be here forever. However, in the back of our minds we know we won't. We hope to live to see our children at least through childhood and young adulthood. It is agonizing for all parents to entertain the idea of leaving their child. And it is horrifying to imagine losing our children. And yet, it happens.

How we approach death in our own lives and how we engage with children around it is important. Each of us has our own ideas about death based on personal experience, religious or spiritual beliefs, dreams, science, or nature. We each find our own way to address death based on our beliefs and life experiences. And for many of us our views about death are still forming. Life teaches about death and this uncertainty can also be reflected in conversations with children.

Talk to children about death in ways that seem appropriate and understandable for your child's age, interest, and sensibilities. In my view, it is important to view death as a natural process, to notice and speak about it, even when children are young. Nature is our greatest teacher. Living plants and creatures die, new ones are born. Pets, friends, and family members die. Children are naturally curious about death. They actually enjoy talking about it and have loads of questions.

Obviously, death in war torn and impoverished countries is different. It is more of an everyday phenomenon. In some ways, it is more complex, and in other ways, so painfully simple in its everyday presence. In addition, those who have experienced a lot of tragedy around the death of loved ones, or have grown up in violent neighborhoods and social environments, have to grapple with the violence, agony, and fear this generates. For the scope of this book, I will not focus on dealing with such tragedy; there are many books that address grief, trauma, and loss in regard to children.

I do want to address the basic wonder that most kids have about death even before they are faced with the actuality of loss. Death comes up in fantasy and play quite often. Many parents and teachers get uncomfortable and try to change the subject. I want to support parents to not fear the conversation but to be able to engage with it in a meaningful way. Death also gives perspective to life; it brings wisdom from other worlds, wisdom that your child may in fact possess.

CREATING COMMUNITY

I remember a boy in a first grade classroom who was sharing his journal entry about his grandfather who died. The teacher quickly changed the subject, hurrying to get to the next student. However, it would have been more helpful if the teacher could have used that experience as a teaching and a vehicle to create community.

Take, for example, a video I watched of an extraordinary teacher from a Japanese classroom who demonstrates an opposite approach.[5] The video shows Mr. Kanamori, a fourth grade teacher, whose classroom is a "school of life." Children read letters each day in which they share the events of their lives and their genuine feelings. The class discusses the experiences that emerge and together search for ways to understand and cope with troubled relations, bullying and unhappiness, and the loss of loved ones. In this clip, a boy has come back to school after some days of absence and talks about the death of his grandmother. Mr. Kanamori and his fourth graders are courageous as they share personally how death has touched their lives. A girl who locked away the painful experience of the death of her father comes out of her shell and shares her experience. By sharing with the class, she finds comfort and friendship. In this classroom, there is no taboo against speaking about death. There is room for grief, personal experience, and the expression of shared feeling. What emerges is a sense of community. The grieving children are held by the warmth and focus of their classmates. This is essential education where children learn lessons about life and death, compassion, deep sharing, and the value of community.

The day we had to put our cat down, our son had to come home from school because he was so upset. That morning he had wanted to go to school, but then later, the kindergarten teacher called to tell us that Theo was upset and crying. We had misread him. He wanted to be involved and part of Eli's transition. At home, he joined us being with Eli's body, touching and talking to the body, and remembering his spirit. It was his decision not to cremate the body, but to bury Eli in the backyard. We created a ritual together, digging the grave, sharing special stories and memories, and lighting candles. We said goodbye to our beloved feline companion.

The next day at school, I was so impressed with the teacher who helped with Theo's transition back to the classroom. She invited him to talk about his experiences and asked other kids if they had lost a pet, encouraging them to share how they had felt. A few of the kids even drew pictures of the cat and offered them as gifts. That kind of community support is essential learning.

DEATH AS A METAPHOR

Recently a child I was working with said, "Let's smash our house down." The mother said, "That would be terrible." I said, "Oh, how interesting, let's smash it." I was interested in his experience. I didn't want him to literally destroy his house, but was curious about his underlying need.

Together we smashed the "house" using pillows. When we finished, I asked him what would happen next. He said, "Everyone would be dead."

I said, "Okay, let's imagine that. Let's imagine being dead. What would that be like?"

He said, "Well our bodies would be like in a museum and we could look inside of them."

"How interesting," I said, "let's look inside of those bodies now; what can we see?" We then proceeded to look inside of his mom's body.

He said, "I can see little stars in Mommy, they are shining so brightly and flickering like dancing light."

Mom's face became flooded with feeling, moved that her child would see her like that. Her son was seeing the deepest part of her, a part of her that lives forever even after death, the essence of her being. Her son was showing his depth and his interest in relating to his mom, and others, from a really deep place. Death had to happen to alter his normal way of looking at and living life. This is why he wanted to smash the house in his fantasy. Everyone in the house died, meaning, symbolically, that the everyday way of being died so that something more transcendent could live. Death became a great teacher in helping this boy and his family to relate to each other more from their deep inner states.

CHILDREN'S FANTASIES OF DEATH

Many parents get nervous when their children speak about death or play games that include death. However, death is a metaphor, a symbol for change, for learning about the mystery of life. Children have unique insights and fantasies about death. Sometimes they will offer them or they will ask you about your own. Feel free to share your own views, but do leave room for theirs.

When our son was five he said, "I am going to give you a shot in the tummy. It's not for sickness, but it's for death. What happens is when you die I wait two minutes, and that's not a very long time, and then you are alive again in my heart." He wasn't just sharing a fantasy about our actual deaths, but revealing his view of death as an eternal relationship experience. He "just needs to wait two minutes," meaning he needs enough time to switch realms from everyday reality to another kind of reality where he is in touch with the eternal spirit of our relationship.

Because losing a parent is such a tragic and painful occurrence, helping your child find your presence within them is crucial. You are more than your physical body; you are an eternal spirit that lives in your child, one that he will hopefully be able to access and stay in connection with, regardless of your physical presence.

WORKING WITH GRIEF

Grief needs time and space to be heard and held. Telling kids to be strong and not cry is not very useful. In my mind, strength is the ability to honor and support whatever you feel, in any given moment. We teach children this kind of emotional strength when we model it ourselves. Sharing your own grief and sadness with children is important. Talk about how you feel, take comfort from them. Grief can bring us together and be an opportunity to create better relationship.

It is important to follow the process of the child when she has experienced a loss. Children are generally more fluid in their feelings than adults. They are sad and then are ready to go play. At another moment they will return to grief, they may have a memory, or long to talk about the dead person, or share some of their ideas about death. Spontaneous rituals might emerge; music, dance, art, and creative writing are ways to express our different experiences.

You can make the pain of grief a little easier by helping the child to connect with the missing parent or dead person.[6] Ask a child what the spirit of this person (or animal) was like. Have them get in touch with those qualities.

One teenager told me, "Dad was always supporting me when I was scared." I asked, "How did Dad do that?" Then I listened to the stories of how Dad gave support. This girl shared that when she was afraid of something new, her father encouraged her and believed in her. He would stand by her, put his arm around her, and give her a squeeze. I then encouraged her to feel the arm of her father around her and the squeeze, to imagine that body feeling even without him being present. She closed her eyes and could feel his presence. She said her body felt warm and strong all at once. To anchor this feeling in her body I encouraged her to remember this feeling, to hold it with her. This way her father could always stay present and his spirit accessed as a body experience. Some children may want to carry an object that reminds them of the missing person or the quality they represent. I asked this girl, "Is there an object that reminds you of your dad's support, that warm, strong feeling?" She had a special red rock that her dad had given her. I suggested she carry that rock in her pocket as a way for her to remember that her dad's support was always there.

It is quite powerful to find the inner experience of a dead parent, family member, or friend inside of us. It doesn't necessarily eliminate grief, but it does bring the essence of the person closer to us, which can help to ease our suffering.

FUNERALS, RITUAL, AND CURIOSITY

Children bring out our inherent curiosity. We all have questions about the mystery of death. Kids lead the way by asking naïve questions.

Some will be fascinated by the dead body and will want to touch or move it. Other children might be more fearful of seeing a dead body. As parents, we shouldn't assume how they will feel, but we can anticipate and prepare them.

If you are taking your child to a funeral, a viewing or wake, or if you include your child in watching a loved one take her last breaths, speak to your young child and show him what he can expect. Lie down and show him what a dead body looks like, how still it can be. Tell your child how the body will feel cooler and how the face will be frozen into one expression. Tell her that the face may look a little different to what she was used to seeing. Share how the person will not be able to relate to her anymore in the same way they used to.

Together, you might lie down and imagine what it is like to be dead. This may sound odd or suggestive to young minds, but it is not meant to plant the seed of dying in children. It is meant to help them understand death as an experience, albeit an unknown one, thereby creating more comfort and ease around something that is fraught with taboo. Death is a part of nature and it is a state of mind. We all have "mini-deaths"— experiences where something ends and something is re-born. We dream about death in order to help us make big life changes.

Playing with the experience of death, lying down together, and pretending to be dead can evoke insights and help your child feel closer to the person who has died. For example, you might say, "What is it like to lie so still? As we lie here together pretending to be dead, what do we think Grandma is feeling? Is there something we want to tell her? What message might she give us? Let's listen carefully." Such experiences make death less frightening and enable us to feel closer to the person or animal that has died. For many of us, we never lose the sense of relationship with those we loved. Our relationships continue in some way; we continue to feel connected, hear their voices, and channel them in some kind of way that enriches our lives.

Some parents opt to not include children in funerals or memorials. Each of us will do what is right according to our own value system. However, children can gain from taking part in such rituals. Children also need to say goodbye, to experience community, and express feeling. Besides more conventional or adult rituals, children may want to create their own.

Young children might process death by creating rituals in their play. This is healthy and an indication of the child's use of creativity to explore and come to terms with one of life's great mysteries. Children might let you into their play, and by all means, join in. You might also create more private and intimate rituals with your children using music, dance, art, poetry, acting out memories, talking to the spirits, God, the dead person—it is endless.

Follow the child's process. Some children will want to rapidly focus on everyday life and their routines. This is important, there is a need to also go on with life. Additionally, some experiences are just so painful that a child will repress them. At another point in life, those experiences might come back when the child feels more able to process them. There are cases in which the whole family field may identify with being intensely sad, yet the child might represent part of the field that wants to move on and play. Too often in death we forget joy and play and children will remind us of this.

The loss and tragedy that emerge in experiences of death often create opportunity for learning. Teenagers who usually feel they will live forever suddenly find themselves reflecting on the meaning of life. Death is one of the biggest community creators. We come together meaningfully; we learn about friendship, empathy, and helping others. We learn how to allow ourselves to need help and comfort and we learn about love.

CREATIVITY: CRY ME A RIVER

Cultivating our inner lives makes us more resilient and enhances our ability to deal with life's challenges in a creative way. The arts, such as music, dance, poetry, visual art, and writing are all avenues to help us express and process our deepest experiences.

Take a young boy who at the age of seven was dealing with his father's imprisonment. We were playing and he began to sing a bluesy tune. I sang back, "Let's sing what is in our hearts." The blues poured out of him. "My Daddy is in jail and I miss him," he repeated. "But I am gonna see him one day." The song went on and I was very touched to feel the soul of this young boy as he sang the blues and tried to deal with a situation that no seven-year-old should have to be confronted with. We sang and drummed and although it was sad it was also somehow joyful. He realized that when he sang it brought his father closer to him.

Self-expression in the form of music, art, dance, and writing are healing and fill us with a deep sense of ourselves. Young children spontaneously sing, draw, and dance what is inside of them. Support your children in their creative self-expression.

Many years ago, I worked with a twelve-year-old girl struggling with the divorce of her parents. She was hurting and grieving the loss of her family as she knew it. At one point in our work, she wrote a beautiful poem that I found so inspiring I had to jot it down.

Cry me a river
Cry me a pond
Cry me an ocean
Cry me a blue sky
Cry me

Cry myself to sleep
Cry me
Hold me

Cry me a shower
Cry me a liberation
Cry me a paradise
So I can be free

# the parent path

A Sacred Call

Before you embark on any path ask the question:
Does this path have a heart?
—Don Juan Matus, from the books of Carlos Castaneda

Recently a friend of mine witnessed my son throwing a fit and noticed how I engaged with him. She said to me, "Parenting is so creative for you." I was touched to be seen; she didn't just retreat or become impatient, as many adults do, when a child is upset. It got me thinking. Yes, it is true. I take parenting as a creative challenge. As each day unfolds, I wonder, what will I be met with? What interactions will I be called to have with my child? What will I have to introduce him to? What troubles in the world will he, and therefore, I, encounter? What disturbances will challenge us both to make the world a better place?

Along with my professional and creative accomplishments, I have come to see parenting as an exciting and creative task. When I am challenged by power struggles, temper tantrums, or my fatigue and limitations, something inside of me is inspired to respond and interact with my son in the most creative and meaningful way. I am truly inspired by motherhood and being Theo's mother feels connected to my path in life.

Parenting is one of many life paths, a path that many of us take, often without much forethought or connection to the deeper forces that move us. Throughout the world, people have children for many reasons, not the least of which is to create the feeling of home and security or to experience the love and connection that children bring. Some of us see the child as a product of a loving union. Still others have children for the status it brings, the financial security, or the hope of having others to care for us as we age. Some people reproduce out of obedience to a religious doctrine or value system. Many people have never considered not having children and follow the traditions and expectations of family and culture. And of course, huge numbers of people discover themselves pregnant, having engaged in sex without regard to the life-changing experience of potentially creating a new life. However it happens, parenting is a path, a calling. Each of us has a different path created by our dreams, longings, intentions, and the great mystery of life.

More and more people are choosing not to have children. I find these individuals extraordinarily courageous often having to ward off persistent family and cultural pressures. It is almost viewed as a matter of course that people are, or will be, parents; and those who choose otherwise are often put on the spot to defend their choices. Sometimes I feel they awaken those of us who are parents to reflect on and become aware of why we have children. Parenting is a profound path and, in my view, should not be taken lightly.

When having a child is consistent with our deepest calling and the meaning and purpose of our life then being a parent is a true vocation. We are not in conflict with the parenting experience. Even when it is difficult, we feel enriched, creative, and have a clear sense of being on the right track. Most parents will say that they love their children and could not imagine life without them. What is more difficult for parents to voice is the regret—what they gave up to have children, the feeling that it was too soon or not the right time, or that they had a dream they never fulfilled.

Many realize much later in life that they weren't really present in their role as parent.

Many women speak of the "biological clock" and feel a pressure to conceive before the optimal time for pregnancy passes them by. Biology does press women in a different way than men, at least in terms of carrying a child. That pressure can bring out the deeper dreams of a woman who wants to be a mother but it can also force her into becoming pregnant without enough connection to her life path.

I didn't begin to consider having a child until I was 38. My dream life was full of babies; I would see their beautiful open faces and see the universe in their eyes. Night after night, these divine beings flooded my dreams, filling me with bliss and deep joy. In the daytime, children were always in my view. Suddenly the world seemed full of children to me. Had I not noticed them before? My eyes were transfixed by nursing mothers sitting in coffee shops, lost in the open gazes of their babies.

Being a psychotherapist, I wondered how I would know if I was meant to actually give birth to a baby, or, if the babies I dreamt of were symbolic of new experiences and parts of myself being born. What was my path? Even as I worked on these dreams symbolically and embraced new experiences and parts of myself, there was one baby's face I saw repeatedly in my dreams: my son. As I looked into his eyes, I felt as if I was looking into a sky of stars, an infinite world of experience that was too compelling to deny. I knew a great spirit was calling me.

The spiritual pull was strong, and yet, I wondered how I would have a baby and still have my work, creative interests, and time for relationships; it was hard to see the everyday world of parenting. Then, I had an awesome dream that brought different parts of myself together and showed me a possible path.

I dreamt that a forty-year-old politician was on The Oprah Show. She was singing a love song and as she sang, she stuck her protruding belly out to make sure the audience could see she was pregnant. I was in the audience and was very moved by her love song and inspired by her pregnancy. As I watched her sing, I felt that I could do it, too. I too could be pregnant.

The dream gave me another dimension to my calling as a mother. The spiritual call had been clear to me, but I now realized that it was also a socio-political act to have a child. Thus, the politician singing a love song on Oprah! My child would have two mothers; and as a mother in a lesbian relationship, I would be standing for love in all of its diversity and mystery. The dream showed me that my motherhood would be public in order to show the universal nature of love.

I am still unfolding this dream. As each day goes by, I feel incredibly inspired by my path to mother my son. The depth of feeling and love that has been brought forth has transformed me to my core. I have been creative in ways that I couldn't have predicted. I feel absolutely challenged and excited interacting in my day-to-day exchanges with Theo. I am newly inspired in my work as it now focuses more on children, families and parenting, and education. This is how parenting is a social and political act for me; raising a child is like raising the world.

On October 31, 2011 the world population reached the 7 billion mark.[1] Our population is exploding at a faster rate than ever. With such a rapid rate of population growth, many fear that we do not have the resources to continue in the same vein. Many people in the world already go without the basic necessities of clean water, food and shelter, and too many children roam the planet uncared for.[2] These statistics should awaken us all to the need to consciously decide to have children and to see parenting as a deliberate calling. And ultimately, for our own joy and well-being, it is my hope that exploring our unique path of parenthood is a rich and meaningful adventure.

For these reasons, I would like to re-connect us to the idea that parenting is a *calling*. Something deeper than our conscious intent moves us to make big decisions in life, like to have a baby. Aboriginal Australians believe the spirit of the child calls the parents. The spirit-child is present in dreams, remarkable events, experiences with animals, and in signs and events in the natural world.[3] Though in our more material developed world, we may not think of it this way; in private moments, however, some parents share uncanny dreams or experiences in which they felt called by their child.

The path to parenthood can also develop over time. I remember working with a woman who couldn't get pregnant after trying for some time. She dreamt that there was a child wandering the streets looking for parents.

The wandering child in her dream symbolically represented how she treated herself. She was the abandoned child. She neglected her feelings and disregarded her needs. We began to work on her self-neglect, helping her notice when her feelings were hurt or when she needed something. With time this pattern began to change, and after a few months, she dreamt that she was in a lush forest, and the green foliage turned into an arm that pulled her close. She got scared and woke up. We explored the "arm" of the green foliage and I had her show me how it pulled her. As she did it, instead of being something frightening, it held her close. She said it felt like a mother from the earth, holding her in a deep and eternal embrace. The next month she became pregnant. In this woman's process, part of her path to motherhood involved developing the "mother" within. In her second dream, a mother was born.

Dreams help us learn more about our development as a parent. They show us where we are growing and can also be healing. I recall a woman who was very distraught after a miscarriage. After comforting her and grieving together, I asked her if she had a dream. She dreamt that all of the people in the town she grew up in were in a hot air balloon. Suddenly, the bottom of the basket opened up, and the people started to fall out. A teenager was able to save herself by holding on to the sides.

When I asked her about the teenager, she said that girl reminded her of someone she went to school with who was always a little outside of the crowd. She was really smart, and my client had always wondered what happened to her. I asked her about her hometown, and she said she grew up in a small town in which she felt constricted, unable to express her individuality. You can see two parts in the dream—the constricting hometown and the individual or unique teenager.

As we continued to work on the dream, it became clear to her that she felt constricted and needed to literally drop some attitudes and behaviors that were too conventional. She needed to identify more with the teenager on the fringe. When we explored the energy of the teenager, she sat upright, and took up more space. She stood up and began to strut around my office, as if exploring it for the first time. She said that this energy was about freedom and exploration. She suddenly realized that as much as she had wanted a child something about it had felt constraining. Even though she really did want a child and loved her husband, it felt surprisingly relieving to her to let it drop for the time being. She felt renewed vigor to discover herself outside of her role as wife and potentially as mother. She began to venture out creatively and take more chances in life.

Some of us just know we are meant to parent. It feels right and indisputable. However, for some, it's important to explore this direction more deeply. How do we know we are meant to parent? What is our calling to parenthood? What does this path want from us? Can we get in contact with our deepest aspirations? Is there a message coming from another realm that is moving us? Many of us might search for our direction or connection to another realm in nature or a vision quest. Can we hear or sense the calling from the natural world? What do the trees, the seas, or the mountains want from us?

For many people this kind of questioning seems quite unusual and too far-out. Yet indigenous peoples throughout time have asked nature for guidance concerning child bearing.[4] Many indigenous cosmologies understand that the spirit of one's child calls from another realm. Parents hear the song of their child wanting to be born or feel the ancestors call them into parenthood. Christianity tells the story of Mary, a mother who is impregnated by the Holy Spirit, called by God to carry the Christ-child. Regardless of one's spiritual or religious beliefs, there is great mystery in conception and life, which are aspects of the deep powers of our universe. Throughout the ages, people have created stories, myths, and religions that reflect their experiences. These stories and myths represent the profound and spiritual calling that invites us into our roles as parents.

A woman who was considering motherhood told me that she went to one of her favorite spots along the Pacific Northwest Coast. She walked along the beach until she came to a place where she felt a sense of well-being. She then followed the signs of the natural world as she asked about her path to become a mother. It was a foggy and windy day and she felt as if the winds mirrored her own inner uncertainty. Then suddenly, the fog lifted, and the sun came through. She felt the warmth on her body. In her meditation, she imagined becoming the sun. She stood up and stretched out her arms. As the sun, she heard the words, "I am life." Tears streamed down her face and she felt the sun was giving her life and was simultaneously calling her to become a mother.

When we pay attention, the universe provides us with the most unpredictable and uncanny messages. At one point in my own journey, my partner and I were sitting in our car in a parking lot discussing how we would imagine our relationship with a child. Like many couples, we were concerned about the changes that happen to the adult relationship when kids enter the picture. The car was very low to the ground and suddenly we looked up to find a two-year-old boy climbing onto the hood, crawling up to the windshield right between us! We were flabbergasted and giddy at this incredibly direct response. Of course, our child would just crawl right in!

Being connected with our path to parent as well as the deeper feelings and callings that create our lives, make life meaningful. If we *are* on our path, we feel that even trouble is somehow exciting. We marvel when something new and unexpected arises. We wonder what we can learn and we approach life with curiosity. We welcome and explore each step as we walk this sacred path bestowed upon us.

the growth of the parent

The Way of the Elder

> The greatest tragedy of the family is the
> unlived lives of the parents.
> —C. G. Jung

The act of parenting awakens us to who we are. We learn about ourselves when we are at our limits and when we are challenged by the independence and unique nature of our child. For many of us the most profound learning will be in our capacity to love and be loved. We tend to think of parenting in terms of helping our children grow, and yet, we grow as parents alongside our children. The growth of the parent is a vital and enriching journey.

Along this journey, we might be surprised to learn that we are children as well as parents! Many parents awaken to childhoods that were never enjoyed and now, revel in the laughter, fun, and delight that children bring. Some of us learn to be more flexible, less in control, and others may be challenged to be firmer and more direct. We may discover more about our own spontaneous nature, learn to work on conflict in a new way, or how to express ourselves more fully. Children may confront us with parts of ourselves that we have been too shy or fearful to look at. Kids can bring us into contact with interests and parts of the world that we have not experienced. And children can inspire us to think more about the world we want to live in and cause us to reflect on the deeper questions about the meaning of life.

Parenting is not only a process of observing, nurturing, and appreciating our children's development; it is as much about our own growth as a person, a parent, and an elder.

SEEING THE WORLD THROUGH THE CHILD'S EYES

Many parents experience the delight of seeing the world through their child's eyes. The openness of young children, shown in their unique perceptions and capacity to see what we often miss, is inspiring. Their pure and uncomplicated view of life and their curiosity and ability to love teaches us basic life lessons. Our everyday concerns seem less significant; nature becomes more vibrant, and social interactions may feel more intense or fascinating. Young children show us how to be more present in each moment and to live fully. Suddenly, the world is an adventure and the mundane can become profound.

This is why many spiritual and religious traditions elevate children. Christianity celebrates Baby Jesus, Buddhism tells us to return to the open state of a newborn, and indigenous people the world over see children as especially sacred. The young child's world-view is our teacher.

BEING OPEN

The openness of babies and young children make them irresistible. The loving and accepting demeanor of these young beings draws us in; their trust and curiosity can inspire us in our own development. We all aspire to be the best parents possible and we have ideals that we strive to uphold. As we grow as parents we may find that our children question our beliefs and values and those are also challenged by new life experiences. Being open means being aware of our parenting ideals while at the same time meeting new experiences and challenges with an open mind. That is easy to give voice to, but quite another to live.

Take the case of a mother who wants to leave her alcoholic husband and take her twelve-year-old son with her. The son does not want to leave because he feels responsible for his father. He worries about what will happen to the father if they both leave. The mother feels she has stayed in an abusive household for too long and she must protect herself and her son. Her values rest in wanting to protect her son; it is essential to her to step up as a responsible adult. She feels her son shouldn't have to take care of his father.

However, being open means considering the boy's experience as well. He feels responsible. We can think that he is too young to be responsible and try to convince him that his father's alcoholism is not his responsibility. Yet, if we opened up to his feelings, maybe there is something for us and for him to learn. Can his mother do both—hold onto her value of protecting her son, while at the same time be open to her son's experience?

This boy needed to speak to his father and express his sense of responsibility and love. He needed to tell him he was scared to leave him with no care. Being able to express his love and concern for his father is part of his personal development. With support, the boy pleaded with his father to get help and to stop drinking. I then asked the boy if he could be even more responsible and create the conditions in which he and his father would have contact. The boy said he wanted to live half time with each parent. However, he could only live with his father if his father stopped drinking. Through the son stepping up and valuing his sense of responsibility, this twelve-year-old was able to challenge his father, perhaps in a way in which no one else could. What a boost it was to his own inner esteem and what a great teaching for him to be able to interact so genuinely and powerfully with his father.

However, in order for the son to have this experience he needed the openness of his mother. The mother was about to sweep him away because she was only aware of her need to protect herself and her son. As she opened up to her son, she allowed him the opportunity to express his deepest feelings and gave him the freedom to step into his sense of responsibility.

PARENT'S EDGES

Children bring us to our edges, to the obstacles and belief systems that inhibit us from learning and experiencing more of who we are.[1] In such cases, they can be our greatest teachers; they become our role models and show us ways of being in the world that might be new or challenging.

Take Lukas, an eight-year-old, who wanted to earn money and became quite the entrepreneur. He had ideas about how to make jam and sell the jars in a park. He wanted to go to the beach and sell cold drinks. His mother was ambivalent and discouraging. Some of her hesitancy was quite reasonable; it could have ended up being a lot of work for her that she didn't have time for. The ingredients could have cost more than he would have been able to recoup. These were all good thoughts that needed to be explained to her son.

However, when we dug deeper into her discouraging feeling, we discovered she was very shy about self-promotion. In fact, she was self-employed as a massage therapist and needed to market herself, but felt she could hardly do it. Lukas was doing something that she needed to learn. He was enterprising, full of ideas, and self-promoting! Incorporating such behavior into her life was a development she needed to make.

Sometimes kids get stuck in life just where their parents are also stuck. Owen was in his senior year of high school, half way through the school year, and wanted to drop out. Laura, his mom, was terribly upset about this. Owen said that school wasn't important to him; he was bored and wanted to get a job. He wanted to earn his own money and live on his own.

Laura told him how few options he would have without a high school diploma, how his earning potential would diminish, and how he would be stuck and bored in a low-paying job. He snapped back and said, "Like you? You don't do a job you like. You are always complaining and look unhappy." Laura started to cry and said that he was right. Out comes her story about how she married young and, with two young children to support, she had to take any job she could find, and give up her dream to be a veterinarian. Owen piped in with great enthusiasm, "She is amazing with animals. You would be a great vet, Mom!"

"I think it's too late for me, now," Laura said. Here was the parent's edge, the place where she felt she couldn't go any further. She was stuck in her current identity and was unable to embrace something new. She had done what she feared Owen would do: she had settled for a job she didn't like and gave up on her dreams. Owen was now stuck in the same place, unable to formulate his dreams and believe in them.

"Yes, you can Mom. I know you can. Why don't you go back to school?" The encouragement that Owen gave his mother was heart-warming and Laura was visibly moved. "I think I will look into it. You are right; I gave up my dreams. But what are your deepest dreams, Owen? Let's do this together." Now Owen was at his edge! He shared something that Laura had never known about him. He said he wanted to study psychology but felt that there was no way he could ever afford it. His mother was thrilled to hear this and said they both had to investigate how to afford school. They both needed to go for their dreams.

SOLUTIONS FROM OUR CHILDREN

When parents get stuck or have a conflict, kids often have the solution. Sometimes it is hard to notice, but if we stay alert, we might see something we need to learn. Take the case of Jack and Paul, two dads who were arguing about finances. In the midst of their argument, their five-year-old gave each of them a toy. They were taken aback, looked at each other sheepishly, and despite their intent to continue their argument, they began to giggle. The wisdom of the child was not lost on them. They both saw how they had not been in contact with a deeper feeling of generosity between them and how they were both too one-sided in their viewpoints.

The freedom of younger children and their uncanny way of bringing something surprising and seemingly irrational into our interactions is a rich resource for our own growth. Watch what your children do and see if you can pick up on their teachings!

We tend to keep our conflicts private from children. I appreciate the need for privacy and intimacy between parents. However, in day-to-day life, conflict happens and kids are present. Their presence can give us a different kind of awareness. Some of us might not want to be as harsh in front of our children as we would be without them; we may temper our language and feel more protective. We may say we do this, "because of the children," however, we might consider that *we* are also the "children." We, as parents, are also the children who are too sensitive and easily hurt. This might teach us to bring more of our sensitivity into our relationships! Having a third person present, whether child or adult, can press us to be more conscious in the way we relate.

FORGIVENESS AND LEARNING

Sometimes when we look back on our parenting choices, we're horrified. We're filled with regrets over the moments we were hurtful or unnecessarily harsh. We wish we could take back our words and actions. We wish we had taken time to listen and tried to understand our children. We wish we could have those moments back when we missed something important because we were absent, preoccupied, or just distracted by life. These regrets may be painful and they are also signs that we have changed and grown. Growth needs to be valued. It is more troublesome when we remain stagnant and rigid.

Share your learning and regret with your children. Be open about your limitations and challenges and disclose how you have changed. Apologize to your children. As adults, many of us still wait for parents to apologize, to soothe and heal past hurts. Children can be quite understanding and flexible if we can show them our remorse, the learning we gained, and our desire to change.

Sometimes our regret lingers. The abuse we have carried out onto others persists internally. The intense self-hatred, inner criticism, and sense of unworthiness may have become pervasive. We also need to forgive ourselves. We need to see that being too harsh on ourselves is a form of inner parenting that is just as abusive as what we did to our children. It must stop.

Forgiveness happens through learning. If we can learn about ourselves and make a genuine change, we can forgive ourselves. If we can be genuine with the people we have hurt, apologize to them, and feel remorse for the suffering we have caused, we can move on. If we have hurt others, this also indicates that we, too, have been hurt, but probably are not aware of it. Exploring our own personal history brings deeper understanding. Feeding the cycle of inner abuse and torment is not good for us or our children.

EXPLORING OUR OWN PERSONAL HISTORY

It is important to become aware of our basic parenting beliefs and explore how they came to be. It's not uncommon to suddenly realize we sound like our own parents in the comments we make to our children. However, most often we are less aware of *how we parent ourselves*. Our internal dialogue—the way we speak to ourselves—often reflects the way our parents spoke to us. For many of us, these internal messages are not very positive. Sometimes our inner dialogue is elusive. We don't consciously hear it, but we feel depressed or hurt and don't know why. Our inner dialogue is often full of internalized negativity, lack of confidence, feeling insignificant, or just inner neglect. How we fail to parent ourselves shows up as:

- Disavowing feelings.
- Not giving time to unfold unknown experience.
- Only valuing outer success and outcomes.
- Criticizing ourselves relentlessly.
- Hating our bodies.
- Not allowing ourselves to try new things.
- Seeing ourselves, others, and the world as absolute and unchanging, destined to fulfill our worst expectations.
- Not trusting or believing in love; being cynical, and settling for second best.
- Not going for our dreams.
- Pushing away something foreign or different.
- Not loving the struggle or having compassion for ourselves and where we are in our growth.
- Not valuing dreaming reality, the experiences that don't fit into everyday consensus reality experience.

When we prepare for parenthood, it is essential that we explore our own history and become more aware of how we parent ourselves. This awareness translates into how we will parent our children.

CROSSROADS OF PERSONAL HISTORY AND PARENTING STYLES

What are your deepest parenting beliefs? How did you learn about parenting? Most of us learned about parenting by becoming parents. We didn't give it much thought until we were suddenly thrown into it. Parenting is such an awesome task, yet most of us meet it with little preparation, except for our own experience of being parented. That, however, is no small preparation. It is important to be aware of how our own experience of being parented influences our parenting.

Many of us unconsciously adopt parenting attitudes from our own parents; we end up talking to ourselves and treating ourselves the way they treated us. This happens so unconsciously that we don't recognize the depth of these internalized parental voices, values, and beliefs. And these in turn govern how we parent our children and parent ourselves. Often times, if we had negative or difficult experiences as children, we become *compensatory* parents. Compensatory parenting creates edges or beliefs against certain behaviors and paradoxically leaves us less equipped to deal with experiences that have hurt us. It's almost like we take an oath: "I will not be like my parent." We are on a mission to avoid whatever our parents did. We take a vow to never do that to our own children. However, compensatory parenting creates its own set of troubles. We can see this with many parents who raise their children as "free spirits" in reaction to a culture they feel is rigid and too rule-oriented. The free spirits then have troubles living in a culture with boundaries and don't know how to set meaningful and useful boundaries for themselves.

Similarly, a young woman I worked with felt so criticized by her mother that she vowed she'd never be critical of her daughter. As a result, the daughter grew up with a lot of praise and positive feedback, but she never really trusted her mother. She felt her mother lacked critical abilities and ran away from difficult conversations, glossing over anything that felt like a potential conflict or challenge. As a result, the daughter began to feel critical of her mother—she picked up the ghost of the critical one! The daughter grew up feeling like anything critical was forbidden. Thus, she didn't know how to give or receive criticism. She watched her mother unable to do things in the world because of self-doubt and criticism, which her mother never interacted with.

Another common example is the case of a man I worked with who had a terribly abusive father. Similarly, he vowed he'd never be like that himself. As a result, he was very mild-mannered but also out of touch with his own vitality, passion, and physicality, because it was all associated with abuse. These qualities that he disavowed included some of his own much-needed energy to feel impassioned and connected to his life force.

Another aspect of compensatory parenting is when we parent our children the way we wanted to be parented. We become the parent we wish we had. This can be quite transforming to become the parent we always wanted but never had. We create an environment for our child that we also would have liked and, at the same time, we heal something from our own past. However, this often happens unconsciously; we don't notice that our style of parenting is more about us than about our children. We might not even notice the fact that our kids aren't into the way we are parenting them.

For example, I worked with a young mother who suffered from a very somber and serious upbringing. She never got to be light and playful as a child so she made it a point to be playful with her young son. She would dance around and act silly and he would just stare at her and tell her to stop. He was a very serious boy who liked reading and was very internal. While the mother needed lighthearted play, her son was more reflective and serious and needed to be parented to fit his nature.

And still, another common fall-out from personal history is the parent who asserts: "This is the way I learned it, and this is how I will teach my children." Of course, this is a beautiful heritage to continue if the child (and later the adult) thrives. However, this philosophy is often adopted even if the way the parent learned it hurt them. It is almost vengeful, "This is the way it is, we all go through it, and you will too." In these cases, the parent needs to focus more on their own childhood experiences including the hurt and anger long buried, which are unconsciously passed down to the next generation.

THE INNER ELDER[2]

How can we learn to be better parents especially if we were so hurt as children? Is it even possible? Some people feel they won't ever have children in order to stop the cycle of generational abuse. My view is that regardless of whether or not we parent children, we are all meant to connect to the deepest part of who we are, to the one who is beyond our personal history and family experience, and who deeply supports and cares for us inside.

I see this aspect in each of us as an inner elder or even a divine parent, something larger than life, bigger than our small view of ourselves. So many religions give rise to divinities as parental figures and eternal caretakers. In my view, this is an attempt to connect us each to something incredibly fundamental. Despite our religious or spiritual views the human spirit seems to long for an inner experience of love, compassion, and guidance. This experience is available to each of us regardless of our background and the role we play in life.

It is imperative that we connect to the inner experience of this generous and open elder in ourselves—the part of us who can hold the ups and downs of life, who can weather storms and still maintain a center, who is open and curious to that which is less known, and who is interested in growing. This inner elder has transpersonal qualities. It is the sense of yourself that is somehow eternal; that which supported you to breathe your first breath and will be present at your deathbed. As an everyday experience, this inner parent sees your wholeness, can protect you from internalized negative tendencies, and reveals your deeper, more compassionate nature. Having contact with this divine inner parent allows us to meet experience with pure eyes and an open heart, encourages exploration, and holds us as we tumble and soar through life.

When we as parents feel close to this essential elder or divine parent we feel better. We have the inner sense of being deeply cared for which allows us to better meet life's challenges. We can parent our children with more ease and our children hone great lessons by observing how we parent ourselves. Growing into this inner sense of eldership is a profound personal development and might be the most fundamental change that we make as a parent.

EXERCISE: FINDING THE INNER ELDER[3]

The purpose of this exercise is to connect to these deep states of consciousness that are potentially present for all of us—if we only tapped into them. The inner elder gives us the necessary emotional intelligence and reveals the wisdom we need to better parent ourselves as well as our children.

1. Remember a time when you were really down and out.
2. Reflect on how you parented yourself during that time. How did you talk to yourself and treat yourself? What were the beliefs you had around the experience? Sometimes this is quite subtle.
3. Now put this memory aside. Close your eyes, relax, feel your body, and notice your breathing.
4. Ask yourself: Where in my body is the deepest part of me? If the deepest part of you were to be located in a part or area of your body where would it be? This is an irrational question so just allow yourself to feel into your body and notice what comes up.
5. Focus on that body part or area by breathing into it. Notice the sensations you have in that area of your body.
6. Amplify your body experience by feeling it more. Feel the sensations, temperatures, pressures, and feelings that arise.
7. Now ask yourself: If that experience were a place on earth, where would it be?
8. Go to that place in your inner mind and feel the quality of that earth-spot. Feel it inside of you and make a movement that gives you a sense of it. Shapeshift into that earth-spot so you can really embody its essence.
9. Hear the voice from this earth-spot. Let it speak to you and through you. What are its deepest parenting ideals? This is the inner elder, the divine parent, or eternal self—a part of you that is always there, who parents you and others, and is connected to the earth.

10. What does this voice say to you about your initial difficulty?

11. Imagine parenting your children from this state of mind.

For many, this kind of exercise will feel very foreign. Let me give you an example. A woman I worked with recalled a recent divorce. She was devastated and terribly hurt. At the time, she was parenting herself by simultaneously criticizing herself and fighting her ex-partner. In the exercise, she sat back and focused on her body, and after a few minutes, shared that the deepest part of herself was in her upper stomach. She put all of her attention on that area, breathed into it, and felt the area was warm and solid. She then imagined a place on earth that embodied those same qualities. She said it would be a special rock in a field near her house. In fact, she often went there during the painful break-up. When she became this rock, she stood up and swayed from side to side, very slowly. She felt solid and felt the warmth of the sun. The suffering one was no longer present, but instead a very different experience was emerging. Speaking from this new experience, she said, "I am here. No matter what, I am here. Fall back on me. I will comfort you. It doesn't matter who was right or wrong in your marriage. We are all growing and learning. You are on a path and I am here to support you." The woman was brought to tears hearing this message. An old wound felt healed and she birthed a part of herself that she hadn't had much contact with.

She then imagined how she would parent her children from this state of mind. She said she would be more relaxed in regard to the new family arrangement and felt more empowered as a parent. Since the divorce she had been tense and often on edge, ready to do battle. This newly discovered part of her had more ease with life's difficulties and could model a calmness and sense of security for her children.

The inner elder is our most profound teacher and offers a more balanced and unifying viewpoint. When we are able to connect with this part of ourselves there is more ease in ourselves and in our parenting. Parenting is full of unforeseen delights and challenges that open us up and press us to grow beyond our known worlds. Our ability to embrace our learning, particularly when we feel troubled and challenged, is paradoxically, one of the greatest gifts we can give our children.

parenting at odds together

Common Couple's Challenges

> *No one wins a relationship battle*
> *without injuring the relationship.*
> —Arnold Mindell

Many of us learn more about our significant other when we parent children together. Core values and principles emerge more clearly even though they were already present. Similarities and differences come to light and often times get amplified in our different approaches to parenting. Sometimes we feel enriched by the differences and other times these differences create conflict and distress. Every couple will be confronted with their own unique experiences, however there are some common challenges that emerge. In this chapter I will address some of the typical conflicts that come up within the parenting relationship and offer guidance.

DIVERGENT PARENTING PHILOSOPHIES

As couples raising children together, it is useful to speak about your differences and explore the core beliefs upon which they are based. For example, try and name some of your basic parenting values. Often these have not been stated directly yet they unconsciously drive many of our interactions with children and with each other. Get to the depth of your viewpoint—what is it based on and how has your belief emerged? Is your viewpoint based on a principle? Where and how did you develop it? Is it from your family background? Is it something you heard your parents say—do you agree with it and if so, why? Many of us parent based on principles that we never examined. We need to explore the intensity and energy that drives our viewpoint. Often we don't go deeply enough into the emotional core of what moves us.

For example, take a couple that was in conflict around how to raise their son. The father said, "Our son needs to be more independent." The mother felt the father was being too harsh. They had a big distance between them on this point. In our work together, we explored the father's principle. He had a lot of feeling and was adamant about his view: boys should be independent and he felt that the mother was too coddling. The mother brought out her view and stood for her emotional connection to her son.

At this point, I asked the father how he developed his view about boys being independent and why that was important to him. The father said he was raised with this view and he felt boys had to defend themselves. If they were too soft, he feared, his son would be bullied. Suddenly, he got teary as he remembered some rough moments from his childhood and how he was happy he could defend himself. He got more choked up and shared that he did not want his son to be defenseless. We can see that the father had a strong principle around raising boys and he had a lot of emotional charge around it that went back to his own childhood.

When the mother saw all the feelings the father had, something changed in her. She moved towards him and the distance between them diminished. She didn't want her son to be bullied either and agreed that she wanted him to be able to defend himself. She explored her view and said she felt it was artificial for her to just push her son away. From her view, she felt strongly that boys should be more sensitive and that she was fighting against a sexist principle.

She reflected on her own personal history around male figures in her life and how she promised herself she would raise her boy differently. She spoke with great passion about her vision of a world where men and boys could express feelings and relate with more sensitivity. This moved the father; in fact, he loved it when she related sensitively to him. Exploring their parenting philosophies in more depth brought them closer together. They agreed they both wanted to raise their son to be independent and be able to defend himself while simultaneously supporting his feeling life and sensitivity.

This example is a particularly common experience. Many of us discover differences in how we parent girls and boys and it gives us a great opportunity to learn more about our views and the culture we live in. What does it mean to defend oneself? Do girls need self-defense and a sense of independence as much as boys do? Do boys need strong connections to their feelings? Many of our most adamantly held parenting beliefs are formed around our personal backgrounds and social norms. The point is not to find out whether one view is correct, but to explore the views in more depth. The exploration brings greater understanding and more emotional connection for the parents. Additionally, by examining our deepest held parenting beliefs, we might find that they no longer serve us.

THE ROLE OF NEEDS

One of the biggest challenges in the parental relationship is getting our own needs met. The child is so central and dominates the role of the needy one in the family system. As parents we must tend to the needs of our children: survival needs for food and shelter, emotional needs for love, comfort and attention, as well as the social need to get along in the world. We drive them around, educate them, and try to create opportunities for them. We nurture them often more than we ever nurtured ourselves. We are present for the day-to-day practical needs from changing diapers, to reaching for things on higher shelves, to reading directions on toy boxes, and doing laundry. Particularly with young children, domestic life becomes very time consuming. Our own needs are continually put on hold.

An interesting study was recently published about the effect being in the workforce has had on women's needs.[1] Popular opinion held that having more women in the workforce and less full time mothers in the home would have reduced the total time spent with children. Surprisingly, the study revealed that mothers spent just as much time with their children as their 1960s counterparts. The difference is that working mothers today spend significantly fewer hours doing housework and sleeping. Culturally, we certainly have loosened up in our standards for clean and tidy households; however, the need for sleep is a health issue. For parents with young children, sleep is a precious commodity, a huge need that is often put aside.

Sleep-deprived and consumed by the role of caretakers, parents often find themselves bickering over who gets a free hour, who gets to go to the gym or the bookstore, or which parent gets the night off. From an outside perspective, it is obvious that both parents are in need. Parents need to appreciate and see their role as caretakers, and at the same time, they need to share the role of the needy one with the child. Kids tend to express their needs so well that they inadvertently dominate that position. Then we explode and get mad at them, "Don't you see how much we do for you!" Tension escalates with our co-parent as we keep tabs and resent the one whose needs got met.

It is crucial to appreciate the difficulty of this process which so many parents go through. Instead of fighting, care for yourself and each other. Appreciation goes a long way and tends to create an opening where parents then *want* to give to each other. Parents might not see or value all of the tasks that the other is doing and instead become moody, snappy, or hurt. Parents need to see what the other does, and strives to do, and value each other.

The next step is to talk openly about our deepest needs and discuss how we can support each other in getting them fulfilled. Needs are quite diverse; some parents have an exercise need, others a need for absolute quiet, doing nothing, going out on the town, reading a book, doing creative work, meditating, or just having down time to connect to the deepest part of themselves. Relationship needs are also often overlooked including time for romantic connection, sexuality, going out, or having an intimate conversation.

As a family, it's important to sit down together and discuss needs. Parents often don't express their needs directly and congruently enough or with real emotional need, but kids can understand statements such as, "Mommy has been playing all day with you and I really need some alone time." Your child might actually surprise you and give you the precious time you so much desire. Too often, our needs become so pent up that when they finally are released, it is with such volatility that we end up being hurtful to our children.

EXPLORING JEALOUSY

Jealousy is a common dynamic within the family system that isn't sufficiently addressed. More attention is given to jealousy between siblings, yet there are times when parents get jealous of each other and this impacts their relationship. We might feel the child loves or favors one of us more. We might wish we had the kind of connection that the other has or we might feel jealous of a quality that our partner has in relationship to the children.

As parents we don't talk enough about this dynamic, but our kids bring this up. Younger children are quite free and expressive. They blurt out, "I love you the best," "I don't want to be with you," "I like you better," etc. They don't do it maliciously but are quite neutral in their presentation. These words shock and hurt us and the effects usually create conflict between parents. Different dynamics arise; for example, one parent might minimize the child's comments while another might use those comments to further fuel the jealousy. The preferred parent might feel self-righteously elevated whereas the other might sink into self-doubt and inferiority or become defensive. It is important to be aware of those relationship dynamics and discuss them candidly. There are, in fact, ways to approach and explore jealousy that can make the experience useful instead of just painful.

A parent in this situation might ask herself: What quality does the other parent have that I might need to develop in myself? Rarely do we use jealousy as an inspiration for our personal growth. Many people suffer terribly from jealousy, tear themselves apart, and sometimes destroy their relationships. Another way to view jealousy is that we are jealous of a quality in the other that we just don't know enough about in ourselves. Jealousy is an awakener. It awakens us to something that is actually in us that we may be ignorant of or haven't developed enough.

In the parental relationship, it can be quite humbling to become aware of a quality that you see in your partner that you would like to develop in yourself. Instead conflict usually erupts; typically the jealous parent does not admit she is jealous, but instead accuses the other of being, for example, too nice or too permissive. She may then assert that the other should be stricter, like she is. The jealous parent does this because she too wants to feel valuable as a parent—and she is. Two points in this dynamic are important. The first is the need for each parent to name and support their own parenting style and their unique qualities. The second is for the jealous parent to see the quality in their partner they are jealous of as a piece of their own development. From this perspective the emphasis is on learning—not on whose way is right or better. Here is a fun exercise you might try alone or with your partner:

1. What are the parenting qualities or qualities in general that you value about yourself? If you are not a parent of a child, think of how you parent young people in your life, or yourself, friendships, colleagues, or communities.

2. Name a quality that you might be jealous of in your parenting partner? Or if you are not actively parenting a child, notice if you might be jealous of someone who elders or supports others in a way in which you aspire.

3. Try and open up to the possibility that the quality you are jealous of in your partner is also a part of you. This is a big feeling step; see if your mind will allow you to explore it.

4. Study in your inner mind how the partner or other person behaves. See if you can sit like them, feel like them, hear their voice, make small movements like them. Become them as much as you are able to. This experience is also you—embrace it!

5. Imagine bringing this aspect of yourself into your parenting.

If you do this exercise with your partner, share your experiences and teach each other about the qualities you would like to develop. This changes the tenor of the conversation from conflict to learning and enriches the relationship. For example, take a couple in which the mother was jealous of the way the kids listened to the father, without arguing back. She felt everything was a power struggle with the kids, and she ended up losing it and screaming at them. Later, she found herself seething with jealousy and fury that the kids so easily listened to him without any argument. Occasionally the kids had made comments that they liked Dad better or she noticed they would ask him for something and not her.

Together we explored her husband's behavior as potential qualities inside of her. She noted that he seemed calm when he spoke to the kids. On the other hand, she felt tense and ready for a fight. He seemed confident and at ease. Doing this exercise with her husband's support, she imagined being him. She stood up much taller and felt a calm and inner strength inside of her body. As they explored more about how the husband interacted with the kids they noticed that when he would ask or tell the kids to do things he would always give a reason. He would calmly answer all of their questions until they understood. It seemed like the kids didn't listen to Mom because they either disagreed with her or didn't understand her reasons. Dad took more time to go into the disagreements and gave explanations, making it easier for the kids to agree. He also would take time and make eye contact and/or physical contact when he spoke with them. This was useful for Mom to learn. It immediately alleviated the conflict with her husband, helped her to develop an important part of herself, and improved her relationship with her kids.

A different dynamic can emerge with older children. Older children are more aware of the effect of their words and preferential statements are often made with the intent to hurt. Paradoxically, the child's motivation is often a desire to improve the relationship, to impact the parent she has injured, and to effect change. Indeed the child can unconsciously wish for the parents to conflict in order to work out a disagreement that she actually has with one or both of her parents. The child feels that if she hurts one parent by preferring the other, the parent would want to change and become more like the preferred parent. Additionally, one parent can unconsciously make a coalition with the child against the other parent. This dynamic frequently creates terrible tension between parents. All of these instances signal that the whole family system is challenged to learn more about working out conflict directly. Parents need to be more direct with each other and not unconsciously use their children to support their views. And, the preferred parent needs to support the child to work things out with the other parent instead of polarizing one parent against the other.

In those instances, parents need to express their hurt. Additionally, we might understand the child's outburst as an unspoken request for better relationship. Rarely do parents grab this moment as opportune because we are so hurt. However, we might say, "Oh, that really hurts. I feel you wanted to get at me and you did. I am devastated and I must have also hurt you. How have I done that?" Or, "I wish we were closer. I just don't know how to do it." Or, "I would like to improve our relationship. We are both hurt. I want to listen to what upsets you and also be heard." This would be a different kind of response than the hurt and escalation that often occurs.

CONFLICT ON THE HOME FRONT

Many parents hide conflict from their children. Others, although they try, still end up conflicting in front of their kids. Many parents think that children should be protected from conflict. Conflict is seen as dangerous instead of a place where kids can learn. As I have previously mentioned in this book, the result is that most of us do not learn how to have a conflict that resolves fruitfully. So when conflict does emerge, most of us don't do it well. When I teach a class on conflict work I often ask if anyone grew up in a home where they saw conflict worked out and resolved in a way where everyone felt well. I rarely see a hand go up.

Kids witness tense atmospheres in which conflict is avoided and everyone walks on eggshells or where sudden explosions occur when the tension is finally too big to contain. Some children grow up in family situations where nothing is ever resolved and there is a lot of volatility, roughness, and sometimes, even abuse. Other family atmospheres with unprocessed conflict can be cold, distant, snappy, or depressed. Considering these experiences, I can understand why we want to protect our kids from our conflicts.

How can kids learn about conflict if we don't show them how to have conflict? Naturally, there are some parental conflicts that you would want to address privately. And there are everyday conflicts that always come up in family life. They are usually the ones that seem like they are about nothing, like fighting over directions in the car, how something is cooked, who should clean up, or deciding which movie to go to; yet, within such conflicts much more is being said. As parents we are our child's first role models and how we disagree and get along with each other serves as a first imprint. The most basic viewpoint, sorely lacking for many, is that conflict is valuable; it is an opportunity for learning where our differences can be creative. Just opening up to this notion creates a different feeling in how we approach conflict.

THE UNITED FRONT

The united front is a strong parenting philosophy for many. The premise that parents must be consistent and of one mind so that children know what to expect and do not play one parent against the other has its obvious value. And yet, this view also has its limitations.

One of the problems with presenting a united front is that it communicates to children that parents are a force to contend with. Children then learn that they must battle us in order to get their point across. Or, they become hopeless about dealing with power, feeling that there is no use in saying anything because the parental unit is so strong. The other problem with the united front philosophy is that parents often do not feel united or strong. And, our children are quite savvy; most of the time they see right through the united front. They see the diversity in their parents and notice the conflicting communication signals between partners.

The alternative to trying to present a united front, particularly, when you don't feel one, is to have an open discussion about the various viewpoints on the issue. Learning together through exchanging viewpoints gives value to each person and allows people to learn from each other, to express their views, and to open up to other points of view. Listening and appreciating differing viewpoints can also bring surprising solutions and furthers the building of consensus. This does not mean one parent undermines what the other has said. If Mom says, "Jim, you can't go out," and then Jim goes to Dad who says, "He can," there is a problem. Instead when Jim comes to Dad and complains that Mom won't let him, Dad should encourage Jim to discuss the issue with his mother. This furthers Jim's relationship with his mother. Jim might need support and

Dad could certainly encourage Jim to bring out his viewpoint with Mom and to listen to hers.

This is a very typical dynamic: one parent will complain, "He doesn't back me up; I say one thing to the kids and he lets them go." What needs to be backed up is the relationship interaction, not necessarily the content. One parent should not protect the child from interacting with the other parent. This is where backup is really needed—in the relationship interaction with the parent the child is having difficulty with. Thus, Dad needs to send Jim back to Mom to continue the discussion.

Let's take this scenario further to model how parents can bring out differing views in a way that doesn't undermine their relationship. Imagine this: Mom, Dad, and Jim are sitting at the kitchen table together.

Mom: I don't want you going out tonight, Jim.

Dad: What is your thinking around that? I feel it would be okay under certain conditions, but maybe I am missing something in the discussion.

Mom explains her thinking and then asks what Dad's conditions are. Jim listens to them discuss their viewpoints and also joins in. Jim says Dad's conditions sound fair to him and then he answers one of Mom's concerns. This partially satisfies Mom, but then she adds another condition. Dad says that he hadn't thought of that concern, and it makes sense to him. Everyone agrees, Jim is allowed to go out, and everyone consents to the parameters the family came up with. This is ideal—everyone learning, discussing, hearing each other, and being able to be flexible as well as state their view.

Such interactions support children in their learning to appreciate a variety of voices and to be able to facilitate the vast amount of opinions and viewpoints that come their way in life. This also teaches kids to stand up to power, not to fear it or to become hopeless in the face of it. It teaches them to not just follow blindly, but to question others, which prepares kids for dealing with peer groups and other group scenes where individual voices are often missed or fear prevents them from being voiced.

My view is the reason the united front became such a strong piece of parenting advice is because parents felt undermined by each other. This only happens if the relationship is undermined. Kids must learn to go back to parents who differ from them and engage in the relationship, instead of pulling the other parent in to release them.

CONFLICT AS ROLES

We tend to see conflict personally and one-sidedly and fail to recognize that it is also an expression of two roles in the family system that are interchangeable. Any one person in the family can identify and step into any role in a given moment. We know this in practice but don't always notice our own fluidity in the heat of the moment. We get set in what we feel. In the example above, the role of the one setting limitations was ultimately shared by all. The permissive one and the conditional one were roles in the family that all could appreciate. This is where a united front limits the diversity of the family field from coming forward. Differing viewpoints get repressed. However, bringing forward different views and using the concept of roles can help everyone see their wholeness.

For example, take two moms and their eleven-year-old Cleo, who got an average report card. One of the moms, Bev, says Cleo can do better and she feels the other mom, Sandy, is too lax with their daughter. So, we have two roles. Bev feels Cleo can do better and is more achievement and success-oriented, while Sandy is more laid back and less concerned with grades.

The issue is a personal conflict between them, but it is also a conflict in the larger system, which shows up between the two women, within the daughter, in the school, and the world we live in. Instead of keeping it personal, we played with the interaction as roles and let them speak strongly, sometimes in an exaggerated form.

Bev: I think she can do better. I want her to be excellent. She is
         lazy. I want her to succeed, be tops, perfect.

Sandy: She is great how she is. She will find her own way. Grades
         aren't so important. Relax; you are so uptight.

Bev: I have to be uptight because you are so relaxed!

Sandy: Well, I have to be so relaxed because you are so driven and
         perfectionistic.

Then came the moment of change—they both started laughing! When I asked why they were laughing, they said because they actually agreed with each other. They made jokes how one was a perfectionist in many ways and the other was more laid back. These roles were familiar to them in many of their day-to-day interactions and they agreed they were often polarized against each other.

The laughter was a good beginning that broke the intensity and seriousness of their polarization. However, something else had emerged in this role-play. Each one implied that she would be less relaxed or less on task if the other were to pick up her role. This is so often the case when our relationships become polarized. I then encouraged Bev to experiment and step into Sandy's role of being relaxed in the moment. Could she imagine what that would be like? She slumped down in her chair, took a big breath, and said it was a relief. Quite spontaneously Sandy said she felt more at ease seeing Bev like that. She then shared that in her private thoughts she did wonder if she was too lax with Cleo and would like to be more on task with her.

This created a change within the relationship. They both appreciated the other for their more usual styles, but also realized how the relationship felt better when they could share those roles. They realized that the experience of doing one's best in life as well as being easy and relaxed were qualities they both wanted and had and that their daughter needed and wanted them as well.

Seeing conflict in terms of roles helps conflict resolve; we learn about ourselves by noticing that we do possess both viewpoints and that they belong to the family field. It is difficult to have this view in the midst of conflict, but if you do, you can make your conflicts more enjoyable. Acting out viewpoints as roles gives us distance; it lets us exaggerate them and say the unspeakable. As roles, we have more freedom to interact and are less prone to become frozen because we don't take it personally. We can switch roles as we feel ourselves change inside or we can switch simply because we want to get to know the experience of the other side. Authentic transformation can arise during these role switches. It takes an open mind and a sharp awareness to notice these subtle feeling changes, those moments of laughter, de-escalation, and sharing common ground. It also takes some courage and practice to embrace and explore many viewpoints!

BRINGING IN THE KIDS

Most kids love to be involved in role-play and enjoy observing, directing, or stepping into roles. Creative solutions often come from the kids themselves. Sometimes parents get stuck in their own tailspin and cycle endlessly in the back and forth dialogue between two roles. Try asking your child what they think should happen; you might be surprised with their solution!

I remember one family where the mother felt she was always nagging the kids to do homework and she was upset with the father who didn't involve himself. She felt she had to be the heavy one. They took over the roles in front of the two kids: "You have to do your homework; it's important to do well in school!" Then the father's role: "I don't really want to be involved. I hate to argue and pester the kids, I just prefer to stay out and not conflict." The mother got angrier in her role, "Well you have the privilege to not conflict because you are not around! I really hate having to pester them too! I wish you would care more about me being stuck in my position and about the kids getting their work done." At that moment, the ten-year-old came in and said, "Well, I think we do need to do our homework. But Mom, you are too worried about school. How about we make a deal: we agree to do our homework every day before dinner and no one bugs us?" That was a solution everyone could agree to!

Sometimes even our youngest children give us clues. I remember working with a couple and their four-year-old daughter around toilet habits. The child was not using the toilet, but instead doing her business wherever she was. The mother had developed a strong parenting philosophy to not be authoritarian towards her child; she herself had been really hurt by a strict mother and compensated by being extremely loose. So, when her child began to poop on the floor she wouldn't tell her to use the toilet. Even telling her daughter to use the toilet felt too authoritarian and strict for this mother. The father felt differently, but didn't feel strong enough to assert himself. He was really upset, but yielded to the strong parenting philosophy of the mother, deferring because he thought maybe she knew better. I then asked the father point blank where he felt his daughter should poop and he said, "the toilet." I asked the mother the same question, "Where do you think your child should poop?" There was a blank stare. Just then, the daughter who was watching it all, said, "Daddy wants me to poop in the potty. Mommy, where do you think I should poop?" This question snapped Mom out of her trance. Finally it became clear to the mother that her daughter was looking for guidance and direction. I then said to the mother that her daughter was asking for direction and that if she did have a preference deep inside it would be good to tell her daughter so she would know. The mother then said, yes, she, too, would prefer that the child use the toilet. This cleared up the problem and was a relief to the entire family. In this case, the daughter resolved the tension between the two conflicting roles. This was also a revelation to the mother; she learned that guidance and direction did not mean being heavy and authoritarian, as she had feared.

SEPARATION AND DIVORCE

Separation and divorce is a big topic that really needs its own book. I can't do justice to the topic here, but do want to mention some food for thought. Divorce and separation are often difficult for the family, and yet, that assumption can also be a hypnosis. Sometimes divorce can be good for the family! It is not unusual for older children to say to divorced parents, "We wished you had done that a while ago." Many children suffer from the tensions between their parents and experience the separation as a relief.

With that said, regardless of circumstance, separation and divorce is a huge change for everyone and can challenge the parenting relationship. Some couples make a total cut in their relationship and would prefer to have no further contact. And yet, the parenting relationship keeps them involved. That is a challenging fate. Other couples part amicably and feel that their parenting relationship was one of the better parts of their contact. Obviously these parents have an easier time continuing what they had always done so well together.

However, many of us don't part so well and our own relationship issues do get in the way of how we parent. Children prevent us from totally severing our ties. We must have some involvement together as parents and, as a result, we are challenged to continue to work on our relationship at least in our capacity to parent well together. Those of us who don't work on our relationships create a difficult situation for our children.

Those parents who do tackle their relationship issues with ex's, teach their children that conflict is something to explore and learn from. They teach their kids that you can move on in life, that people do grow apart, that there are different kinds of relationships at different times in life, and that this is okay. We model that we can get along and get through hard times, hurt, and angry feelings. We show our children that we are always their parents and that the presence of conflict does not mean the absence of relationship and love. This is a profound lesson for many children and, despite the possible loss of their dream of an intact nuclear family, they may also be enriched by these major life experiences.

Even though it is obvious, it must be said that we need to be aware of and refrain from using children to work out our own stuff. Don't put kids in the middle of the crossfire and don't use them to get back at the other; don't withhold them from their other parent, don't neglect to keep custody agreements, or show up late, etc. These things mostly hurt the children. Additionally, don't use your children as "third parties." For example, "Tony said he didn't like the toy you got him." Tony can tell that to his parent himself. If you have a beef with the other parent, speak directly to her without using the children to inadvertently inflate your view. Using the children will only hurt their relationship with both parents and create a lot of communication chaos. Additionally, try and inhibit yourself from prying information from your kids regarding your ex-partner's new partner. If you want to know, ask your ex and leave the kids out of it.

It is important to let children develop their own relationships with each parent. Children need to believe in and have their own experiences. They don't need to be pumped full of venom against the other parent even though we might feel it. Let them discover the other parent on their own. Listen to them and encourage them to have a direct relationship with the other parent. Of course, if you believe your child is in danger with your ex, you need to find out and involve yourself.

Another suggestion rarely mentioned is to consider including children in the discussion of separation. Obviously, there is a private discussion between parents that needs to happen. However, at a certain point discussing it as a family can be enriching. The concept of family needs to be valued and preserved. This is important to children and probably to the parents as well. The feeling of connection and home is important to us all. Having a conversation about creating a new kind of family can be very supportive to your children. They then feel that they are not losing family, but creating something new. Talk about what family and connection mean. Discuss the feeling of home. Home is an inner as well as an outer experience. Inside it is the feeling of comfort and security, love, and a sense of value, regardless of outer circumstance. Outwardly, it is the structures that uphold and support those basic values. How will you now support those values with the changing family structure? Each family will have their own unique solution. Some parents who separate feel strongly connected by their family bond. They celebrate special occasions together, move in and out of each other's home with ease, and have dinner together. Some nurture family by building on these values and bringing others in, thereby extending the family. Children can also develop two strong families where there are more adults and children in their lives. The possibilities are endless.

Children can also be included in the conversation by inviting them to speak about things they would like to separate from. We tend to think only of parents separating. However, many children can enjoy thinking of things they would like to leave as well! One boy told me he was happy to leave an atmosphere of constant fighting. Some children might want to leave a certain style of interaction or communication, an old bedroom, or place. Such a conversation involves and empowers kids so they are not just victims of their parent's decisions; it may even lead to a surprising feeling of relief or celebration.

We must remember that even though as parents you can be at odds, you are together in your fate as parents.

 **parenting the planet**

Beyond Your Own Family

There is no single effort more radical in its potential for saving the world than a transformation of the way we raise our children.

—Marianne Williamson

Although this book focuses primarily on parenting children, the deeper vision that inspires me is that of parenting our planet. Parenting children sometimes narrows our focus to our nuclear family, but it can also inspire us to see our roles as parents outside the parameters of the nuclear family. Indeed, having children implicitly motivates adults to think beyond their lifetimes. Parenting children *is* parenting the planet. Children who have positive parenting experiences are better equipped to take care of themselves and others. Those children have the inner love and self-esteem to look beyond themselves and see each person as a part of the global family.

Parenting the planet means parenting for the future. It means caring for our environment, our educational systems, our political systems, and global relations. It means caring for our inner lives and deepest dreams and nurturing our relationships. It also means stepping into a parenting role in moment-to-moment situations—on the playground, at work, in our relationships, on the streets, and in our neighborhoods. Some of us who parent in this sense are grassroots community workers, mentors, teachers, social workers, and neighbors who are the backbones of our communities. These elders are sorely needed. Eldership does not refer to age, but to the sense of caring for the whole. The elder reaches out to others, encourages diverse viewpoints, and makes a home for all. In fact, an elder *is* a home for all; we gravitate towards such people because they make us feel well.

The elder makes room for the dreaming background of life. She befriends that which seems foreign or unknown. Just as a mother will meet her young baby's gibberish with delight and curiosity, the elder meets what he can't quite comprehend with that same spirit of curiosity and affection. Indeed, life is more than a one-dimensional material world; we sorely need those who can parent and discover the dreaming background, the incomprehensible or irrational, and the unspoken emotional and feeling atmosphere of a situation. People who have historically cared for this realm of life have been called shamans, healers, prophets, or sages. Yet, these qualities are in each of us; we just need to hear the call.

One of the worst nightmares for parents is the thought of losing their child or their child dying prematurely. It is a common fear that I have explored over the years with many new parents. A recurrent theme that often arises and brings some comfort is the sense that there is something greater than us as parents, something like the elder, or a world parent. Through connecting with deep inner states, dreams, and a sense of the ineffable, parents discover that they are part of a universal mother or father, a parent that is always caring for all children. Women and men who discover this in themselves find an inner calm that relaxes their fear. It connects them to a deep sense of parenting the world and a profound knowing that their child is cared for, regardless of circumstance. When we get in touch with this sense of parenting the planet, we know that our family is not just the one we live with, but a sense of family that extends outside of those boundaries. Parenting is that sense of eldership that deeply nurtures, uplifts, and follows the unique nature of all beings.

EVERYONE IS A PARENT

The process of "parenting" is both an inner experience and a literal calling. We are all called to develop a parent inside of ourselves. We all long to find in ourselves a good parent, a wise guide, or calm center—whatever we may call it. In this sense everyone is called to parent, though not everyone is called to have children.

The parent, or the elder, is always trying to come to life in us. Too often our culture thinks about birth as only related to babies. I also think of the birth of parents. For those of us who work in the field of psychology or focus on our personal growth, we know that the experience of developing an inner parent and/or transforming internal negative dialogue is deep and profound. Such transformations obviously translate to the parenting of our children.

"Parents" emerge in our dreams as mythical figures, nature spots, or inner experiences that embrace our totality. Many of us feel parented by spiritual beliefs or religious figures, sages, or Gods. As children, some of us developed parental relationships with guardian angels or spirit friends. Some of us feel parented by nature, communities or organizations, or feel that there are other individuals besides our birth parents who are our parents. I remember a wonderful story from Eli. At three years old Eli said to his American mom, who had adopted him from India as an infant, "I always knew you were my real mother. I remember being inside another mother's tummy, but I knew that I had to get to you." Many of us will discover that our deepest connection to being parented didn't necessarily come from our birth parents. Perhaps the paradoxical advantage of having a parent that has been inadequate is that we are pressed to discover an inner parent. It is this profound experience of parent or elder that many of us long for. We feel a deep sense of well-being inside when we are connected to this aspect of ourselves. I believe that when people have this inner experience they become better parents to children.

IN HOMAGE TO THE CHILD

Too many parents feel they have lost time or missed important experiences with their children. The errands and "doings" of our day-to-day lives can consume us until we realize we have missed these precious moments with our children—the expressions of love, uncontrollable giggles, moments of silence and intimacy, or a wondrous new discovery. Suddenly the milestones of graduations are upon us and our children are adults and out of our homes. It is my hope that this book encourages us in our busy lives to take time for these precious moments, cultivate them, and nourish the inner lives of our children.

Having a child is a sacred responsibility; we are meant to nurture and shepherd the body, mind, and spirit of new life. And, having a child is a gift; we not only reap the rewards of that intimate relationship, but we are inspired to deeply connect to the open and ineffable spirit of new life and the child residing in each of us.

 **notes**

introduction

1. Dr. Arnold Mindell, author of numerous books, founded process-oriented psychology or "process work." Process work is an innovative and comprehensive psychotherapeutic modality that encompasses body, mind, spirit, and world processes, and has its roots in the teleological thinking of Carl Jung, the non-judgmental and meaning-based view of Taoism, the dreaming wisdom of indigenous peoples, the signal-based methods of communication theorists, and non-locality principles of quantum physics that reveal the complex interconnectedness of all things.

2. Benjamin Spock, *The Common Sense Book of Baby and Child Care* (New York: Duell, Sloan, and Pearce, 1946). As quoted in Wikipedia, accessed on May 20, 1013, http://www.en.wikipedia.org/wiki/Benjamin_Spock#cite_note-bbc-.

the inside scoop

1. This book is not meant to discuss the concept or the history of emotional intelligence; for further information please see: Daniel Goleman, *Emotional Intelligence: Why It Can Matter More Than IQ* (New York: Bantam, 1995).

2. "The second attention focuses upon things you normally neglect, upon external and internal, subjective, irrational experiences. The second attention is the key to the world of dreaming, the unconscious and dreamlike movements, the accidents and slips of the tongue that happen all day long." Arnold Mindell, *The Shaman's Body: A New Shamanism for Transforming Health, Relationships and Community* (New York: Harper Collins, 1993), 24-25.

3. Arnold Mindell describes three different realms of awareness or realities. consensus reality reflects the material world that we all more or less

agree to. It is the world of facts, rational and linear thinking, and objective material reality. Dreamland or the dreaming world is the experience of our more subjective experiences that are often expressed in feelings, irrational thoughts, fantasy and in experiences that we marginalize. The world of the essence is reflected in the larger spirit or intelligence in the background of all experience, or what Mindell calls the Process Mind. Essence experience is at the heart of all spiritual tradition; it is the sense of unity and unbroken wholeness. See: Arnold Mindell, *Process Mind: A User's Guide to Connecting with the Mind of God* (Wheaton, IL: Quest Books, 2010).

4. C. G. Jung first spoke of a central childhood dream and its connection to a life myth. See: C. G. Jung, *Psychological Interpretation of Children's Dreams*, Zurich lectures, (unpublished) 1938-1939. Arnold Mindell took this idea further connecting childhood dreams and chronic body symptoms. See: Arnold Mindell, *Working With the Dreaming Body* (London: Routledge and Kegan Paul, 1985); Arnold Mindell, *Process Mind: A User's Guide to Connecting with the Mind of God.* (Wheaton, IL: Quest Books, 2010), 31; and Alan Strachan's studies, accessed on May 20, 2013, http://www.alanstrachan.com/Dreaming_Childhood.html.

5. For more information on how bodies dream, see: Arnold Mindell, *Working With the Dreaming Body* (London: Routledge and Kegan Paul, 1985); and Arnold Mindell, *The Dreambody: The Body's Role in Revealing the Self* (Santa Monica, CA: Sigo Press, 1982).

6. Arnold Mindell's ground-breaking work and early discovery of the "dreambody" connects body and mind and demonstrates how body experiences are reflected in dreams and vice versa. See: Arnold Mindell, *The Dreambody: The Body's Role in Revealing the Self* (Santa Monica, CA: Sigo Press, 1982), and *Working with the Dreaming Body* (London: Routledge and Kegan Paul, 1985).

7. My son said this at the age of four and then turned it into a little song. In 2006, I performed a one-woman show, *MamaSpeak*, about my journey of motherhood and the deeper sense of "mother" that carries

us all. This song was included in the show. Segments of the show can be found on my website, http://www.dawnmenken.com. This particular segment can be found under the *Inner Life of Children*, the direct link: http://www.dawnmenken.com/multimedia_mamaspeak_inner.html.

heart and smarts

1. The term "emotional intelligence" has been more popularly recognized in the work of Daniel Goleman, author of *Emotional Intelligence: Why It Can Matter More Than IQ* (New York: Bantam Books, 1995). However, for a more thorough historical credit, please see: http://en.wikipedia.org/wiki/Emotional_intelligence, "The first use of the term "emotional intelligence" is usually attributed to Wayne Payne's doctoral thesis, *A Study of Emotion: Developing Emotional Intelligence* from 1985. Prior to this, the term "emotional intelligence" appeared in Leuner (1966). Stanley Greenspan (1989) also put forward an EI model, followed by Salovey and Mayer (1990), and Daniel Goleman (1995). The distinction between trait emotional intelligence and ability emotional intelligence was introduced in 2000." In addition see: John Gottman, *Raising an Emotionally Intelligent Child: The Heart of Parenting,* (New York: Simon and Schuster, 1997).

2. There are so many children's books that teach kids language to express their feelings. Here is one I like: Saxton Freymann, *What Are You Peeling? Foods with Moods* (New York: Arthur A. Levine Books, 1999).

3. Rachel Simmons, *Odd Girl Out: The Hidden Culture of Aggression in Girls* (Orlando, FL: Harcourt Books, 2002).

4. J. K. Rowling, *Harry Potter and the Philosopher's Stone* (UK: Bloomsbury, 1997), 299.

5. Carlos Castaneda, *Journey to Ixtlan: The Lessons of Don Juan* (New York: Pocket Books, 1974), 214-230. Carlos Castaneda describes his encounters with the worthy opponent in his mentorship with the Yaqui Indian shaman Don Juan Matus.

power at play

1. Arnold Mindell, *Sitting in the Fire: Large Group Transformation Using Conflict and Diversity* (Portland, OR: Lao Tse Press, 1995). Mindell's seminal book differentiates different kinds of rank and power, particularly in regard to understanding group and world dynamics.

2. Arnold Mindell, *Sitting in the Fire: Large Group Transformation Using Conflict and Diversity* (Portland, OR: Lao Tse Press, 1995), 49-73.

3. C. G. Jung first spoke of a central childhood dream and its connection to a life myth. *Psychological Interpretation of Children's Dreams*, Zurich lectures, (unpublished) 1938-1939. Arnold Mindell took this idea further connecting childhood dreams and chronic body symptoms. See: Arnold Mindell, *Working With the Dreaming Body* (London: Routledge and Kegan Paul, 1985). See: Arnold Mindell, *Working With the Dreaming Body* (London: Routledge and Kegan Paul, 1985); Arnold Mindell, *Process Mind: A User's Guide to Connecting with the Mind of God.* (Wheaton, IL: Quest Books, 2010), 31; and Alan Strachan's studies, accessed on May 20, 2013, http://www.alanstrachan.com/Dreaming_Childhood.html.

4. Gerard Jones, *Killing Monsters: Why Children Need Fantasy, Super Heroes and Make Believe Violence* (New York: Basic Books, 2002).

5. Ingrid Rose, *School Violence: Studies in Alienation, Revenge, and Redemption* (London: Karnac Books, 2009).

6. See Chapter 5 for a more in-depth discussion on bullying.

your child in the world

1. I am well aware of the revisionist history movement, those who ignore historical fact, gloss over pain and struggle, and recreate it to justify or glorify past events. Here I am referring to history as a present-day reality, where the themes and emotions of the past are still present. Therefore, history can also be an opportunity to create new interactions and possibilities that can be potentially enriching, instructive, or even healing.

2. On Thanksgiving 2008, I was grateful that the *Oregonian* newspaper published an article by Prof. Karl Jacoby of Brown University, reviewing the real history of Thanksgiving. Americans would be surprised to discover that Thanksgiving was created in the middle of the Civil War in 1863 when President Lincoln declared the last Thursday in November a holiday. His intent was to give thanks to the advancing Union troops, as well as the harvest, and to send prayers to all those suffering from the losses of war. Northerners donated turkey and cranberries to the Union troops and Jefferson Davis created a special Thanksgiving holiday for the Confederacy. During reconstruction, Southerners were averse to celebrating a "Yankee holiday," so the Thanksgiving story from 1621 was unearthed. During that year, fifty colonists survived a brutal winter; they had a successful harvest and feasted (not on turkey and cranberries) with a group of Wampanoag Indians. Fifty years later, the colonists seized Wampanoag land and set off a brutal war in the Northeast. Hundreds of colonists and thousands of indigenous people were killed and many were sold into slavery in the British West Indies. The colonists prevailed and in 1676 they declared a public day of Thanksgiving to celebrate "the subduing of our enemies." What I find so fascinating in this history is, indeed, Thanksgiving is all about the deeper dream of America, our dream of unification, of being a home for diverse and marginalized people. And yet, that history also includes the one who fears difference, who wars with it, and enslaves and conquers. After the Civil War, the country was at a great crossroads to genuinely reconcile our racial divide. We were not really able to do so and instead looked at another time in history romanticizing the history of Europeans and Indians. Unconsciously, we longed for and dreamed of unification and created an entire history of sharing and harmony. In so doing, we marginalized the suffering and real history of Native Americans. And obviously, the painful history of race in the U.S. is still palpable. However, psychologically, this story informs us about the hope of reunification, of understanding the other, and of the simple lesson of a six-year old: sharing.

3. Todd Parr, *It's Okay to be Different* (New York: Little, Brown and Company, 2001), and *The Family Book* (New York: Little, Brown and Company, 2003).

4. Please see the following link for Anderson Cooper's interview with President Barack Obama, posted on July 15, 2009, accessed on May 20, 2013, http://www.cnn.com/video/#/video/bestoftv/2009/07/15/ac.obama.intv.cnn?iref=allsearch.

5. I am grateful to my friend Raija Sirra from Finland who shared with me that in Finnish there are no gender pronouns. There are gender-neutral words to describe people without connotation of gender. I wondered what it would be like to grow up in a culture in which gender was not emphasized. Raija told me that her experience was that jobs and behavior did not appear to have such a strong gender association as they do in other cultures. In addition, my thanks go to Julie Diamond for calling my attention to Geert Hofstede's research http://geert-hofstede.com/dimensions.html in which he shows to what degree a culture displays socially determined "masculine" or "feminine" traits. Finland and other Scandinavian countries are some of the most "feminine" cultures on the planet.

bullies, victims, and bystanders

1. There are many studies that discuss how parental involvement helps reduce bullying. Here are two: "Parental Involvement Key to Preventing Child Bullying." *ScienceDaily*. Reprinted from American Academy of Pediatrics. Posted on May 6, 2010, accessed on June 17, 2013, http://www.sciencedaily.com/releases/2010/05/100503074239.htm. "Poor Parenting–Including Overprotection–Increases Bullying Risk." *ScienceDaily*. Reprinted from University of Warwick. Posted on April 25, 2013, accessed on June 17, 2013, http://www.sciencedaily.com/releases/2013/04/130425214005.htm.

2. William Golding, *Lord of the Flies* (New York: Perigee Books, 1959 [1954]).

3. Ingrid Rose, *School Violence: Studies in Alienation, Revenge, and Redemption* (London: Karnac Books, 2009). This book researches the dynamics associated with school violence and bullying.

growing through conflict

1. See Chapter 5 on Bullies, Victims, and Bystanders.

2. Double signals are those often subtle, non-verbal communication signals that are unintended. We do not identify with the feelings and experiences embedded in those signals, which is why they are unintended. See: Arnold Mindell, *Working with the Dreaming Body* (London: Routledge and Kegan Paul, 1985); Arnold Mindell, *The Dreambody in Relationships* (London: Routledge and Kegan Paul, 1987); Julie Diamond and Lee Spark Jones, *A Path Made by Walking* (Portland, OR: Lao Tse Press, 2004); Joe Goodbread, *The Dreambody Toolkit* (Portland, OR: Lao Tse Press, 1997).

3. The edge is what prevents the identity from embracing and exploring that which is unknown. Please see: Arnold Mindell, *River's Way: The Process Science of the Dreambody* (London: Routledge and Kegan Paul, 1985); Julie Diamond and Lee Spark Jones, *A Path Made by Walking: Process Work in Practice* (Portland, OR: Lao Tse Press, 2004).

4. See: Arnold Mindell, *Working with the Dreaming Body* (London: Routledge and Kegan Paul, 1985); Arnold Mindell, *The Dreambody in Relationships* (London: Routledge and Kegan Paul, 1987); Julie Diamond and Lee Spark Jones, *A Path Made by Walking* (Portland, OR: Lao Tse Press, 2004); Joe Goodbread, *The Dreambody Toolkit* (Portland, OR: Lao Tse Press, 1997).

5. Arnold Mindell, *Dreaming While Awake: Techniques for 24-Hour Lucid Dreaming* (Charlottesville, VA: Hampton Roads, 2000). Arnold Mindell offers exercises like this to guide the reader to pick up dream-like signals. Also see, Arnold Mindell, *Earth-Based Psychology: Path Awareness from the Teachings of Don Juan Richard Feynman, and Lao Tse* (Portland, OR: Lao Tse Press, 2007).

6. Please see: Arnold Mindell, *Earth-Based Psychology: Path Awareness from the Teachings of Don Juan, Richard Feynman, and Lao Tse* (Portland, OR: Lao Tse Press, 2007) and Arnold Mindell, *Process Mind: A User's Guide to Connecting with the Mind of God* (Wheaton, IL: Quest Books, 2010). Mindell demonstrates how connecting with the deepest part of our body also connects us to an earth spot and to the "Process Mind," a part of us that feels connected to all, feels more unified, and less polarized. Thus, it is central in resolving conflict.

7. Here is an exercise you might try to connect to your deepest nature. There are many iterations of this exercise that can be found in: Arnold Mindell, *Process Mind: A User's Guide to Connecting with the Mind of God* (Wheaton, IL: Quest Books, 2010) and Arnold Mindell, *Earth-Based Psychology: Path Awareness from the Teachings of Don Juan, Richard Feynman, and Lao Tse* (Portland, OR: Lao Tse Press, 2007).

i. Relax your body, close your eyes, and ask yourself: where in my body is the deepest part of me? This is an irrational question, let your mind relax and follow what spontaneously comes up.

ii. Feel that part of your body and notice the sensations. Notice pressures, temperatures, feelings, and subtle movements. For example, a woman felt the deepest part of her was in her lower abdomen and felt a sense of warmth and strength.

iii. Amplify those feelings and sensations and try to feel them throughout your body perhaps making slight movements that correspond to the feeling. If we go further with our example, the woman above felt the warmth and strength and could feel it radiate through her whole body. She stood up and felt a slight swaying motion.

iv. Imagine this body feeling as a place on the earth. Imagine an earth spot or nature place that would somehow feel like your body experience. In the example above, the woman described her earth spot as a special place on the Mediterranean Sea.

v. Allow yourself to embody the essence of that earth spot. Feel it, move like it, and most importantly let your mind perceive from the perspective of this earth spot. Feel and see the world through its eyes. What message might it have for you? The woman who experienced herself as the Mediterranean Sea, continued her swaying motions, felt the warmth of the sea wash over her. The message from the sea was, "I am the great mother. I take care of all my children. I hold everything."

vi. The last step is to remember and use this experience of yourself in the midst of conflict. Let this deep part of you guide you in your relationships with children and everyone. The woman imagined a very difficult conflict with her teenage daughter. With this state of mind, she felt more detached and had more perspective. She found herself feeling less angry, more able to listen, and more reflective. She then reported back to me a week later that she could connect to this larger earth spot in herself and that, as a result, conflicts that usually escalated were easier to resolve. She reported that she felt more loving towards her daughter and that this was often missing when they would argue. As a result, she reported that her daughter was also kinder and less combative.

the big questions

1. Tobin Hart, *The Secret Spiritual World of Children* (Novato, CA: New World Library, 2003).

2. Jack Kornfield, *Stories of the Spirit, Stories of the Heart: Parables of the Spiritual Path from Around the World* (San Francisco, CA: Harper Collins, 1991).

3. In memory of Sara Halprin. Included here with permission from her husband, Herb Long.

4. See: Arnold Mindell, *Earth-based Psychology Path Awareness: from*

the Teachings of Don Juan, Richard Feynman, and Lao Tse (Portland, OR: Lao Tse Press, 2007), an instructive and inspiring book that demonstrates our connection to the dreaming earth. In addition see how Mindell's thinking expands in *Process Mind: A User's Guide to Connecting with the Mind of God* (Wheaton, IL: Quest Books, 2012).

5. I am grateful to Makiko Tadokoro who alerted me to this video, which is part of a larger documentary titled *Children–Full of Life: Learning to Care*. It follows the fourth-grade classroom of Mr. Kanamori. The program is an intimate portrait of a teacher and his classroom that prepares children for life's challenges. Mr. Kanamori's "school of life" classroom encourages children to share life experience. The documentary won the Japan Prize in Education for 2003. Read about the documentary at: http://www.nhk.or.jp/jp-prize/english/2003/jyusyou_05.html. The snippet showing Mr. Kanamori's discussion about death can be seen (with English subtitles) at: http://www.wimp.com/homeroomteacher.

6. I am grateful to Arnold Mindell and his teachings about death and dying and working with grief. He has shown in his work how grief seems to be somewhat alleviated when we are able to connect with the spirit or the qualities of the person whom we miss.

the parent path

1. See statistics by the United Nations Population Fund at: http://www.unfpa.org/swp/.

2. It is estimated that there are at least 143 million orphans in our world although many children go uncounted. See: http://www.orphanshope.org/our_vision.html.

3. I am grateful to Colleen Clarke who supplied me with the following references: Ronald M. Berndt and Catherine H. Berndt, *The World of the First Australians Aboriginal Traditional Life: Past and Present* (Canberra: Aboriginal Studies Press, 1964), 150-157; Sylvia Poirier, *A*

*World of Relationships: Itineraries, Dreams and Events in the Australian
Western Desert* (Toronto, NY: University of Toronto Press, 2005), *67-68
& 132-141.*

4. Ibid.

the growth of the parent

1. Arnold Mindell, *River's Way: The Process Science of the Dreambody*
(London: Routledge and Kegan Paul, 1985), 25-26; Julie Diamond and
Lee Spark Jones, *A Path Made by Walking: Process Work in Practice* (Portland,
OR: Lao Tse Press, 1985), 125-145.

2. Arnold Mindell uses the term "elder" or "eldership" in many of his
books. He repeatedly refers to the elder as someone who is able to hold
and facilitate many points of view, one who can facilitate tension and can
bring in the deepest dimensions of experience, particularly that which
has been disavowed or is least known. The elder is a grand facilitator who
sees the world as her child. Eldership is an attitude of openness, compassion, and gives us a sense of home. Mindell has mostly used this term in
reference to group facilitation, conflict work, and dealing with challenging
world issues. Please see: Arnold Mindell, *Process Mind: A User's Guide
to Connecting with the Mind of God* (Wheaton, IL: Quest Books, 2010);
*Sitting in the Fire: Large Group Transformation Using Conflict and Di-
versity* (Portland, OR: Lao Tse Press, 1995); *Earth-Based Psychology Path
Awareness: From the Teachings of Don Juan, Richard Feynman, and Lao Tse*
(Portland, OR: Lao Tse Press, 2007); *The Leader as Martial Artist: Techniques and Strategies for Resolving Conflict and Creating Community* (San
Francisco, CA: Harper Collins, 1992).

3. This exercise has been inspired and adapted from Arnold Mindell's
groundbreaking work on the Process Mind and its connection with earth
spots. The Process Mind is the deepest part of each of us, the intelligence
behind our dreaming. There are aspects to Process Mind which feel parental in that the experience is one of great eldership and care for all living

things. This exercise has its foundation in many of the exercises created by Mindell in the following books. Please see: Arnold Mindell, *Process Mind: A User's Guide to Connecting with the Mind of God*, (Wheaton, IL: Quest Books, 2010); Arnold Mindell, *Earth-Based Psychology: Path Awareness from the Teachings of Don Juan, Richard Feynman, and Lao Tse* (Portland, OR: Lao Tse Press, 2007).

parenting at odds together

1. See: Katy Abel, "Working Moms and Kids," *Parent Education*, accessed on May 19, 2013, http://life.familyeducation.com/working-parents/child-care/36454.html; Liana C. Sayer, Suzanne M. Bianchi, and John P. Robinson, "Are Parents Investing Less in Children? Trends in Mothers' and Fathers' Time with Children," revised version of paper presented at the American Sociological Association annual meeting, August 2000, Washington, D.C. (University of Chicago, 2004), accessed on May 19, 2013, http://csde.washington.edu/downloads/bianchi_AJS_paper.pdf. Lecia Parks Langston, "Mom at Work: Guilty or Not Guilty? What is Your Verdict?" accessed on May 19, 2013, https://jobs.utah.gov/wi/pubs/womencareers/qualitytime.pdf.

# bibliography

ABEL, KATY. "Working Moms and Kids." *Parent Education*. Accessed on
   May 19, 2013. http://life.familyeducation.com/working-parents/
   child-care/36454.html.

BERNDT, RONALD M., AND CATHERINE H. BERNDT. *The World
   of the First Australians: Aboriginal Traditional Life: Past and Present.*
   Canberra, Australia: Aboriginal Studies Press, 1964.

CASTANEDA, CARLOS. *Journey to Ixtlan: The Lessons of Don Juan.*
   New York: Pocket Books, 1974.

———. *The Teachings of Don Juan: A Yaqui Way of Knowledge.*
   Berkeley, CA: University of California Press, 1968.

CHIAWEI O'HEARN, CLAUDINE, ed. *Half Half: Writers on Growing Up
   Biracial and Bicultural.* New York: Pantheon Books, 1998.

CLUNIS, D. MERILEE AND G. DORSEY GREEN. *The Lesbian Parenting
   Book: A Guide to Creating Families and Raising Children.* New York:
   Seal Press, 2003.

DIAMOND, JULIE, AND LEE SPARK JONES. *A Path Made by Walking:
   Process Work in Practice.* Portland, OR: Lao Tse Press, 2004.

DREXLER, PEGGY AND LINDEN GROSS. *Raising Boys without Men:
   How Maverick Moms are Creating the Next Generation of
   Exceptional Men.* New York: Holtzbrinck Publishers, 2005.

FIELD, EVELYN. *Bullying Busting: How to Help Children Deal with
   Teasing and Bullying.* Sydney: Finch Publishing Pry Limited, 1999.

FREYMANN, SAXTON. *What Are You Peeling? Foods with Moods.* New
   York: Arthur A. Levine Books, 1999.

GALLAS, KAREN. *Talking Their Way into Science: Hearing Children's
   Questions and Theories, Responding with Curricula.* New York:
   Teachers College Press, 1995.

GOLDING, WILLIAM. *Lord of the Flies.* New York: Perigee Books,1959
[1954].

GOLEMAN, DANIEL. *Emotional Intelligence.* New York: Bantam, 1995.

GOODBREAD, JOE. *The Dreambody Toolkit.* Portland, OR: LaoTse
Press, 1997.

GOTTMAN, JOHN. *Raising an Emotionally Intelligent Child: The Heart
of Parenting.* New York: Simon and Schuster, 1997.

GREENE, ROSS W. *Lost at School.* New York: Simon and Schuster, 2008.

HART, TOBIN. *The Secret Spiritual World of Children.* Novato, CA:
New World Library, 2003.

HOWEY, NOELLE AND ELLEN SAMUELS, eds. *Out of the
Ordinary: Essays on Growing Up with Gay, Lesbian and Transgender
Parents.* New York: St. Martin's Press, 2000.

JONES, GERARD. *Killing Monsters: Why Children Need Fantasy, Super
Heroes and Make Believe Violence.* New York: Basic Books, 2002.

JUNG, CARL GUSTAV. *Psychological Interpretation of Children's Dreams.*
Zurich lectures, (unpublished) 1938-1939.

KOHN, ALFIE. *Unconditional Parenting: Moving from Rewards and
Punishments to Love and Reason.* New York: Atria Books, 2005.

KORNFIELD, JACK. *Stories of the Spirit, Stories of the Heart: Parables of
the Spiritual Path from Around the World.* San Francisco, CA: Harper
Collins, 1991.

LANGSTON, LECIA PARKS. "Mom at Work: Guilty or Not Guilty?
What is Your Verdict?" Accessed on May 19, 2013. https://jobs.
utah.gov/wi/pubs/womencareers/qualitytime.pdf.

MARTY, MARTIN E. *The Mystery of the Child.* Grand Rapids, MI: Wm.
B. Eerdmans Publishing Co., 2007.

MCGRAW, JAY. *Life Strategies for Dealing with Bullies.* New York:
Simon and Schuster, 2008.

MINDELL, AMY. *Metaskills: The Spiritual Art of Therapy.* Tempe, AZ:
New Falcon Press, 1995.

MINDELL, ARNOLD. *The Dreambody in Relationships.* London:
Routledge and Kegan Paul, 1987.

———. *The Dreambody: The Body's Role in Revealing the Self.* Santa
Monica, CA: Sigo Press, 1982.

———. *Dreaming While Awake: Techniques for 24-Hour Lucid
Dreaming.* Charlottesville, VA: Hampton Roads, 2000.

———. *Earth-Based Psychology: Path Awareness from the Teachings of Don
Juan, Richard Feynman and Lao Tse.* Portland, OR: Lao Tse Press, 2007.

———. *Process Mind: A User's Guide to Connecting with the Mind of
God.* Wheaton, IL: Quest Books, 2010.

———. *River's Way: The Process Science of the Dreambody.* London:
Routledge and Kegan Paul, 1985.

———. *The Shaman's Body: A New Shamanism for Transforming Health,
Relationships and Community.* New York: Harper Collins, 1993.

———. *Sitting in the Fire: Large Group Transformation Using Conflict
and Diversity.* Portland, OR: Lao Tse Press, 1995.

———. *Working With the Dreaming Body.* London: Routledge and
Kegan Paul, 1985.

NEILL, A. S. *Summerhill: A Radical Approach to Child Rearing.*
London: Hart Publishing Company, 1960.

PANTLEY, ELIZABETH. *The No-Cry Sleep Solution.* New York: McGraw
Hill, 2002.

PARR, TODD. *It's Okay to be Different.* New York: Little, Brown and
Company, 2001.

———. *The Family Book.* New York: Little, Brown and
Company, 2003.

PIPHER, MARY. *Reviving Ophelia: Saving the Selves of Adolescent Girls.*
New York: Ballantine Books, 1994.

POIRIER, SYLVIA. *A World of Relationships: Itineraries, Dreams and
Events in the Australian Western Desert.* Toronto, NY: University of
Toronto Press, 2005.

REISS, GARY. *Families that Dream Together: Process-Oriented Family Therapy and Community Based Healing.* CreateSpace Independent Publishing Platform, 2013.

ROSE, INGRID. *School Violence: Studies in Alienation, Revenge, and Redemption.* London: Karnac Books, 2009.

ROWLING, J. K. *Harry Potter and the Philosopher's Stone.* London: Bloomsbury, 1997.

SAYER, LIANA, C., SUZANNE M. BIANCHI, AND JOHN P. ROBINSON. *"Are Parents Investing Less in Children? Trends in Mothers' and Fathers' Time with Children."* Chicago: University of Chicago, 2004. Accessed on May 19, 2013. http://csde.washington.edu/downloads/bianchi_AJS_paper.pdf.

SEARS, WILLIAM AND MARTHA SEARS. *The Attachment Parenting Book: A Commonsense Guide to Understanding and Nurturing Your Baby.* New York: Little, Brown and Company, 2001.

SIEGAL, DANIEL J. AND MARY HARTZELL. *Parenting from the Inside Out.* New York: Penguin, 2004.

SIMMONS, RACHEL. *Odd Girl Out: The Hidden Culture of Aggression in Girls.* Orlando, FL: Harcourt Books, 2002.

SPOCK, BENJAMIN. *The Common Sense Book of Baby and Child Care.* New York: Duell, Sloan, and Pearce, 1946.

THOMPSON, MICHAEL, CATHERINE O'NEILL-GRACE, AND LAWRENCE J. COHEN. *Best Friends, Worst Enemies: Understanding the Social Lives of Children.* New York: Ballantine, 2001.

THOMPSON, MICHAEL AND DAN KINDLON. *Raising Cain: Protecting the Emotional Life of Boys.* New York: Ballantine Books, 2000.

VITALI, KEITH. *Bullyproof Your Child.* New York: Skyhorse Publishing, 2007.

YOGANANDA, PARAMAHANSA. *Autobiography of a Yogi.* Los Angeles: Self–Realization Fellowship, 1990 [1946].

index

 **about the author**

Dawn Menken, Ph.D., is a certified process worker, therapist, conflict resolution educator, group facilitator, and mother. After graduating from college, she had the good fortune to be one of Dr. Arnold Mindell's first students and was a founding member of the Research Society for Process-oriented Psychology in Zurich, Switzerland, where she lived for ten years. In 1989, Menken earned her Ph.D. in clinical psychology. In 1990, she moved to Portland, Oregon and co-founded the Process Work Institute, a vibrant center for process-oriented psychology attracting a diverse, international student body. She is a senior faculty member at the institute and was a co-creator of both the Master of Arts degrees in Process Work and in Conflict Facilitation and Organizational Change, serving as academic dean for the conflict facilitation program for the last decade.

A worldwide conflict resolution educator and group facilitator, Menken teaches workshops on all aspects of process-oriented psychology, runs life skills programs in schools, facilitates dialogues in agencies, organizations, and communities. She is a presenter at conflict resolution, leadership, and youth conferences.

In September of 2006, Menken performed her one-woman show, *MamaSpeak*, at a local theater, based on her personal journey and celebration of motherhood, highlighting the universal mystery behind birth, and the sacred calling to parenthood. Motherhood continues to be a source of inspiration in her life, has informed her creative approach to working with children, families, and groups, and has brought new direction to her enduring vision to create a global community. She offers workshops on parenting, family work, youth leadership, and bully prevention and brings her love of children and fresh ideas into the classroom. She dreams of a day when conflict work and community building are central components to every school curriculum and is dedicated to creating home lives and school environments that support the deepest learning spirit in each of us.

Menken is also the author of *Speak Out! Talking About Love, Sex and Eternity*, a book of personal essays that explores themes of marginalization, relationship, and the basic essence of community. She maintains a private practice in Portland, Oregon and works with adults, children, couples, and families. Learn more about her work at www.dawnmenken.com.